Find out what it's like to grow up in one of the nation's most famous families in the finale to Joanna Philbin's irresistible Daughters series

"Who knew? Stars' daughters—they're just like us."
—*Publishers Weekly*

"An addicting read filled with drama and friendship."
—Teensreadtoo.com

"[T]his noteworthy series . . . feels less mean girls and more girl power, with messages of honesty, respect, [and] being true to oneself."
—*VOYA*

"Philbin excels at portraying teens honestly and there isn't a fake note in this entire book. The drama in the boy department doesn't disappoint either."
—Bookfinds.com

"As if navigating their high school hallways weren't enough, these girls have to do so under the entire world's watchful eyes!"
—Seventeen.com

"In The Daughters, you'll read about best friends . . . as they navigate normal high school life (drama and all!), along with the glitz and glamour of red carpet events."
—*Twist* magazine

"An insider's glimpse into the gilded world of those born to be famous."
—Alyson Noël, author of #1 *New York Times* bestselling The Immortals series

the
daughters
join the party

the daughters join the party

JOANNA PHILBIN

poppy

LITTLE, BROWN AND COMPANY
New York   Boston

Poppy

Hachette Book Group
237 Park Avenue, New York, NY 10017
For more of your favorite series and novels, go to www.pickapoppy.com

Poppy is an imprint of Little, Brown and Company.
The Poppy name and logo are trademarks of Hachette Book Group, Inc.

The publisher is not responsible for websites (or their content) that are not owned by the publisher.

First Hardcover Edition: November 2011
First Paperback Edition: May 2012

Library of Congress Cataloging-in-Publication Data

Philbin, Joanna.
  The daughters join the party / by Joanna Philbin. — 1st ed.
    p. cm.
  "Poppy."
  Summary: Emma's senator father is running for president, and when her rebellious style and indifference to rules and convention create problems, she relies on her good friends, who are also the daughters of well-known people, to help her gain perspective.
  ISBN 978-0-316-17968-3 (hc) / ISBN 978-0-316-17961-4 (pb)
  [1. Politics, Practical — Fiction.   2. Individuality — Fiction.
3. Friendship — Fiction.   4. High schools — Fiction.   5. Schools —
Fiction.   6. Family life — New York (State) — New York — Fiction.
7. New York (N.Y.) — Fiction.]   I. Title.
  PZ7.P515Dbj 2011
  [Fic] — dc23

2011019222

10 9 8 7 6 5 4 3 2 1

RRD-C

Book design by Tracy Shaw

Printed in the United States of America

To every daughter

chapter 1

Emma Conway stood up, looked carefully around, and stepped away from the clump of bushes in front of Flanner Hall. Nobody had followed them, thank God. The main quad was still, except for the night sounds of crickets and sputtering sprinklers, and the August sky was awash with stars. Emma felt a warm breeze caress her face and let her breath return to normal. In almost twelve months of living and studying at the Rutherford School, she'd never seen it look so beautiful. She wondered why she'd never snuck out of her dorm before.

"Okay, guys, we're cool," she said.

Behind her, Tiffany and Rachel stood up slowly from the bushes. Tiffany smoothed her perpetually messy blond ponytail and looked uneasily over her shoulder. "I thought I heard someone," she said. "You sure no one's following us?"

"We're fine, Tiffany," Emma replied.

There was a hooting sound, and Tiffany quickly squatted back down.

"Oh my God, Tiffany," Rachel said in her condescending voice. "That was an owl." She flicked her glossy Brazilian blowout–treated hair out of her eyes and turned to Emma. "So, now what? You promised us a party. Where is it?" Rachel's attitude could be a little much, even if she was the bravest girl at Rutherford — besides Emma, of course.

"First I have to get inside," Emma said, gesturing to Flanner Hall.

"Wait. How?" Tiffany asked, wide-eyed.

"I've got to climb in," Emma said.

"You're going to *climb* in?" Tiffany asked. "How are you going to get up there?"

Emma eyed Jeremy Dunn's window. It was the one with the peeling Obama sticker, directly above the front door. She hadn't remembered it looking that high before. Earlier that day, Flanner Hall had looked almost friendly, with its cheerful red bricks, its white windows, and the antique weather vane that spun in the wind. But now, in the moonlit darkness, the dorm looked as immense and forbidding as a Gothic castle. "It's not that bad," she bluffed. "I've climbed trees that were higher than that."

"And then what?" Tiffany said. "What do we do once we get in there? What if someone *hears* us?"

"Calm down, Tiff. You're summer students. I'm the one who actually goes to school here. I'm the one who could really get in trouble." *Yeah, right,* Emma thought. The most that could possibly happen to her was another detention. And she'd done enough of those already that she didn't care about another lost hour. "Okay, when I say 'go,' we run."

"Again?" Rachel asked. "I'm wearing platforms."

Tiffany just sighed heavily and nodded.

Emma crouched down into ready position. "Get ready," she said. "Get set...Go!"

She took off in a sprint across the quad, her bare feet sinking into the dirt. She could almost see herself as if she were in a movie: her dark brown, shoulder-length hair waving in the wind, her heavy brows knit together, her dark blue eyes ringed, as usual, with a little too much purple eyeliner. *Finally,* she thought, *freedom.* For a solid year, she'd lived on the most regimented schedule imaginable. Seven hours of class, two hours of sports, then three hours of study time, then sleep — that was the Rutherford schedule, six days a week. There were fifteen minutes before dinner when people could socialize on the quad — if the weather was nice — and a half hour in between study time and lights-out for visiting people's dorms, but other than that, students had to be busy and occupied. Sunday was the only free day, but there were usually hours of homework, and nowhere to go except for the sad excuse for a mall in town. She'd thought boarding school would be an escape from rules and chores and parental supervision — not to mention her painfully small and snobby private school in New York City. Instead, Rutherford had been anything but an escape. Except for this moment, right now.

She stopped a few feet from the front of the building and leaned over her bare knees, panting. Her favorite denim cutoffs dug into the tops of her thighs. Sweat trickled down the back of her neck. It had felt so good to run, but now she hoped she didn't smell. Discreetly she sniffed the armpit of her Cheap Trick T-shirt. No offensive odor. She was ready.

3

"I think I twisted my ankle," Tiffany said, hobbling to a stop.

"Oh, please," Rachel muttered.

"I think I really did," Tiffany said, limping a little on her Keds.

"I'm sure you'll be okay," Emma said. She looked up. Every window in Flanner Hall was dark, including Jeremy's, which was directly above her. For a moment she wondered if he'd forgotten about their plan.

Suddenly the window jerked open a few inches, then a few more, until a head stuck out in the dark. "You coming up or not?" Jeremy whispered in his sexy, sarcastic voice.

"Be right there," she whispered back.

Jeremy Dunn was the only thing that had made summer session tolerable. She'd noticed him that first day, at lunch, on line in the dining hall. Then again, she'd noticed lots of other guys that day, too — the freakishly tall guy with Taylor Lautner's eyes in her World History class, and the boy with the floppy strawberry-blond hair who'd quietly sketched X-Men all through Art class. But the moment she'd seen Jeremy, as she walked over to the salad bar, there had been something fascinating about him. Maybe it was what he wore: green camouflage-patterned flip-flops and a T-shirt with a picture of Bert and Ernie from *Sesame Street*, designed to look like Starsky and Hutch. Or maybe it was his longish, straight, sandy-colored hair, which he tucked behind his ears. Or the focused way he used the salad tongs to drop falafel onto his plate one by one, as if he were conducting a science experiment.

She made her move at the soup station. "Gross," she said, looking at the cream of broccoli soup, which had formed a solid, congealed surface of oil and cream. "That's, like, the most disgusting thing I've ever seen in my life."

"I'll eat a bowl if you will," he dared. He turned to look at her. His eyes twinkled in a way that made her momentarily speechless.

"You're on," she said. She reached for the ladle, dumped some in her bowl, and then handed it to him.

"Hey, you didn't get enough gelatinous surface in yours," he said, dumping more soup into her bowl. "We have to make this fair, after all."

They sat down together at an empty table, which was fine with Emma. She didn't really have a regular group of friends.

"Okay, you ready?" he asked, his spoon poised.

Emma looked at the green lumpy soup. "I think I might throw up."

"Come on," he said with mock seriousness. "No pain, no gain."

Thirty minutes and the most disgusting bowl of soup in her life later, Emma was in love. Jeremy was the guy she had been waiting to meet at Rutherford — funny and reckless and genuinely smart. He lived in Boston and had come to Rutherford to pull up his grades. Like her, he'd been called an "underachiever" by more teachers than he could count. Also like her, he loved Led Zeppelin, thought Twitter was lame, and knew every line from *Superbad*. Starting that first day, they ate every meal together, hung out on the quad together before dinner, and used enlargers that were right next to each other in Photography 2. And Jeremy seemed to like certain things about her, too. Or at least, he didn't question them. He never asked her why she wore so much eyeliner, or what she thought of her senator dad, who everyone was already saying should run for president, or why she spent so much time alone, or why she sometimes wore tiny skull earrings instead of the hoops all the other girls wore. And for the half hour every night that the inmates of Rutherford were allowed to visit one another's dorms, she and Jeremy would curl up on the sofa in their respective common rooms, cracking up over funnyordie.com.

In short, they were practically going out, except for one thing: Jeremy hadn't kissed her. Yet. And as the last week of summer session began, Emma knew that she needed to help things along.

"So am I coming to *you* tonight?" she'd asked him earlier that day, as they lay on the quad before dinner. Even though their arms weren't touching Emma could feel the warmth of his skin, just inches away.

"This dorm-visiting thing is so lame," Jeremy moaned, picking at a handful of grass. "Nine to nine thirty? Even on Saturday night? I just wish we could do our own thing," he said, his hand edging closer to hers on the grass. "No signing in, no watching the clock."

Emma's heart skipped a beat. Was he saying what she thought he was saying? Did he wish he could be alone with her? "What if I came over tonight?" she heard herself ask. "After lights-out?"

"You mean, what if you snuck out?" he asked, sounding unsure.

"Yeah." She'd been wondering what his room looked like for weeks. She could just picture his desk spread with books, his clothes hanging out of the dresser drawers, his bedspread and sheets in a ball on his bed...

"Well, you'd have to come in through the window," he said,

6

sounding more excited about the idea. "Vince's room is right next to the door."

Vince Truffardi was the head prefect of Flanner and a notorious discipline freak. The rumor was that he'd deferred college for a year so he could stick around Rutherford and continue busting kids for minor infractions.

Emma turned over onto her stomach. "You're the Obama sticker, right?" she asked, pretending she didn't know which window was his.

Jeremy turned over onto his stomach, too. Now their fingers were practically touching. "Yup. Second floor."

Emma stared at the window, thinking of all the times she'd imagined climbing through it. "No problem. I used to climb trees all the time at our old house upstate."

"You want to bring friends?" he asked. "And I'll have some of the guys there?"

Her heart sank a little. A party hadn't been what she'd had in mind. "Sure," she said.

"Cool." He stood up and held out his hand to help her. "Come at eleven," he said.

"Eleven fifteen," she said, standing up and wiping the back of her shorts. "And you better be there to let me in."

"Absolutely," Jeremy said, grinning.

Emma's heart skipped again. She'd been right all along: He definitely liked her.

Except now, standing under his window, she wasn't exactly sure if this was going to work out.

"Just climb *that,*" Rachel said, gesturing to the drainpipe that

7

shot up the wall toward the roof, through a patch of ivy. It ran alongside Jeremy's window. "And pull yourself up with those." She pointed to a metal hook that curved around the pipe, bolting it to the building. There seemed to be a hook every three feet.

"And we're supposed to do that, *too*?" Tiffany asked.

Emma ignored her. "Okay, I'm going," she whispered, grabbing hold of the first-floor windowsill. She climbed onto it, saying a prayer that this wasn't Vince's room.

"Shhh!" Tiffany hissed.

Standing on the windowsill, Emma reached for the metal hook. Then she swung herself over the pipe and hugged it with her legs. She pulled one foot up the wall and then the other, so that she was in rock-climbing position. The metal piece groaned under her weight. With one tentative arm she reached up for the next hook and grabbed it.

"Good job," she heard Jeremy whisper in the dark, just as she felt the hook come loose in her hand. With a creak, one end of the drainpipe swung away from the wall.

Tiffany screamed. Emma realized that she was falling.

Pain shot up her spine as she landed on her butt. The ground beneath her felt wet. "Ow!" she exclaimed, a little too loudly.

Lights blinked on in some of the windows. Including Vince Truffardi's. Emma heard Vince scramble to his feet out of bed. Tiffany and Rachel turned and ran, just as the door to Flanner flew open. "Who's out here?" Vince's voice was loud and strident.

She stood up and brushed herself off. "Over here," she said. There was no use trying to hide.

The beam of Vince's flashlight hit her square in the face. "Hi, Vince," she said cheerfully. "What's up?"

His flashlight traveled up and down her body. "Whose room were you trying to climb into?"

"Nobody's."

The flashlight shone straight into her face again, making her squint. "Nobody's?"

"I have a problem with sleepwalking."

He clicked off the flashlight. In the moonlight, Emma could just make him out. Vince was short, with chicken legs and overdeveloped arms, and his hair was already thinning. It was no surprise that he seemed irritated all the time.

"You're in violation of code five-two-four," he barked. "Trying to gain unauthorized access to another student's room."

"Vince, do you really think I can climb a building?"

"At this point, Emma, I wouldn't be surprised," he said. "Let's go. Time to see Dean Ward."

"Awesome," Emma said. "I can't wait."

He grabbed her arm and with a sharp yank pulled her across the wet grass. Emma thought about Jeremy at his window, watching all of this. She knew what he was probably thinking: *Yeah, that's Emma. Not afraid of anything. Getting busted and keeping her cool.*

But just before they turned left on the path, Emma glanced back over her shoulder. To her surprise, Jeremy wasn't in the window. It was dark. And someone had even drawn the curtain.

chapter 2

"I'm going to ask you one more time," said Mr. Moyers, tapping his meaty fingers on his desk blotter. With his pale face, hangdog eyes, and rainbow-striped necktie, the headmaster of Rutherford looked like a very sad clown. "Who were you trying to see in Flanner Hall last night? And be honest, Emma. For both our sakes."

Emma shifted in the leather wing chair across from his desk. She could easily just tell him. Jeremy Dunn hadn't shown up for breakfast, and when she'd passed by him on the quad on the way to first period, he'd actually looked right past her. But she wasn't a tattletale. "Nobody. I was having trouble sleeping, so I just felt like taking a walk."

"A walk," Mr. Moyers repeated doubtfully. The afternoon sun poured in through the tall window behind him. Through it Emma could see two girls walking to the Art Building past the massive elm trees. She wished she were with them.

"I couldn't sleep," Emma said. "Doesn't that ever happen to you?"

"Emma, do you like being in this office?" Mr. Moyers asked, leaning forward. "At this point, I feel I have to ask."

She took in the framed degrees in education from Yale and Columbia, and the cheesy poster of a rainbow with a quote that read: *There is nothing impossible to him who will try. — Alexander the Great.* And of course the electric guitar leaning against the wall, which Mr. Moyers supposedly used for "jam sessions" with some of the faculty members. Just thinking about that made her cringe. "I guess it's kind of cozy," she said. "Though you might want to think about redecorating soon."

"Emma." Mr. Moyers sighed. "We're going to have to discuss your future here at Rutherford."

"My *future*?" she asked.

"Yes," he said soberly. "Your future."

Those ominous words still hung in the air when a brisk knock on the door made her jump. "Yes?" Mr. Moyers called out.

His assistant, Kathy, stuck her gray, permed head into the room. Emma always got the impression that Kathy was secretly listening on speaker to everything that went on in Mr. Moyers's office. "Senator Conway is here," she announced. "And his wife."

"My *parents*?" Emma exclaimed, sitting straight up in her chair. "But they're on vacation. At Lake George. Nuclear fallout wouldn't get them to leave."

Mr. Moyers coolly flapped his rainbow necktie. "They didn't seem to have a problem coming in. Especially when I told them the gravity of the situation."

A shiver ran through her as she gripped the chair's armrests. She wasn't going to just be getting detention. That much was clear. "Can I speak to them first?" she asked, getting to her feet.

Mr. Moyers blinked, surprised.

"They're my parents. Isn't that my constitutional right?"

"Go ahead," he said with a resigned shrug.

She opened the door. Her dad was talking to Kathy. He held a miniature bronzed football that he'd picked up from her desk, and his large green eyes were lit up, the way they always were when he talked to a voter. "You said your husband's a Giants fan?" he asked her, a faint New York accent curling around his words. "Well, you tell him from me that I think they're going to have a terrific season. And if they don't, I will *personally* —"

"Dad?" she interrupted.

His expression went from folksy to furious. "Hello, Emma," he said soberly. He put down the football and crossed his arms over his barrel chest. Adam Conway was just over six feet, but he could suddenly appear several inches taller if he wanted to, especially if he was annoyed. "I take it you're here to plead your case?" he asked.

Kathy stood up from her chair. "I'll just leave you two alone," she said, and ducked out the door.

"Where's Mom?" Emma asked, looking around. Mr. Moyers's waiting room was permanently dim, even in the middle of the day.

"She's in the ladies room," her father said. He cocked his head to the side. His thick, wavy brown hair had yet to go gray, but it

12

seemed to be getting lighter at the temples. And it was always strange to see him out of a suit, and in a blue polo and khakis.

"First of all, this has gotten *way* blown out of proportion," she said. "It was barely anything. I didn't even make it into the dorm. Nothing happened."

"Whatever happened, it was bad enough to get your mother and me in a car at eight thirty this morning."

"I'm just asking you to have an open mind. The way you would if Remington got into trouble."

Her dad gave her a searing look. "Your brother doesn't get into trouble," he said, just as the door to the office opened and Emma's mother entered.

"Hello, honey," she said, reaching out her slender arms. Even in a crisis, Carolyn Conway could be counted on to look good — no, impeccable. She wore a yellow silk top and navy blue capris with gold ballet slippers, and she'd pulled her thick black hair back into a casual but chic ponytail. She didn't wear makeup, and she was too practical to indulge in jewelry. But she did like handbags. Today she carried a bright pink Kelly bag in the crook of her arm, and it banged against Emma as she gave her mom a hug.

"Hi, Mom," Emma muttered, getting a noseful of citrus-gardenia perfume. "Sorry about this."

Carolyn pulled out of the hug and frowned at Emma. "So. You snuck into a boys' dorm."

"I *tried* to sneak in," Emma said. "Huge difference."

Her mom seemed about to say something when she noticed

Emma's T-shirt, silk-screened with Edie Sedgwick's face, and her black skinny jeans.

"Sorry I'm not decked out in J. Crew," Emma said.

"Nice earrings," Carolyn said. "Skulls really send a great message."

"Okay, let's get this over with," said her dad, heading toward Mr. Moyers's office. Her mom followed.

Emma trailed behind them with a sinking feeling in her chest. She had a strong hunch that this wasn't going to go very well.

When they walked inside, Mr. Moyers almost leaped out of his chair. "Senator, Mrs. Conway! It's so nice to see you again," he said, approaching them with his hand extended.

"Same here," said Senator Conway, shaking Mr. Moyers's hand. "And please, call me Adam."

"Then call me Jim," Mr. Moyers said, so excited that his eyes seemed about to bulge out of his face. "Mrs. Conway," he said, turning to Emma's mom.

Carolyn shook his hand. "Hello, Mr. Moyers," she said in her brisk lawyer's voice. Unlike her husband, she had little talent — or use — for chitchat. She sat down next to Adam on the couch.

"Emma?" Mr. Moyers said. "Do you want to join your parents?"

Emma realized that she was still standing by the door. She perched herself on the arm of the sofa and winced. Her butt still hurt from last night's fall.

"So, uh, Jim," her father said. He leaned forward so that his elbows rested on his knees. She'd seen him sit this way in some of the photos on his Senate Web site. SENATOR ADAM CONWAY CARES

14

ABOUT NEW YORKERS, read the banner at the top of the page. "What can we do to help?"

"Well, I believe you know what happened here last night," Mr. Moyers said, settling into his chair. "Leaving one's room after lights-out, and then trying to enter another dormitory, is a serious violation of the Rutherford student code."

"So what's the punishment?" asked her mom. "This can't be the first time someone has done this."

"It's the first time someone has violated as many codes as your daughter has," Mr. Moyers said.

"How many are we talking about?" Emma's father asked, casting an alarmed glance in her direction.

"Well, let's see here…" Mr. Moyers picked up the file on his desk. "January tenth, Emma showed up in homeroom with purple hair."

"What?" her mother exploded. "She *dyed* her hair?"

"Yes. Purple."

"Burgundy," Emma cut in.

Mr. Moyers gave her an annoyed glance. "February fourteenth and twenty-first, she cut first and second period to sleep in."

"I was sick," she argued.

"When the RA went to her room," Mr. Moyers said, "she found Emma watching a movie on her laptop."

"Which was for class," Emma said.

"Emma," her father warned.

"March fifth," he went on, "Emma was caught in the pool, with a boy, after hours."

15

Emma let that one pass. Her dad sighed deeply and looked at the carpet.

"April seventeenth," said Mr. Moyers, "Emma started a food fight in the dining hall."

"I flung a piece of bread at someone," she said.

"Which hit Miss Wilkie, the math teacher," Mr. Moyers added. "May tenth —"

"Okay, we get the picture," Adam interrupted, holding up his hand. "And then last night —"

"Our head prefect heard Emma first try to scale the boys' dorm, and then fall on the ground." Mr. Moyers closed the file. "Which leads me to conclude that this might not be the best place for your daughter." He cleared his throat and swallowed. "We think it best she explore new possibilities for the coming school year."

Her parents looked dumbfounded. "Are you saying you don't want her to continue here?" her mom asked.

"I don't believe Emma wants to be here, Mrs. Conway. And I think she's doing everything she can to let us know that."

"You know she's dyslexic," her mom pointed out, in a way that made Emma cringe.

"We have plenty of other students with learning disabilities who don't have the...behavioral issues that Emma has." Mr. Moyers swallowed again. He seemed uncomfortable. "Emma's bright. She has the capacity to be an excellent student, despite her learning disability. But she doesn't take school seriously. In fact, she doesn't seem to take anything seriously."

"That's not fair," Emma argued. "What about my A in Swimming? And Photography? And the social service I did at the animal shelter?"

"Emma," Adam said sternly.

Carolyn reached over and put her hand on Emma's arm.

"I'm sorry," said Mr. Moyers. "But we think it's best that you find Emma another school."

Emma fumed silently. *Come on, Dad,* she thought, staring at the carpet. If he could get the Republicans and Democrats to agree on a health-care bill, he could get Mr. Moyers to keep her here. But instead of saying something persuasive and charming, her dad simply looked at her mom and held up his hands.

"All right, then," Carolyn said, reading his signals. "We'll take her home."

Emma got to her feet. "It was Jeremy Dunn," she confessed. "That's who I was trying to see last night. He's on the second floor of Flanner. Summer student, from Boston. Just ask him —"

"Thank you, Emma," Mr. Moyers said, scribbling something on a pad. "And good luck."

"That's it?" she asked. "I just gave you a name."

Mr. Moyers sighed. "Good-bye, Emma."

She went straight to the door, not even waiting for her parents. This was a joke. If this school wasn't going to give her a second chance, if it was going to kick her out for *attempting* to sneak into someone's room, and if it wasn't even going to give her a break for naming names, then she didn't want to be here anyway.

She hurried past Kathy, who she knew had probably heard every word, and threw open the door to the hall. All she wanted to do was run back to her room, slam the door, and try to think. She just needed to be alone. Even though she knew that would be impossible. Behind her she heard her parents walk into the hall.

"Well, I guess we shouldn't be too surprised," Emma heard her dad say. "It was a matter of time."

"You're the one who thought she was ready for boarding school," her mom replied.

"I just said we should try it," he said. "I didn't say it was going to be the perfect solution."

Emma whirled around. "Can you stop talking about me like I'm not here?"

"What would you like us to do?" her father asked. "You're walking ten paces ahead of us."

"You didn't even try to talk him out of it!" she said. "You didn't even defend me."

"Defend you?" Her mother's voice was uncharacteristically loud. "For dyeing your hair purple? Causing food fights?"

"Of course you'd believe all that," Emma muttered.

"Are you aware of what's going on with your father these days?"

"No, I have no idea," Emma said sarcastically.

There was no way she couldn't know. For the past six months, whenever she walked by the huge flat-screen TV in the student lounge, he was all over the news. *If Conway runs for president… Senator Conway put in another appearance today… The crowds showing up for Conway today were in the thousands… Sources close to the Senator say he is definitely eyeing a run…* She'd see a snippet of her dad making a speech in front of a crowd, or being applauded as he walked from his town car into a building, and it would all feel like she was watching someone else. It was too surreal. But ever since he'd won the Democratic New York seat for the second time, he'd practically become a celebrity.

First there'd been the health-care bill that he'd shepherded through the Senate, the one that nobody thought would get passed. Then there'd been his book, *Bridging the Divide,* about his plans for a *"united* United States of America," which had hit the *New York Times* bestseller list the day it was released and hadn't dropped off since. Then there'd been the interview on *60 Minutes,* where, when Morley Safer asked him about his plans for a campaign, he said, "I definitely haven't ruled it out," which only got every on-camera pundit and political blogger more obsessed over whether he might run. She would've had to have been trapped under a rock not to know what was going on with her dad. "Of course I know," she said.

"Well, there's more," her mother said. "When we get home —"

"I'm not going to live at home."

"Emma, your mother is trying to tell you something," her dad said somberly.

"And I am *not* going to Chadwick," Emma added. "You are not going to make me go to Remington's school. I *refuse.*"

She turned and headed for the door that led out onto the quad. She needed to get some air. *Expelled,* she thought. It was such an ugly word.

She pushed through the doors and there, on the veranda of the administrative building, stood a man talking on a cell phone. "Yeah, we had a quick change of plans this morning," he said in a raspy voice. "Now we're at their daughter's school." His slicked-back, dark hair was beginning to thin on top, and he wore an expensive-looking black suit. He looked up and saw her. "Lemme get back to you." He clicked off the phone. "You must be Emma," he said, holding out his hand. "I'm Tom. Tom Beckett."

Emma shook his hand. There had always been people hovering around her family — mostly anxious men in their twenties, who were always waiting to ferry her dad to appearances or to hand him a speech. But none of them had ever seemed this confident or well-dressed, and none had ever come with her parents to her school. "Hi," she said uncertainly.

Just then her parents came through the doors. "Who is this?" she asked them, turning around.

"This is Tom, my chief strategist," said her father.

"Chief strategist for what?" she asked. "You just got reelected last year."

Her dad paused for a moment. "I'm running again, honey."

Emma blinked. "You're running again? For what?"

"For president."

For a moment the words didn't compute. She watched as he put his hand on Tom's shoulder. "Tom here is the best," her dad went on. "Came highly recommended to me by Shanks. Where is he, by the way?"

"Out by the car, on the phone," said Tom. "He's lining up that Parks Department event for you tonight."

Emma tried to think of something to say. Anything.

"It all just happened," her mother put in. "Tom came up to the house yesterday for a meeting with a few people from his team. We were going to tell you when you came home next week."

"Come on," her father said. "Let's go pack up your things."

Emma began to follow them across the quad. She was supposed to be leading them, but she was too distracted to do anything but put one foot in front of the other.

Tom Beckett slipped on a pair of black wraparound sunglasses that made him look like a cross between an alien predator and Tom Cruise. "Everything okay?" he asked her parents.

"Not exactly," her father said, giving Emma a disapproving glance. "But then again we're all a little used to that by now."

chapter 3

As they walked the curving path to her dorm, certain images kept popping into her mind: Cameras. Crowds waving. Halls packed with people and decorated with red, white, and blue bunting. Burly Secret Service men following her every move, for the rest of her life... *Okay, calm down,* Emma thought. *First you just have to get through this day. Then you can freak out about the rest of your life.*

At her dorm she swiped her key through the slot and pulled open the door. She led the way up the staircase and unlocked the door to her single room. She tried to step in front of the terrarium on the floor and kick it under the bed, but she was too late.

"A snake?" her mom said. "You have a *snake* in your room?"

"That's Archie. I found him outside the dorm," Emma said, sliding the top door aside to pet the green garter snake.

"He's staying here," her mom said firmly.

"But who's gonna take care of him?"

"It's a snake, Emma," her father said curtly. "It can take care of itself."

"I'm bringing him," she insisted. "There's no need for him to be traumatized, too." That's when she noticed Tom Beckett staring at her and trying not to laugh. She glared at him.

"I'll go bring the car around the back," he said, excusing himself.

Adam bent over the mattress and began to pull it off the frame.

"Dad," Emma said, "the mattress stays here. I just need the sheets."

"Oh," he said.

He pushed the mattress back onto the frame, and Emma and her mom pulled off the hot pink and white batik sheets. It didn't take long to pack up the rest of her stuff: her posters of PJ Harvey and Lou Reed, her clothes, her Doc Martens, her favorite rainbow-colored hook rug, her purple beanbag chair. She dumped all of her Clairefontaine journals into a shopping bag and held on to it, in case it wound up in her dad's hands and, God forbid, one of the journals fell out and he glimpsed a page. Her mom zipped up her bulging suitcase and then picked up a framed photo of her parents and Remington, taken at Lake George several years earlier. "You don't want to forget this," she said, and put it in her purse.

When everything was finally packed, Emma picked up Archie's terrarium and closed the door behind her. *So long, Rutherford,* she thought. *It's been real.* On her way past Tiffany and Rachel's room she thought about scribbling a sarcastic message on their Dry Erase board — something like "Bye, guys! Vince Truffardi should be calling u later!" — but then thought better of it. The two of them weren't worth it.

She walked across the parking lot behind the dorm toward a black SUV in the guest spot. She supposed the SUV was Tom's — it looked like the kind of car he would drive. Emma opened the backseat door, slid Archie's tank onto the floor in front of the seat, and then swung herself up and into the car, next to her mom and dad. Tom Beckett sat behind the wheel and beside him in the shotgun seat was another man, older than Tom and much heavier, with a mop of gray hair and a large mustache. All of his attention was focused on a small laptop resting on his knees.

"Emma, this is Michael Shanks," her father said. "He's my chief of staff at the Senate."

Shanks turned around and offered Emma his hand. "Hi there," he said in a gravelly voice. "I've heard a lot about you."

"I haven't heard a thing about you," she replied with a smile, and felt her mom elbow her softly.

A few moments later they were headed south on the highway, whizzing past green trees and the occasional roadside Denny's. It was annoying to have these two strangers in the car. She wished she could at least have half an hour alone with her mom and dad. "So, why now?" she finally asked.

"Your father set up an exploratory committee," her mom said. "It's a group of people in charge of finding out if it's a good time for a candidate to run. They call people and do polling, and in the case of your dad, the response was enormous. A lot of people thought he should run for president."

"And then there's been the response to the book," her father added.

"And the health-care bill," Tom added.

"It just seemed like the right time," her mom said.

Emma didn't say anything. It seemed ludicrous to think that her dad should have consulted her about this first, but she almost wanted to ask him why he hadn't.

"So, as we were saying," Tom said, looking at Adam in the rear-view mirror, "the first thing you'll want to do is get to the steak fry in Iowa next month."

"Already?" her mom asked. "The caucus isn't for almost a year and a half."

"You can't start courting Iowa too early," Tom said. His blue eyes were harsh and glittery in the rearview. "Most of the other candidates have already made inroads there."

"Wait. A steak fry is important when you're running for president?" Emma asked.

"He's not going there for the steak; he's going there to speak," Tom said condescendingly. "It's an enormous Democratic event."

"Emma," her mother said, taking her hand. "You can't tell anyone about this. Not a soul. Your dad won't be announcing this until January, at the earliest. So we have to keep this in the family."

"Fine," Emma said. "Does Remington know?"

"We called him yesterday," her mom said. "He should be home by the time we get there. His plane lands at three."

Of course he'd gotten a phone call, she thought. Her brother would always beat her in everything — grades, popularity, *and* parental attention, even when he was overseas. "How'd he like Cambridge?" she asked.

"You know Remington," her dad said. "Sounds like he loved it."

"He took post–World War Two European History and English," said her mom. "With that and his AP classes he's almost got the first year of college covered. Isn't that amazing?"

Emma fought the urge to roll her eyes. Only her brother would already be started on his college courses while he was still in high school.

"We should invite some press to this event tonight," Shanks piped up from the front seat.

"Let's ask Bernard Summers at the *Times*," Adam said. "We went to college together."

"Don't you know his daughter?" Carolyn asked, turning to Emma. "What's her name? Lucy?"

"Lizzie," Emma said. Lizzie Summers wasn't her closest friend in the world, but they'd attended each other's family Thanksgivings and Christmas parties. Lizzie was one of the nicer girls Emma had known when she lived in New York.

"Right. She goes to Chadwick, doesn't she?"

Emma gripped the armrest of her seat. *Don't say anything,* she thought. "Yes," she managed to say.

"Well, then at least you'll know someone there," her mom said, taking out her BlackBerry.

"Wait. I have to go to this tonight?" Emma asked.

"Well, since both you and Remington will be home, yes," she said. "And maybe you and Lizzie can talk about Chadwick."

Emma squeezed the armrest harder. "I told you I don't want to go to Remington's school. Can we not talk about this like it's a done deal?"

"Emma, it's August fifteenth," her mom said, fixing her with a glare. "School starts in three weeks. Where on earth do you think I can get you in by then?" Her mom pressed a button and put the phone to her ear.

Emma wanted to grab the phone, or at least yell and plead her case. But then she remembered Shanks and Tom in the front seat. She couldn't say anything — not with them there. *How convenient,* she thought. Her parents had probably brought them on purpose.

With a sigh, she grabbed her iPod out of her backpack. When they got home, and they were finally alone, she would try to get her mom to listen to her. *If* they were finally alone. She was starting to think that the little privacy they'd had as a family was now going to disappear.

It was late afternoon when they crossed the Henry Hudson Bridge into Manhattan. As they drove down the West Side Highway, the Hudson River looked as smooth as glass. Beside it a steady stream of bicyclists and Rollerbladers rode up and down the path, luxuriating in the beautiful summer day. Emma remembered her dad teaching her how to ride a bike on this path. Remington had tried to teach her how to Rollerblade, too, but it had been a disaster. She'd refused to wear kneepads and skinned both her knees pretty badly. But for the few moments before she'd fallen, she'd loved the feeling of skating near the water, and being a part of the city. She'd never loved New York the way her brother did, but now, as they drove, it felt good to be home.

Home, specifically, was a bright, sprawling apartment on Eighty-ninth between Lexington and Third, not too far from where her dad had grown up, in an even more sprawling apartment on Park Avenue. Adam Conway came from money — lots of it.

His father was Remington Conway, a brilliant lawyer who founded one of the first literary agencies in the country. Along with his two older brothers, Adam attended Andover, summered in Southampton, and made annual trips to Italy and the South of France to brush up on his language skills. It was expected that he'd go to work for his dad, or at least become a lawyer. But when he decided to run for president of his class at Harvard Law School, and won, everything changed. He decided to go into politics.

At first his parents were aghast. But Adam Conway's career took off right away. At twenty-six he won a spot on the New York City Council. At thirty, he was elected to the New York State Senate. Despite his upper-class background, he quickly earned a reputation for being hardworking, committed, charismatic, and brilliant. The newspapers called him the "Camelot Kid," comparing him to another politician who also had looks, ambition, and loads of charm. It was only a matter of time until he ran for the United States Senate. But there was still something of the black sheep about her father, despite his success. His wife — whom he'd met at Harvard Law — was the one who became a lawyer at a fancy midtown firm.

When they reached their apartment building, Tom double-parked and stayed behind the wheel. Her mom dialed someone on her BlackBerry. "Remington? Could you come down here? We just pulled up. Emma has a lot of things she needs to bring in." She paused. "Yes, Emma's home. It's a long story." She hung up.

Great, Emma thought. Of course she would have to get expelled on the same day Remington came home from Cambridge. She leaned down and grabbed Archie's tank. Suddenly all of her limbs felt weary. None of this was going to be easy.

Outside on the street, Emma helped Tom and her dad pull her belongings out of the back of the car and onto the curb. It was a messy pile of stuff, and Emma caught her dad eyeing the snake tank in her arms with irritation.

"You guys need a hand?" asked Shanks as he got out of the car. Emma finally got a good look at him. He had a mustache and a pot-belly and a permanently distracted air, as if he were late for three things at once.

"No, we're good," Tom said, hefting her suitcase down onto the sidewalk. He seemed to be eager to impress her dad. Just as the suitcase touched down the zipper opened slightly, showing the lace-edged back of one of Emma's bras.

"I got it!" she yelled, frantically stepping in front of the suit-case. Why were there always so many people around? Why couldn't they just be alone once in a while?

Remington walked out of the building and stopped short at the sight of Emma, stuffing her bra back into her suitcase with her foot. "You okay, Em?" he asked. "Need some help?" Her brother was extremely, ridiculously handsome, with light blue-green eyes, wavy chestnut hair, and a cleft chin.

"Nah, I'm good," she said, finally managing to get the bra out of sight. "Hi," she said, giving him a quick hug.

"How are you, sweetie?" Carolyn asked her son as she hugged him. "How was your flight?"

"It was okay," he said. "Not too bad. Here, Em. Let me take that."

As he picked up her suitcase, Emma noticed that he'd lost weight over the summer. His favorite Harvard crew shirt seemed a bit big on him, and his legs looked thin under his khaki shorts. Whenever he stopped his swim team training, he always got skinnier.

"Good to see you," Adam said, giving his son a hug, too. "We missed you."

"I missed you, too, Dad." Somehow Remington was able to say things like that without sounding totally cheesy. "So, what are you doing home, Em? I thought we wouldn't see you until next week."

Emma felt Tom and Shanks looking at her. "Um..." she began.

"And is that a snake you have in there?" he asked.

She knew that he'd changed the subject on purpose. "This is Archie," she said, holding out the tank. "I rescued him."

"Interesting," he said. "Hey, Michael," he said to Shanks. "Good to see you again."

"Remington," Shanks said with obvious respect, nodding back at him.

"I'm Remington," he said to Tom, extending his free hand.

"Good to meet you," Tom said, shaking it. "I've heard a lot about you."

Remington glanced at Emma. "That's cool," he muttered.

Emma wondered how he felt about being the perfect kid sometimes. In some ways her brother's intelligence was fascinating. He was smart enough to get straight A's and ace every AP class he took. But didn't that also mean that he knew getting perfect grades was all kind of meaningless, too?

"I'm gonna go park this," Tom said, getting back behind the wheel. "But you should all be ready to leave here by six o'clock."

"We'll see you at six," Adam said.

Note to self, she thought, as they walked into their building. *Do whatever you can to get out of this thing tonight.*

The lobby was still badly furnished — a chintz-covered couch flanked by spindly wood chairs with needlepoint seat covers — but there was something comforting about the fact that it all looked exactly the same. The two doormen, Gus and Jairo, gave Emma high fives as she walked by. They'd covered for her one weekend a year ago, just before she'd gone to boarding school, when she'd had a few people over without her parents knowing about it. She'd definitely lucked out by having cool doormen. Not everybody did.

"What's going on tonight?" Remington asked, as they walked into the elevator.

"I'm speaking at an event for the Parks Department tonight," her father said, as Shanks squeezed into the elevator with them. "Shanks figured it would be a good opportunity for press."

Her brother nodded as if he understood completely. "Good idea," he said.

They walked into their apartment, and Emma was hit with the familiar smell of garlic and onions from the neighbors cooking in the apartment downstairs. On one side of the foyer, French doors led to a dining room, which was lit by a perpetually flickering chandelier, and on the other side was a living room that nobody ever used — mostly because of the stuffy furniture given to them as a gift by Adam's parents. At the far end of the creaky wood floor was a den that both of her parents used as a home office, and beyond

31

that, a hallway that led to three bedrooms. Like the lobby of their building, the apartment was in desperate need of a makeover, but neither Adam nor Carolyn seemed to notice. Both of them were way too busy.

Emma and Remington walked to her room. As she opened the door, she was relieved to find that it was just as she'd left it, with its black-and-white fleur-de-lis patterned duvet, black lacquered desk, white chair, and bright yellow leather ottoman. Her mom hadn't been so keen on giving her a black-and-white bedroom when she was in the sixth grade, but Emma had insisted. There was also a trio of black-and-white photos she'd taken of a cemetery during a school trip to Boston in seventh grade. Four headstones sunk deep into the ground, tilting in all different directions. Her mom called the photos morbid, but Emma thought they were beautiful.

"So what happened?" her brother asked as he placed her suitcase on her bed. "It's bad, isn't it?"

She put Archie's tank on the windowsill. "They kicked me out."

"Oh, God, Emma," her brother groaned. "Are you serious? For what?"

"I snuck out of my room. I was trying to visit someone."

"*Someone?*" Remington asked. "Like, a guy?"

Emma felt herself blush. "It's not like I was trying to have some X-rated night or anything. It was just this guy who was really cool, and we just wanted to hang out together in his room —"

"His *room*?" Remington repeated.

"Don't look at me like that," she said, picking up one of the throw pillows from her bed and throwing it at him. "Do you have any idea how strict that place was? How many rules there were?"

"So naturally you decide that you're going to break every one of them and somehow *not* get in trouble," her brother replied, leaning against her desk. "Didn't you think about the consequences?"

"Whatever, it's over," she muttered. "That place wasn't right for me, anyway."

"So now where are you going to go?" he asked.

"Where do you think? Mom's dead set on sending me to Chadwick."

Remington shrugged. "Well, I've been trying to get you to go there for years. I think you'd love it."

Emma flopped on the bed and faced away from her brother. She'd never been able to explain to Remington why she didn't want to go to his school. It was too embarrassing. "What about Dad's campaign? I almost threw up when they told me."

"I wasn't that surprised. Dad's been talking about this for months."

"But what does this do to us? Are we going to have Secret Service trailing us around? Are we going to have to drop out of school? Are there going to be death threats?"

"Emma, you're getting way too ahead of yourself. As usual." He stifled a small yawn with his fist.

"I just feel a little freaked out. Like I just got signed up for something I didn't want to be a part of."

There was a knock on the door, and their dad peeked his head in. "Hey, pal," he said to Remington. "Can you look over this speech

33

for tonight? Tell me what you think?" He handed her brother some stapled pages. "I'd appreciate it. Tom just had it sent over."

"No problem," Remington said.

"Oh, and you and Emma meet your mom and me at the Boathouse," he said. "Tom wants us to do an interview at Fox on the way."

"Sure thing," said her brother.

Her father closed the door and there was an awkward silence. Emma tried to imagine her father asking her to proofread one of his speeches. Her mind drew a blank.

"I just think this whole campaigning thing is going to change all of our lives," she said.

"Well, that's kind of the point, isn't it?"

Emma saw him become instantly absorbed in the speech, the way he did any time he was confronted with the printed word. "You can go read that. I should get unpacked."

"Okay," he said. "And I'm sorry about Rutherford. But don't worry. I have a feeling that everything is going to be just fine. You're gonna love Chadwick." He smiled, and then he was out the door.

Emma looked out the window and sighed. *Easy for him to say,* she thought. Her brother had never had to worry about anything. Things just came to him — straight A's, friends, opportunities to shine. And now she was going to be trapped in the same house, and possibly the same school, with him for the next year, until he went to college. Unless she could go talk some sense into her mom right now.

She left her suitcase unopened on the bed and went to the kitchen, where she found her mom making a pitcher of iced tea.

"Mom?" she began. "About the whole Chadwick thing…You didn't call the school from the car or anything, right?"

Her mom stirred the tea vigorously with a wooden spoon. "I spoke to Mr. Barlow," she said. "He's going to look at your transcript, but it looks like you'll be starting at Chadwick on September fifth."

"What? I thought we were at least going to talk about it!"

"Emma, there is way, way too much going on in this family right now for you to be calling the shots. Especially in light of what you've done." Her mom poured the iced tea into a tall glass. "Chadwick is one of the best schools in the city. And if it weren't for the fact that your brother is such a good student, this would not have been so easy. I hope you remember to thank him."

"*Thank* him?" Emma exploded. "So I can have a daily reminder that I'm not as brilliant and wonderful as he is? I should feel grateful for that?"

"Emma, please stop." Her mother sighed and looked at her watch. "It's time you got in the shower. There are going to be press people there tonight, so I'd like you to look like you made an effort. Do you have a dress?"

That was the final straw. Emma turned on her heels and stormed out of the kitchen.

"Emma!" her mom yelled after her, but Emma kept walking. She'd been home less than twenty minutes and she already wanted to scream. She slammed the door and stood in the center of her room, so angry she was shaking. She should never have tried to sneak into Jeremy's room; she knew that now. But her mom wasn't helping. And here she was, being dragged out to one of her dad's stupid events on top of it, so people could take his picture and go on and on about how great his speech was. And so she could look like the perfect little daughter. Like she'd made an *effort*.

An idea suddenly came to her. She went to her suitcase and unzipped it. Inside she found her toiletries bag and, inside that, the extra box of the purple hair dye she'd used earlier this year. BERRY WONDERFUL, read the name on the box. The picture showed a woman with dark auburn hair, but Emma knew that if she left the color on long enough it would turn out three times that bright.

She picked up the box and glanced at her watch. There was just enough time. She walked into her bathroom and turned on the shower. Her mom wanted her to make an effort? Done.

chapter 4

"I can't believe you did that," her brother said as they walked along the jogging path toward the Central Park Boat Pond. "You've been home for, like, an hour."

Emma ran a hand over her eggplant-colored locks and breathed in the soft summer air. "It's hair dye, Rem. It's not like I got a tattoo on my face."

"Doesn't matter. Mom and Dad are going to freak. And your outfit isn't exactly helping."

Emma glanced down at her super-short metallic skirt and ultra-casual, striped, long-sleeved, boatneck T-shirt. "What you don't know is that this is all very Alexa Chung."

"Who?" Her brother asked.

"Forget it. It's way over your head, Mr. Men's Wearhouse."

Remington smiled at this. He knew that he wasn't the world's hippest dresser. But he looked pretty good tonight, in his dark blue suit. "Just be careful, Em," he said, straightening the knot of his tie.

"You can be your own worst enemy sometimes. We both know that."

Emma let this last comment pass and gazed at the lake up ahead. Its surface was broken here and there by the last few rowboats of the day, skimming across the silvery water. It would have made a gorgeous photo, and she almost took out her iPhone to snap a shot of it. But Remington wouldn't understand what she was doing. For all his brilliance, he could walk out of a Picasso exhibit at MoMA or a Kurosawa movie and have absolutely nothing to say.

At the entrance to the Boathouse restaurant, Remington flashed the invitation their parents had given them. Two hefty security men nodded them in. The room was thick with adults mingling among white linen–covered tables set with flickering hurricane lamps. Inside, a banner hung across the restaurant proclaiming A WEN FUTURE FOR CENTRAL KRAP. Emma focused on the words until she guessed what they really said: A NEW FUTURE FOR CENTRAL PARK. Sometimes being dyslexic was like being a word detective. She just had to make her best guess as to what things actually said.

"I think they're probably in the back," her brother said, taking the lead through the crowd.

As Emma followed she remembered the first time her dad had run for the Senate, when she was seven. The whole family had driven from town to town all over the state, making stops at diners or town halls or even someone's house. She and her brother would play with the other kids while her father spoke to a group of five or fifty. He never got tired, never got bored, even when they hit four different towns in a day. People would tell him terrible things about taxes and unemployment and health care, and he'd listen with superhuman focus and attention. Then he'd give a speech and make people laugh. Even if people started out angry, the event would usually end with them surrounding him, just wanting to shake his hand.

Just like now, Emma thought, as they found him on the patio of the Boathouse, shaking hands, laughing at jokes, and generally spreading his charm around like gooey hot fudge. There were adoring, almost goofy smiles on some of the people's faces tonight, as if her dad were a rock star. Had they done that a year ago? She didn't think so. Then again, the last time she'd seen her dad speak to a crowd had been at West Point, where she'd been too distracted by the male cadets to really notice the way anyone was looking at her father.

"What are we supposed to do?" she asked Remington as they waited outside the patio doors.

"Just wait here," he said. "That way at least we buy some time." He pointed to her hair.

Just then Emma spotted her mom in the crowd. She looked lovely in a sleeveless black shift dress with a gold belt, but she seemed to hang back from her husband. Cocktail chatter wasn't her thing. Her mom was much better at serious talking — deposing a witness, say, or addressing a court of appeals. Emma had no idea how her mom would survive a presidential campaign. A Senate campaign — two of them — had been hard enough on her. New Yorkers had criticized her for having such a high-powered career, for not wearing enough makeup, even for being too skinny. It would probably only get worse now.

After a few minutes a gray-haired man wearing a gold pin in the shape of a leaf in a circle slipped behind the podium.

"Excuse me, everyone," he said into the microphone. "May I have your attention, please? It is our great pleasure tonight to have Senator Adam Conway with us. He is not only a born and bred New Yorker, but a man who believes in change. A man who has proven himself able to cross party lines and make the promise of change a reality. A man who just might be the best hope for this country in the next election."

He was cut off by applause and foot-stomping and yelling. The noise was almost earsplitting. Emma looked at Remington, wondering if he was as affected by all of this as she was. But he didn't seem fazed by it at all.

"But that's not why he's here tonight," the man continued, looking at her father with adoration. "He's here because he has shown a commitment to the environment that has been unparalleled. And when we were searching for someone to speak here tonight, he was the obvious choice."

Emma turned her head suddenly and saw her mom staring at her with a clenched jaw. Or, rather, staring at her hair. *Uh-oh,* she thought, and looked away.

"So without further ado," the man said, "I give you the junior senator of New York, Adam Conway!"

Emma's dad made his way to the podium, waving and smiling. "Ladies and gentlemen," her father said into the microphone. "Parks Commissioner, and my fellow New Yorkers, thank you for having me tonight. I have to say, I've never seen so many people in town on a Sunday in August. What happened? Did they close down the Hamptons?"

The crowd tittered.

"As New Yorkers we understand the importance of green spaces," her dad continued, "and Central Park is New York's greatest resource. I remember coming here every Saturday with my father, begging him to put me on the carousel. Of course, at that time, in the early seventies, it hadn't worked in almost ten years…"

Emma always tuned out a little when her dad made a speech. She was scanning the crowd, looking for a cute guy, when a girl her age caught her attention. There was something familiar about her — curly red hair, a long nose, and big eyes that also seemed to be checking out the crowd. It was Lizzie Summers, Emma realized. Without hesitation, she left her brother's side and began to work her way through the crowd, toward Lizzie. Normally she would have waited for her dad to finish speaking, but after the day she'd had, she needed to see a friendly face, pronto.

"But in all seriousness," said her father, "I think New York City is the perfect microcosm of this country. Its diversity, its work ethic, its refusal to bow to the daily threat of terrorism. In New Yorkers we truly have the best of what it means to be an American. And not a day goes by that I don't feel fortunate to represent this city, and this state, down in Washington. And in conclusion," Adam said, "I'd just like to say that change is possible. We don't have to resign ourselves to ecological disaster. We can live a better life. Starting now. Starting tonight!"

As the crowd began to applaud, Emma walked up behind Lizzie and tapped her on the shoulder.

"Hey, Emma!" Lizzie said, throwing her arms around Emma. She'd grown taller since the last time Emma had seen her, but her hair was still a gorgeous coppery red color and thick with curls. "I was hoping you'd be here," Lizzie said, pulling away from her. "I haven't seen you in forever."

"I know," Emma said. "Thank God you're here. I think we're the only people in here under sixty."

Lizzie smiled. "Your dad gave a great speech. And hey, cool hair. What color is that?"

"Berry Wonderful," Emma said, surreptitiously scanning the room for her mother.

"I would love to dye my hair," Lizzie said. "But it's so thick and crazy it probably would take a day and a half." She twisted a lock around one finger and then let it go. It sprang back into a curl next to her cheek.

"Maybe for one of your modeling shoots," Emma said. "I saw that story in *Rayon*. It was really cool."

"Thanks, but it wasn't really my scene. The people were kind of shallow. Except for this one photographer I met. She's normal. And cool. And so talented. I still model for her sometimes." Her voice trailed off. Emma could see that talking about herself embarrassed her. "So, is your brother here?"

"Yeah, he's lurking around somewhere. Like I said, we're the only people here under sixty."

Lizzie smiled. "He went to Cambridge this summer, right?" she said.

"Yes," Emma said, rolling her eyes.

"The real Cambridge — not an American program, right?"

"Yup," Emma confirmed.

"Wow. He's shaping up to be Chadwick's resident genius."

"Yeah, I'm sure," Emma muttered.

"How's Rutherford?" Lizzie asked, changing the subject. "The last time we hung out you were on your way there."

Emma hesitated. "It was okay. I actually got kicked out this morning."

"Really?" Lizzie looked horrified. "For what?"

"I snuck out of my dorm. To see a guy. And I got busted."

Lizzie looked slightly impressed. "I got suspended last year. For skipping school."

"You did?"

"For a modeling job," Lizzie said. "My parents totally freaked. And I have to admit, it was a dumb move. So, where are you going to go?"

"Go?" Emma asked.

"To school?" Lizzie asked.

Emma grimaced. "My parents want me to go to Chadwick."

"Oh my God, you have to!" Lizzie said, grabbing her arm. "We'll totally take care of you."

"Who will?" Emma asked, almost alarmed at Lizzie's reaction.

"Me and Carina and Hudson. They're my best friends, they're amazing, and they'll *love* you. You have to come."

"Really?"

Lizzie nodded. "Definitely."

Camera flashes lit up the room, and craning her head, Emma saw her dad, her mom, and Remington posing for pictures.

"Whoops," Emma said. "I think I'm supposed to be over there."

Lizzie turned around. "Yeah, you better go," she said.

"I'll be right back," Emma said as she walked away. Moving through the crowd, Emma couldn't stop thinking about what Lizzie had said. She hadn't expected Lizzie to be so welcoming. Maybe going to Chadwick would actually be tolerable.

"Excuse me," she said to a middle-aged couple blocking her path. "Excuse me, please."

Tom Beckett suddenly stepped in front of her, stopping her progress. "There you are," he said, smiling. "You enjoying the party?" Flashes popped behind him.

"Sorry," she said, trying to pass him, "but I think I need to get over there."

"Just wait here," Tom said in his deep, raspy voice. "They shouldn't be more than a minute."

"But I think I'm supposed to be in the pictures," Emma said.

"Actually, we'd rather you weren't. At least, not tonight." Tom gestured to her hair. "I'm sure you understand."

Emma looked at him. "So *you* don't want me in the picture, or *they* don't want me in the picture?" she asked, pointing to her parents.

He gave her an unbearably fake smile. "Both," he said.

For a moment she was too shocked to speak. And then the words slid out of her mouth. "You're a jerk," she said. She turned away from him and melted back into the crowd.

A waiter glided past her with a tray of champagne flutes balanced on his palm. She grabbed one. The waiter didn't even notice. Emma had never drank alcohol, but now seemed like the right time to try it out. She threw her head back and took a big gulp of champagne. The liquid burned her throat. She bent over, coughing.

Her vocal cords felt like they were on fire. But as soon as she could, she took another gulp, just as her mom walked up to her and grabbed the glass out of her hand.

"Emma," she snapped. "Are you *out* of your *mind*?"

Remington walked up to them. "What's going on?"

"You let your sister come here tonight?" Carolyn asked him in a harsh whisper. "Like *this*?" she asked, pointing to Emma's hair.

"Hey, don't blame me," he said. He glanced at the flute in Carolyn's hand and looked at Emma. "Are you *drinking*?"

Her father approached them. "What's going on, Carolyn?" he asked in a careful voice. He stole a glance at Emma.

"I just caught her drinking," she said.

Her father's face went pale. "Take her home," he said to Carolyn. "Now."

Her mom grabbed her by the wrist and began walking toward the door. "Remington, you, too," she said.

"Why do I have to go?" her brother asked.

"Go with your mother," Adam said, and his voice was so low and furious that Remington followed without another word.

As they walked through the restaurant, people stared openly at Emma and her purple hair. By now they knew who she was.

Emma stared straight ahead, her eyes on the door. Outside she could see night falling in the park, and she wondered, for just a moment, if she could somehow tear off toward Sheep Meadow and leave this family once and for all. After all, wouldn't it just make everyone's life easier if she were gone? Nobody would have to dispatch a guy in a dark suit to keep her out of family photos.

Nobody would have to be scandalized by her taking a sip of champagne.

And then something made her look back.

It was Lizzie, hovering near the hostess stand, watching her. There was no judgment on her face. There was almost no expression at all. But just as Emma passed, Lizzie gave Emma a gentle, sympathetic smile, and Emma could have sworn that she waved.

chapter 5

"It was champagne," Emma said as their cab bumped down Lexington Avenue. "I had a *sip.*"

"In front of all those people there," her mother said angrily. "In front of your father. What is the matter with you, Emma? It's like you're intent on embarrassing yourself."

"I'm not embarrassed," Emma said. "*You're* embarrassed. No matter what I do. You didn't even want me in the photos."

"With purple hair?" her mom asked.

"I know you want me to be fake for these things, but I can't help it if I'm just being myself."

"Right, I forgot," said her mom. "Dyeing your hair purple is really getting to the core of who you are."

The cab made a hard right onto Ninetieth Street and Emma slid into her brother, who was being typically silent.

"It's this awning up here, please," Carolyn said to the cabbie as they turned onto Eighty-ninth Street. "Emma, you're grounded until school starts. Do you hear me?"

Emma looked past her mom and didn't say anything.

"I said do you hear me?"

"Yes," Emma replied thickly.

The cab pulled up to the curb.

Remington opened the cab door and he and Emma got out.

Carolyn stayed in the car. "I'll see you at home," she said. She looked at Remington. "Thanks, Rem."

Remington shut the door and the cab sped off. They stood on the curb in awkward silence. "Happy now, Em?" he asked.

Emma followed him into the lobby. "Don't be like that," she muttered. "I didn't do anything to anyone."

"Right. You never do anything to anyone, Emma. It's always our fault, for getting mad."

They got into the elevator and rode up in silence.

"What do *you* have to be mad about?" she asked as the elevator doors opened and he unlocked their front door.

"Because I'm tired of you acting like this," he said, tossing the keys onto the credenza in the foyer. "I *know* you're smarter than this. But you want everyone to think you're some slacker who's obsessed with messing up her life."

"I'm just trying to think for myself. Which is something you could do a little more of, by the way."

Remington's face darkened. "Fine. The next time you want to 'think for yourself,'" he said, hooking his fingers into quotation marks, "don't expect me to feel sorry for you." He disappeared into the hall. A moment later, she heard him close his door.

48

Emma stood alone in the foyer. Her brother's words hung in the air like a bad smell. She hated him. But she also knew that he was almost, *almost*, right. Anger and shame rose up in her throat, making a terrible ache. She went to her room and slammed the door. Hard. With any luck, she thought, she had cracked the old paint.

An hour or so later, she'd changed into jeans and a T-shirt and had watched enough funnyordie.com to put herself in a better mood. But now, as she lay on her bed, listening to the sounds of cars going down the street, the old, creepy thoughts started to come back. Like what if there was no God? What if it was all some massive science experiment that just barely worked, and one day something would snap and it would all end? What if she was just one of billions of people on a planet spinning like mad in some endless universe? What if everyone was truly, completely alone? Fighting with Remington always did this to her. It made her feel anxious and scared and alone. She knew what she needed to do.

She walked to her bedroom door and eased it open. The hall was dark and quiet, but beyond it she could hear the din of CNN and voices in her parents' study. They were home.

Quietly, she tiptoed to her brother's closed door. "Rem?" she whispered, tapping at his door.

"Yeah?" she heard a voice say.

She opened the door. Her brother was in bed, reading *The Autobiography of Mark Twain*.

"I'm sorry," she said. "I just kind of lost it tonight. It's been a really hard day."

Her brother let the massive book flop onto his chest. "It's just hard for me to stand by and watch you do dumb stuff sometimes. I want to understand. I really do. But sometimes it just doesn't make sense."

She kicked at the wheel of his chair. "I'm sorry. I know."

"Okay. Now, please, get out of here. I need to crash. I'm on England time."

She smiled with relief and closed the door. But then she heard her mother's voice coming from the office.

"What a day. First she gets kicked out. Then she turns herself into something out of a video game. And then drinking, *in public*..."

"We used to think that she'd grow out of it," her dad said.

"Well, she's not growing out of it," her mother said. "It's getting worse."

"Just in time for this campaign," her dad said.

"Has she always been like this?" a voice asked, and Emma knew right away who it belonged to: Tom Beckett. In her parents' office. Talking about her. She couldn't believe it.

"It started when Adam moved down to D.C.," said her mom. "She was always a little headstrong, a little stubborn, but that's when she really started acting out. She worshiped Adam. And when he left I just couldn't fit the bill."

"So this is my fault?" her father asked in an irritated voice.

"All right, guys," Tom said. "She just got home. Maybe she'll settle down."

"Or maybe this isn't the best timing," her father said. "If she's going to be this unpredictable..." His words trailed off. "What can we do, Tom?"

Just then a chiming sound came from her bedroom down the hall. It was her cell phone. Emma ran to her room and shut the door. It was a Facebook alert, telling her that Lizzie Summers had just requested to be her friend. She clicked Confirm and then threw the phone on the bed. She sat down next to it, oddly shaken. She wished she hadn't overheard them. There was something in the way her parents and Tom had been discussing her — as if she were a campaign obstacle instead of a person — that made her feel even more anxious than before.

She reached into the suitcase that she still hadn't unpacked and grabbed her journal. *I HATE MY LIFE,* she wrote on a blank page under the date August fifteenth. She flipped forward to Tuesday, September fifth. For the first time ever, she couldn't wait for the first day of school.

chapter 6

"You're probably going to have Mr. Weatherly for homeroom. He's pretty cool, unless you walk in late," Remington counseled Emma as they walked up Eighty-ninth Street in the sunshine.

It was only eight in the morning but it already felt close to eighty degrees. Emma felt her new seersucker kilt brush against her legs. Her first uniform. So far she'd avoided going to a school that required one. She could practically feel her identity start to disappear.

"And definitely make sure you say hi to Mr. Barlow," her brother continued as they crossed Madison Avenue. "He's the head of the Upper School and a super-great guy. Used to be a Marine, so he's got really straight posture and a commanding voice. He's a lot less scary than he looks."

"Uh-huh."

"And you might have Mrs. Bateman for History," he added as they passed an armada of women with strollers. "She's kind of a piece of work. Just remember: Her bark is a lot worse than her bite. Tell her you're my sister."

"I get it. Everyone there loves you," Emma said.

"It's just a friendly place," her brother explained. "And they like having siblings."

Even when they're not as impressive as their brother? Emma wanted to ask, but she didn't say anything.

Despite her nerves, it felt good to finally be starting school. For the past three weeks, her mom had seen to it that Emma hadn't gone anywhere or done anything fun, aside from going to a hair salon to get her hair dyed back to dark brown, and running around the Central Park Reservoir every morning — neither of which exactly qualified as a rollicking good time. While a steady stream of people went in and out of her parents' office, conducting meetings with her dad before he returned to Washington, she stuck to her room, plowing through the Chadwick summer reading list. She picked the shortest books she could find — *The Great Gatsby, Ethan Frome, Washington Square* — but even those took most of her time to get through. She almost texted some of her old city friends from junior high, but she'd deliberately lost touch with everyone when she went off to Rutherford. She'd expected never to come back here. The only person she contacted was Lizzie, whom she texted to say that she was definitely going to Chadwick. Lizzie had sent back a one-word reply: "AWESOME!!!"

Now they turned onto Ninety-first Street and Emma could see a stream of girls in seersucker kilts and boys in white shirts and black pants walking into the beige limestone building at the corner of Fifth Avenue. Across the street were the lush green trees of Central Park.

"Don't worry, Em," Remington said. "They're gonna love you. Just wait."

She managed to give him a smile. Her brother could be pretty cool, sometimes.

They walked into the brightly lit lobby, and a middle-aged female receptionist waved at them from behind her desk.

"Hi, Remington!" she called out.

"Hey, Dori!" he yelled back, and then waved to the security guard who stood by the stairs. She hadn't even had her first class at Chadwick yet, but she could feel her brother's shadow stretching over her already.

"Is this an old house?" she asked, glancing up at the twenty-foot ceilings as they walked up a grand set of stone steps.

"It's an old mansion," Remington said. "This all used to belong to some guy and his two kids. Some parts of it are supposed to be haunted."

"Seriously?" she asked, as they passed a large library stocked with tables and sofas.

"That's what they say," Remington said.

Then they headed up another set of stone steps, to the next floor. "The Upper School is the third floor," Remington said over his shoulder. "Most of your classes'll be here."

"Got it," she said, hoping that none of the students climbing the steps behind them could hear.

At the third floor, he pulled open a set of doors. "Here it is," he said. "The lockers are to the right."

Emma turned in that direction, eager to get away and find Lizzie. But before she could get anywhere she walked straight into somebody. Out of the corner of her eye she saw a wave of steaming coffee leap right out of a cup and splatter all over a sleeve. "Oh!" she said. "Sorry!"

The sleeve belonged to a tall, wiry man with thinning white-blond hair, piercing blue eyes, and unmistakable ramrod-straight posture. Emma gulped. She had a feeling she knew who this was. "I take it you're Miss Conway," the man said, shaking out his sleeve.

"Uh…yes," she said.

"You certainly know how to make an entrance," he said. He handed her his coffee cup. "Take that, would you?" He pulled a Kleenex from his back pocket and began to blot his sleeve. "I need to mop this up."

Remington appeared at her side. "Hey, Mr. Barlow," he said, looking a little nonplussed. "This is my sister, Emma."

"Let me just say," she started. "I'm so happy to finally be here. I've…uh…heard such great things about Chadwick."

"We're happy to have you," Mr. Barlow said, taking the coffee cup from her. "Even if you pose a threat to people walking around with hot beverages." He gave her a friendly wink. "Have a good day, Miss Conway," he said, and strode off down the hall.

Emma watched him go, feeling slightly mortified. But at least he hadn't said anything about Remington being Chadwick's star student. That she wouldn't have been able to handle.

"Don't worry," Remington said. "I think he liked you."

"Really?" she asked, just as someone came up behind Remington and slapped him on the back.

55

"Walker!" Remington said, turning around. "What's up?"

Emma did a double take. Walker Lloyd, her brother's best friend since the seventh grade, had always been cute, but the guy standing in front of her now was gorgeous. African-American, with large brown eyes and close-cropped hair, Walker looked like he'd shot up at least several inches in the past fifteen months — and packed on ten pounds of muscle. "How was Cambridge?" he said to Remington. "I hope you're glad you took my slot!"

"Hey, you turned *them* down, remember?" Remington said, grasping Walker's hand in a bro-style shake. "How was Stanford?"

"Amazing," he said. "And look who's here," Walker said, turning to Emma. "So your brother finally convinced you to come to Chadwick, huh?" he asked, showing a row of perfect white teeth as he smiled.

"It wasn't easy, but I managed to do it," Remington said.

"Yeah, I finally caved," she said, leaning forward to hug him. "How are you?" As Walker's muscled arms wrapped themselves around her, Emma couldn't help but feel a shiver pass through her. "Long time no see, Walk."

"If you need anything, and your brother doesn't want to help you, just ask. We all know that he can have his head up his butt."

"Hey!" Remington said, punching Walker in the arm.

Walker and Remington had always been competitive, even as kids. Emma could remember each of them trying to outdo the other in everything — doing the biggest cannonball off the dock at the lake house, serving a perfect ace on the tennis court, getting the best GPA every semester. She'd always thought it funny that guys could be that openly competitive with each other and still be friends. Girls could be friends while competing with each other, but not in such a good-natured way.

"Oh, I meant to tell you," Walker said to Remington. "They're not gonna give us the theater. So we're back in the library."

"That's lame," her brother said. "But whatever."

"Are you gonna join?" Walker asked Emma.

"Join what?" she said, too distracted to have figured out what they were talking about.

"Speech and debate," Walker said. "I've seen you argue before. You'd probably be great at it."

The idea of jumping aboard Remington's favorite after-school activity was less than appealing. And it was also embarrassing to remember just how much arguing she'd done in front of Walker, usually with her mom, over clothes and makeup. "No thanks," she said. "Maybe next semester."

"So you'll be okay, right?" her brother asked her. "You know where you're going?"

"I'll be fine," she said. "Bye!"

She walked away feeling light-headed and a little giggly, the way she always did when she was around a cute guy, but she shook it off. This was Walker Lloyd, the guy who had known her only as his best friend's annoying little sister. The guy who had watched her get into a screaming match with her mom at the dinner table about how much lipstick she could wear. The guy who remembered when she wore clear braces. It was ridiculous to have a crush on him, especially when she was surrounded on all sides by new male faces.

With that in mind, she checked out her new schoolmates as

she made her way down the hall. They seemed to be pretty much the same as the kids at boarding school: The girls walked in twos and threes, talking excitedly with one another, while the guys seemed to stay put in clusters here and there, laughing and yelling at the top of their lungs. Everyone seemed so much more keyed up here than the kids at Rutherford. Maybe it was the city. Or maybe it was that people didn't have to spend every waking hour together, like they did at boarding school.

Suddenly she noticed a girl walking toward her, smiling at her as if they knew each other. She had blond-streaked hair and a smattering of freckles on her snub nose, and her brown eyes seemed lit up from behind. "I'm Carina!" the girl said, extending her hand. "Carina Jurgensen. Lizzie told me you were starting today. You're Emma, right? I'm your angel."

"Angel?" Emma asked.

"Don't worry, it's just what they call a guide around here," she said, reaching into her backpack. She pulled out a folded piece of paper and gave it to Emma. "Here's your schedule. We've made sure that you're in class with one of us at all times."

"Us?" Emma asked.

"Me, Lizzie, and Hudson. We're all sort of your angels, I guess," she said, her brown eyes shining.

Jurgensen, Emma thought. She knew she'd heard that name before. And then she remembered: Carina's dad had to be Karl Jurgensen, the man who owned Metronome Media and its gazillion newspapers, magazines, and social-networking sites. "Oh. Cool," Emma said, slightly amazed at how down-to-earth Carina seemed.

"Here's Hudson." Carina started waving her arms. "Hey!"

Emma turned to see another girl walking quickly toward them wearing a huge smile. She was very pretty, with light brown skin, green eyes, and dark, wavy hair. And she'd managed to dress up her blue kilt with purple tights, an ivory-colored blouse with diaphanous sleeves, and dangly silver earrings. *Wait,* Emma thought. *This is Hudson Jones. As in Holla Jones.* She'd seen Hudson's picture countless times in *Us Weekly* and *Star.* And now here she was, standing right in front of Emma. *This is one heck of a school,* Emma thought.

"Hey!" Carina called out to her. "Emma's here!"

Hudson glided up to them. "I'm Hudson," she said, giving Emma a hug. "Lizzie's told us so much about you."

"She has?" Emma asked.

"Sure," Hudson said, as if it were the most natural thing in the world for Lizzie to gush about her. She pushed her hair behind one ear, and Emma saw that her earrings were actually serpents with red stones for eyes.

"You're going to really like it here," Carina offered.

"Yeah, Chadwick is a really friendly place," Hudson said. "Except for a few people," she added as her gaze wandered past Emma. "Incoming."

The "incoming" in question was another girl who strutted down the hall, her extra-short kilt swinging like a bell over her slim, tan legs. Perfect, frizz-free auburn curls bounced up and down on her shoulders, the result of what had to be a professional blowout every few days. "Hey, everyone," she said in a way that seemed to imply that she barely had any time to chat. Even so, she stood right next to them.

"Hey, Ava," Hudson said after an awkward pause. "How was your summer?"

"Oh, you know, Southampton, tennis camp in Florida, blah blah blah," Ava said with a sigh. "But we did take an awesome family trip to Kenya. And I got some super-cool woven bags. Everything's so cheap there."

Nobody seemed to know what to say to this. "This is Emma," Carina said. "She's starting today."

Ava finally looked at Emma and yawned into her hand. "Oh," she said, looking Emma up and down. "Where'd you transfer from?"

"Rutherford," Emma said.

"Really?" Ava asked, sounding shocked. "Why would you leave?"

"I just felt like a change," Emma said coolly.

"She's Remington's sister," Carina added.

"Oh," Ava said, in a much nicer voice. She looked at Emma more intently. "We should have a welcome party for you or something. And invite your brother's friends."

"Uh, sure." *So she's into Remington,* Emma thought. *What a shocker.*

"Hey, Emma. Do you need to find your locker?" Carina asked, already steering her away.

Emma could tell that this was a strategic move to get away from Ava. "Actually, yeah."

"Okay, we'll see you in homeroom," Carina said. "Bye, Ava."

"Bye," Ava said, just as a trio of girls floated over to claim her. Emma didn't get a good look at them, but they all seemed to be wearing the same amount of makeup and jewelry as Ava was.

"Meet Ava Elting and the Icks," Hudson whispered as they walked down the hall. "Ilona, Cici, and Kate. Or Icks for short."

"We were all praying Ava would go to boarding school this year," Carina said as they walked.

"She's totally obsessed with boarding school," Hudson said.

"Well, I can tell you right now, if she'd gone to Rutherford with that hairdo and eye makeup they would have never stopped laughing," Emma said, which caused both Hudson and Carina to crack up.

After figuring out her locker combination, she followed Hudson and Carina to a cluster of desks in homeroom. A quick sweep of the room turned up a couple of cute boys, but nobody as good-looking as Walker. She thought of asking Hudson and Carina about him, but she figured she should wait and feel out the scene first.

Just before the bell rang Lizzie ran in, followed by a cute guy. Her hazel eyes were radiant, and it didn't take Emma long to figure out that the cute guy was Lizzie's boyfriend. "You're here!" Lizzie cried, leaning down to give Emma a hug. "Todd, this is Emma!" she said to the guy. "She's new."

"Hi there," Todd said in a faint English accent. "Lizzie's told me so much about you."

"Thanks," Emma said. She wondered if that included getting marched out of the Boathouse for swigging champagne, but she didn't ask.

"So you got rid of the purple?" Lizzie whispered to Emma, glancing up at her hair.

"I told you, my parents freaked," she said.

61

Lizzie shrugged. "This color looks good on you, too," she whispered, as Mr. Weatherly began to call attendance.

With his pointy chin and long nose, Mr. Weatherly reminded Emma of a character from one of those *Doonesbury* comics her dad used to love. "Angelides," he called out.

From a few rows away, a voice said, "Here."

"Brennan."

"Here," said a boy toward the back of the room.

"Conway," Mr. Weatherly finally called.

Emma raised her hand. "Here," she said.

Mr. Weatherly looked up from his class list. "Emma?" he said, his face lighting up. "Are you Remington's sister?"

"Yes," she said, feeling herself start to blush. Every head in the room had turned.

"Your brother's quite a student," he said. "When I have you next year, I'll be expecting great things."

"I can't wait," she said. She hadn't meant to sound so sarcastic, but it was too late. A few people giggled. Mr. Weatherly frowned and picked up the class list again.

Carina punched her in the arm. "Hi-lar-ious," she whispered, and Emma smiled with relief. People had thought it was funny.

"Did that bother you? What Weatherly said?" Hudson asked after homeroom, as she and Emma walked to their first class.

"No," Emma said. "I guess it just comes up a lot."

"Yeah, your brother *is* kind of a rock star around here," Hudson said. "In case you didn't know."

Emma took out her schedule. "So what's American Political Structures?" she asked, changing the subject.

"Oh. That's Mrs. Bateman. No one knows how old she is. And she calls on people. All the time."

"But it's the first day of class," Emma said as they turned into the classroom. "How much are we supposed to know?"

Hudson made a face. "A lot."

As they filed into the classroom Mrs. Bateman stood with her back to the desks, writing on the board. Tall and solid, with hips that looked like they could do some serious damage to any furniture she bumped up against, Mrs. Bateman wrote quickly, letting the dry-erase marker squeak mercilessly against the board. Her large hand scrawled two words: CAMRALIEB LAUREGISTLE. Emma squinted at them, willing them to rearrange themselves into something she could recognize. But nothing happened.

"All right," Mrs. Bateman snapped, wheeling around on her orthopedic shoes. "We have a lot of material and very little time, thanks to this school's observance of every possible holiday, so let's start." She scanned the room with her deep-set eyes. Emma could see what Hudson had meant about her age: Mrs. Bateman looked like she could have been in her fifties, or so ancient that she could have possibly been friends with Ben Franklin. "Who can tell me the main difference between the House of Representatives and the Senate?" she barked. "Anyone?"

It was an easy question. Emma looked around the room. People doodled on their notebooks or secretly texted on their cell phones, hidden inside their book bags. She caught a dark-haired guy in the corner staring at her. She managed to smile at him before he looked away.

"Miss Conway."

Emma turned around.

Mrs. Bateman fixed her unblinking eyes on her. "Can you enlighten us, please?"

Emma felt her heart start to pound. "Uh, what's the question again?" she asked.

"What is the difference between the Senate and the House of Representatives?" Mrs. Bateman replied.

"Oh, that's easy," Emma said. "Size. The Senate is made up of only two senators per state. The House has a different number of representatives, based on the population of each state."

Mrs. Bateman rocked on her orthopedic shoes. "What else?" she asked, her beady eyes darting around the room to take in other people's reactions.

"Well, they're in charge of different stuff," said Emma. "The House has control over certain things that the Senate doesn't, like spending," Emma said. "But the House always needs the Senate to pass its bills."

"And?" Mrs. Bateman asked, her eyes on the back of the room.

"Senators are elected every six years, and representatives every two."

"And what does the word *bicameral* mean?" Mrs. Bateman asked, pointing to the word on the blackboard that Emma hadn't been able to decipher.

Emma knew exactly what *bicameral* meant, but she'd given enough right answers for one morning. It was time to get out of the spotlight. "I think it means the kind of glasses my grandmother wears?" she asked.

Laughter broke out through the room.

Mrs. Bateman scowled. "No, Miss Conway, it doesn't mean

that." She gave Emma a disgusted look, then turned to the board. "It means two houses, which is exactly how our Congress is structured," she said, drawing a long line down the board. "A House of Representatives and a Senate. Which Miss Conway so deftly delineated for us a few moments ago."

The laughter was still audible, and when Emma glanced behind her she saw the dark-haired boy again. He was still laughing, and this time he looked right at her with a big grin. She smiled at him again. *Whew,* she thought. She'd cut out just in time. One more right answer and people would have gotten the wrong idea about her. They would have thought she was like Remington. And that was the worst thing that could happen. Because then she would have certainly disappointed them.

chapter 7

"I'm home!" Emma let her heavy book bag slide down her arm and land on the floor with a satisfying thud. "Anyone?"

There wasn't a sound. From the foyer she could see the door to her dad's office standing open, revealing a dark, empty room. The dining room table, through the glass doors, was bare, swept clean of papers and laptops. Emma knew that her mom was at work. Her brother had swim practice. Her dad had apparently left to go somewhere with Tom Beckett and Shanks and his army of aides. For the first time since her return from Rutherford, she had the apartment to herself.

She kicked off her shoes, leaving them next to her bag on the foyer floor, and headed to the kitchen. For the past two hours she'd been thinking about the Fig Newtons she knew her mom had hidden in one of the high cabinets. She pulled them off the shelf and shook some onto a plate, then poured herself a glass of iced tea from the pitcher in the fridge. Right now all she wanted to do was veg out in front of the big flat-screen in her dad's office.

She padded into the room. Framed photos of her dad with Bill Clinton, George Bush, and Barack Obama, plus a slew of senators, foreign leaders, and the occasional movie star, hung on the walls. Another frame held a mounted newspaper clipping of the *New York Times* bestseller list, with his book occupying the number one slot. Emma settled herself onto the couch, placed the plate of cookies on the coffee table, and clicked the remote and saw that *100 Craziest Celebrity Feuds* was just coming back from commercial. Sometimes these shows could be incredibly lame, but right now it felt good to just zone out for a few minutes.

She was just getting comfortable when she heard the front door open. "Emma?" her father called. "Are you home?"

"In here!" she yelled.

Her dad came to the door. "Can you come out here, please?" he asked. "There's someone I'd like you to meet."

"But I just started watching this," she said.

Her father looked sideways at the TV. "What on earth is this?" he asked, looking at a clip of two starlets punching each other.

"Nothing, I'm coming," she said as she got up from the couch and walked into the foyer.

Tom Beckett stood next to a woman in her thirties with round blue eyes and perfect, glowing skin. But her boxy red suit and nude stockings screamed Washington, D.C., as did her frosted blond hair, which had been hair-sprayed into a helmet around her face.

"This is Vanessa Dreesen," her dad said, gesturing to her. "Vanessa works with families who are going to be campaigning."

"Hello, Emma," said the woman. She had the confident but slightly abrasive voice of a newscaster. "It's very good to meet you."

Emma just stared at the woman's outstretched hand. Her nails were French manicured. "Hi," she said.

"Vanessa would like to talk to you for a few minutes," said her dad.

"Just me? About what?"

"About whatever you'd like to talk about," Vanessa said with a merry smile.

"She just wants to talk to you," Tom said. "She's very good."

"At what?" Emma asked.

"Use my office," Adam said, pointing to his study. "We'll wait out here."

"Great," Vanessa said. She let Emma walk into the room first and then she closed the door. Emma got a strong whiff of Chanel No. 5. It wasn't Emma's least favorite scent, but this woman wore a *lot* of it. Vanessa dropped down onto the couch and held her large white leather shoulder bag in her lap. "So," she said. "How are you?"

"Fine," Emma said warily.

Vanessa paused. "Is something wrong?"

Emma leaned against her dad's desk.

"I'm just here to talk to you," Vanessa said.

"Are you a shrink?" Emma asked. "Because my parents don't really believe in them."

"No," Vanessa said, smiling. "I'm an image consultant."

"A what?"

Vanessa cleared her throat. "I prepare families — the candidates, their spouses, their children — for campaigns," she said. "It can be quite a stressful adjustment, as you can imagine." She flashed her toothy smile again. "And some people just aren't ready for it."

"So you're here because I'm not ready for it," Emma supplied.

"Very few people are." Vanessa tapped her nails on her bag. "But in this case, your parents are worried you're unhappy. And your father wants to know that he can count on you."

"To do what?" Emma challenged.

"Well, for one thing, to behave in a more appropriate manner when you're out in public." Vanessa crossed her legs and pulled a small pad of paper from her purse. "They tell me that you were caught drinking alcohol at an event a few weeks ago."

"For, like, two minutes," Emma said.

"And that you deliberately dyed your hair before the event," she added. "And that you have a history of being unpredictable when you're out with them. Would you say that any of that is true?"

Emma felt her chest get tight. "Sounds like you're pretty sure of your story."

"I can help you, Emma," said Vanessa. "I've done it for a lot of other people. And if you let me, I can do it for you."

"No thanks," she said. "And I think it's pretty lame that you're here at all. I had no idea my parents were so terrified of what people think."

"What people think has a lot of power, Emma," Vanessa said calmly. "Especially in politics." She pulled an ivory business card from her wallet and handed it to Emma. "Just in case you change your mind…"

"Thanks, but I won't," Emma said, ignoring the business card. She walked to the door and threw it open. Thankfully the hall was deserted. She picked up her book bag, stomped to her room, and closed the door.

She needed to talk to someone. Anyone. She reached into her book bag and grabbed her cell. Carina and Hudson had both given her their numbers earlier at school, and she already had Lizzie's.

But she barely knew those girls. And what if they sided with this Vanessa character? What if they thought that she was weird or out of control? Lizzie had seen what had happened at the Boathouse. And plus, she couldn't tell them about her dad's plans, anyway.

"Emma," her dad said through the door. "Can I come in?"

She opened the door. He stood in front of her, looking guilty. Apparently Vanessa had given him the play-by-play.

"I can't believe you did that to me," she said.

He walked into her room and shut the door. "We just want to help you, Emma. We're all going to need some help once this starts —"

"But me most of all, huh?" she interrupted.

"I'm just trying to make this easier on you," he said, sitting down on the edge of her bed.

"No, Dad, you're trying to make this easier on *you*," she said. "That's what this is all about. She basically told me."

Her father patiently glanced up at the ceiling, as if he just needed to wait out another tantrum. "Emma, please —"

"Do you have to do this right now?" she asked. "I'm *fifteen*. Can't you just wait a couple years? Would that really be the end of the world?"

"When you're older, maybe you'll understand why now is the right time," he said. "But trust me that it is."

"But why do you need to be president? Why can't you just be a senator? What's wrong with that?"

Adam folded his arms and sighed, as if he were almost at a loss for words. "The fact that I've decided to do this doesn't mean I don't love you or care about you," he said carefully. "Your mother and I talked about this at length. We know what the risks are. And we're trying to minimize them."

"Yeah, by getting some Barbie doll to give me a makeover," she said, turning over onto her side.

She heard her father sigh and stand up. "I think we're having dinner early tonight, so get some homework done," he said.

A moment later she heard the door close behind him. Emma stayed on her side for a while, watching a flock of pigeons roost on the windowsill of the opposite building. Had she really thought that she'd be able to change his mind? Of course she couldn't. And like any good politician, he'd totally dodged her last question. *It doesn't mean I don't love you or care about you. We're trying to minimize the risks.* Blah, blah, blah.

She sat up and went over to Archie's tank, then lifted him out gently. She watched him twist and turn for a while on her bedspread. He was so lucky, she thought. Nobody would ever try to change him. Nobody expected a snake to be any different than what it was.

chapter 8

"So...what'd you think of the first week?" Lizzie asked as she and Emma walked out of the Astor Place subway station and up into the hot September afternoon.

Emma blinked as her eyes adjusted to the brightness. There were so many people on the street that it was hard to even see what street they were on. She forgot how crowded it could get downtown on a Saturday.

"I'd say that the first week was pretty good," she said, reaching into her bag and pulling out a pair of sunglasses. "Of course I have you to thank for that."

"Come on. Didn't we have to sit at the same table for, like, three Thanksgivings in a row? It was the least I could do," Lizzie said as she swiped on some ChapStick. "So, we can go down St. Marks Place," she said, pointing across the street. "Or we can go west and check out Joyce Leslie."

Emma felt the sun beat down on her shoulders, exposed by the halter top of her red and blue chevron-printed sundress. When Lizzie had texted her that morning asking her if she wanted to go shopping in the Village, she'd jumped at the chance. This would technically be the first Saturday she was allowed out of the house. Miraculously Carolyn had agreed to let her go, even though she'd made her promise to be home by five.

Emma looked south down the long stretch of Lafayette, past the marquee for something called Buel Man Group. *Blue Man Group,* she corrected herself. "Let's go down St. Marks," she said, stepping off the curb.

"But the light's about to change," Lizzie said.

"So?" Emma grabbed Lizzie's wrist and pulled her into the street. "We can make it!" They ran across just as the light changed and cars began to stream toward them up Lafayette Street.

"We're gonna get hit!" Lizzie yelled.

"Nope!" she yelled, pulling Lizzie up onto the curb just as a taxi raced by. "We just made it!"

"Whoa," Lizzie said, as they walked down the next block. "You should be on the track team or something."

Emma laughed as she caught her breath. "I guess I'm a little impatient," she said as they crossed Third Avenue.

"Uh, yeah," Lizzie said.

"Wait," Emma said, stopping in front of a deli on the corner. "Look at this. Have you ever seen so much of this stuff in your life?"

The racks were hung with more tourist trinkets than Emma had ever seen in one place: I LOVE NY baseball hats, I LOVE NY T-shirts, fanny packs printed with the Empire State Building and

73

the New York skyline, even tube socks printed with the Statue of Liberty.

"It's like a tourist's paradise," Lizzie said.

"I have an idea," Emma said. "Let's buy a bunch of stuff and wear it. Like, all of it."

Lizzie burst out laughing. "Are you serious?"

"Yeah!" Emma said. "Why not?"

"Because we'll look like idiots," Lizzie said.

Emma grabbed an I LOVE NY hat in a blinding shade of white and put it on. "That's the point!"

Ten minutes later both of them were swathed in some of the brightest, whitest, and most emphatic New York tourist regalia on the market. Emma paid for the gear and then adjusted her I LOVE NY hat and her Chrysler Building–shaped sunglasses. "Ready?" she asked just before they walked through the door.

Lizzie twisted her fanny pack to face front and rolled up the sleeves of her Statue of Liberty T-shirt. "Ready."

Emma pushed open the door. A woman walking by with a cell phone to her ear took one look at them and laughed.

"People are looking at us," Lizzie murmured.

"Just go with it," Emma said. "Oh, hold on." She walked straight up to a twentyish guy with a pierced ear and a shaved head. "Excuse me," she said to him. "Would you take our picture, please?"

The bald hipster took a moment to check out her clothes. "O-kaaay," he said.

Emma gave him her iPhone. "We'd just like to remember being here," she said, moving to stand next to Lizzie.

74

He held up the phone to position the lens. "Uh, where are you guys from?" he asked.

"Uptown," Emma chirped.

Lizzie burst out laughing.

The hipster seemed a little confused, but he took several shots of them anyway.

After they'd walked around like that for a couple hours, drawing incredulous stares from most of the people they passed, they peeled off their hats and glasses and went to sit in Tompkins Square Park.

"Okay, that was hilarious," Lizzie said, sitting down on a green iron bench. "I haven't laughed like that in a long, loooong time. You're really funny."

"I try," Emma said, looking down at the shots they'd taken on her iPhone. "These sunglasses are classic. Maybe I'll wear them to school."

"So you like it at Chadwick? Or do you miss Rutherford?" Lizzie asked, twisting her hair into a knot and securing it with an elastic.

"No, I like Chadwick, I think," Emma said. She closed her eyes and heard the sound of an ice-cream truck inching its way up Seventh Street. "The hard part is being at home. I don't really fit in with the family. In case that wasn't obvious."

"I'm sure they don't think that," said Lizzie.

"Yeah, they do," Emma said. "It's like the three of them raided a Banana Republic outlet and I'm the freak in the Doc Martens. They even got this image consultant to speak to me."

As soon as she said it, Emma knew she'd made a mistake.

"An image consultant?" Lizzie asked, turning to face her. "Because of your *clothes*?"

Emma pulled on a strand of hair and began to twist it with her finger. "Can I tell you something? And will you promise to not tell anyone? Even Carina and Hudson?"

"Okay," Lizzie said. From her serious expression Emma could tell that she meant it.

"My dad is going to run for president next year."

Lizzie just looked at her. "What?"

"Yeah. President."

"When is he going to announce it?"

"January, February, something like that."

"Wow," Lizzie said, looking off into the park. Emma noticed that her right leg bopped up and down. "He's not even my dad and I'm in shock."

"I'm trying not to think about it."

"But I still don't get it. Why did they bring in an image consultant?" Lizzie asked.

"Because my dad's evil chief strategist thinks I'm an embarrassment. He wouldn't even let me get my picture taken with them that night at the Boathouse. Like I'm someone who needs to be hidden. And then you might have seen me getting marched out of there for drinking champagne..."

"But an image consultant," Lizzie said. "All because of that night?"

"Well, there's been some other stuff," she admitted. "Like this one time, when I gave a photographer the finger."

"You did *not*," Lizzie said, her hazel eyes widening.

Emma shrugged. "He was being annoying. And then there was this other time that I was texting someone during one of my dad's speeches. Like *that's* a crime against humanity."

Lizzie furrowed her brow. For a moment Emma was afraid she was being judged. "Well, do *you* think you need to change?" Lizzie asked carefully.

Emma shifted on the bench as she thought about it. "I guess it would be nice for them to trust me, and not treat me like I'm some kind of problem kid. But why do I have to pretend to be America's Perfect Daughter so my dad can get elected? It just feels dishonest."

"Is that what they want you to do?" she asked.

Emma wasn't sure how to answer that. She had a feeling they did, but it seemed hard to admit that. Instead she watched a guy on a patch of grass near the dog run, juggling — and dropping — tennis balls. He seemed to be just learning. "All I know is that I refuse to be different just because of my dad and his job. It's not my fault he decided to do this. Why should I base who I am on what he does for a living?"

Lizzie shrugged. "I guess you shouldn't," she said.

Emma took out a pack of orange-flavored Trident Splash and handed a piece to Lizzie. "Have you had this yet? This stuff is the bomb."

Lizzie laughed. "I can't believe you just said 'bomb.'"

"Hell, yeah," she said. "I'm starting to think people don't say that enough. I'm bringing it back."

Lizzie laughed some more as they stood up from the bench and started to walk out of the park.

"Don't worry, I won't say a thing," said Lizzie. "But Carina and Hudson would never tell anyone. You can always tell us secrets. As long as they're totally juicy, of course," she said, laughing. There was a chime, and she pulled her phone out of her bag.

"Who was that?" Emma asked.

"Todd. He's with his mom today." Quickly she tapped out a message to him. "She came in from London for the start of the trial."

"What trial?"

"Todd's dad." Lizzie put her phone back into her bag as they headed toward a cute, French-looking coffee shop. "He was arrested last year for stealing money from his company. Lots of money. Like a hundred million dollars."

"Did he?" Emma asked.

Lizzie shrugged. "He's saying he didn't. But if you go over to his place, it's kind of easy to believe."

"What does Todd think?" Emma asked.

Lizzie sighed. "Todd's not his dad's biggest fan. But he seems to think he didn't do it, either."

They walked into the coffee shop and a wave of frigid air-conditioning hit Emma in the face. A Jack Johnson song came over the speakers. "When does the trial start?" she asked Lizzie.

"Monday," Lizzie said, dropping her voice as they walked to the counter. "I just feel so sorry for Todd. He's trying so hard not to show it, but I know this is all killing him."

As Emma surveyed a row of muffins behind the glass, she tried to imagine being in Todd's shoes for a moment. Having a father who might be a criminal definitely made her situation seem a little trivial.

"Hey, I didn't mean to bring you down or anything," Lizzie said, smiling. "You okay?"

"Sure," Emma said.

Lizzie checked her watch. "Okay. After this how about we stop in Lord of the Fleas?"

"Totally," Emma said, giving her new friend a high five.

"Maybe the best thing you can do right now," Lizzie said, "is *not* go to Banana Republic."

Emma pulled out her Chrysler Building sunglasses and slipped them on. "I hear that."

chapter 9

By the time Emma walked into the lobby of her building, her feet ached so much that she had to sit down on the threadbare sofa and slip off her sandals. She and Lizzie had gone into possibly every cool boutique east of Third Avenue, and in just a couple of hours she'd accumulated three big shopping bags and two blisters. All she wanted to do was take a nice long nap.

But as soon as she opened the door to her apartment she knew that a nap wasn't in the cards. Enormous vases of white roses stood on the credenza and the small table by the front door. The smell of her mom's mushroom puffs wafted from the kitchen. A cream and blue silk tablecloth covered the dining room table. It was pretty obvious: Her parents were having a party.

"Okay, I want these scattered across the table," her mother said as she walked out of the kitchen holding a bag of votive candles. A cater-waiter followed her — a hot cater-waiter, Emma couldn't help noticing.

"Just on the dining room table and in the living room," Carolyn directed, pointing to the living room. "But don't light them yet. People won't be here 'til six." She brushed some black hair out of her eyes and looked right at Emma. "Honey, can you please put on that yellow dress we got you at Banana Republic last year? And those nice gold drop earrings?"

"What's going on?" Emma asked, mortified that the cater-waiter had just heard that.

"We're having some people over," she said. She held out the bag of votives to the waiter, who took them and disappeared into the living room. "People who might contribute to the campaign," she said under her breath.

"Rich people," Emma prompted.

"Potential donors," she corrected. "Tom says this is all your dad should be doing right now. Raising money."

"But why do we have to be involved?" Emma asked.

"Because we're his family," Carolyn said firmly. A sudden clatter came from the kitchen and she grimaced. "Just get cleaned up. They'll be here in less than an hour." She looked down at Emma's shopping bags. "I hope those things were on sale."

Emma rolled her eyes. "They were basically flea markets," she said.

Her mom hurried to the kitchen, and Emma went straight to her brother's door. It was closed, which meant that he was already home. "It's me!" she yelled, pounding the door once with her fist.

Remington opened the door. His hair was still wet from the shower, and he wore a checked blue button-down shirt and dress slacks, which actually looked ironed. "Hey, Em. What's up?"

"Why do we have to be at this party?" she asked, stepping into his room and closing the door.

"Because they want us to be," her brother said. He grabbed a necktie off his desk and walked to his mirror.

"You're wearing a *tie*?"

He gave her a look. "It's a party, Emma. Mom wants us to look nice."

"I just don't get why we have to be part of this," she said. "This is Dad's thing. What difference does it make if we're there or not?"

"Just walk up to people, shake their hands, and talk to them about the weather and what grade you're in," he said, passing one end of his necktie through a knot. "You're better with people than you think. And it's not like you have to say that much at the end."

"What do you mean, say that much at the end?" she asked.

"Dad thinks it would be nice for us to say a few words. You know, about our generation. The problems we face."

"Are you *kidding* me?" she exclaimed, sitting down on the bed. "We have to make a speech?"

"Em, calm down," he said, sitting down next to her. "He just sprang this on me, too. It's not like I have anything great to say."

"Yeah, right, Captain of Speech and Debate."

"Look, just put on a dress, and don't dye your hair," he said, smiling. "You'll be fine."

She went to her room, kicked off her sandals, and shut the door. Talk about her generation? Was he serious? She hated how people talked about generations, as if everyone who was born within the same five-year span was the same person or something. It was ridiculous. On the other hand, maybe she could just get up there in front of everyone and tell the truth: *Hi, everyone. I guess you could say the* real *problem affecting me right now is that my dad has decided to put all of us on the world stage, and I'm about to never have a private moment again…*

After a quick shower she went to her closet and found the daffodil-colored dress her mom had mentioned. Yellow was her least favorite color, but for some reason, her mom loved it on her. Probably because it was exactly like something she would have worn. Sighing, she pulled it off the hanger and slipped it on. But to make up for the dress she gave herself a quick manicure with her favorite polish, which was the color of dried blood. And she gave her eyes an extra helping of purple liner. Her mom could make her put on a dumb dress, but she hadn't said anything about cosmetics.

Out in the foyer, the doorbell rang, and then rang again. She heard happy voices of greeting, mostly male. After listening to the doorbell ring several times, she finally forced herself out of her room. It was time to get this over with.

She reached the living room and edged her way inside. Her parents' guests all seemed to be in their fifties and sixties, and were engrossed in conversation with one another. Her mom and dad stood in the back of the room, chatting with an African-American man who Emma knew was the CEO of a huge Internet conglomerate.

"Mini-quiche?" asked the very cute cater-waiter, stopping in front of her with a tray and a knowing smile.

She grabbed one and a napkin. "Thanks," she said, giving him a smile in return, but he moved on to a woman with a Botoxed forehead.

She chewed her mini-quiche. Maybe if she stood here and ate, she would look like she belonged here. Or maybe if she just slipped out, she thought, nobody would notice. Slowly, she started to creep toward the door. And then she saw Walker come into the room. He looked handsome and grown-up in a purple-and-gray-striped button-down shirt and gray tie, and in his hands he held a bouquet of white roses.

"Walker!" she yelled, causing some of the guests to look her way.

With a smile, he waded past some of the guests and came to stand at her side.

"What are you doing here?"

"Rem invited me. Sorry I'm late." He handed her the flowers. "I brought these for your mom. I know they're her favorite."

As she held them she imagined for a moment that Walker had brought them for her. Then she put the thought out of her mind. "So I take it you know about my dad?"

"Rem told me this week. With your parents' okay, of course. Not that I'm surprised. I mean, we were all kind of expecting it."

Emma just leaned down and smelled the flowers.

"So...um, how was your first week at Chadwick?" he asked, taking a glass of San Pellegrino water from a passing cater-waiter.

"It was pretty good. I think I can see why you and Rem like it so much. I guess I thought it was just for total nerds like you guys," she teased.

He laughed. "So you still think I'm a nerd?" he asked.

"I don't know," she answered. "I mean, you still get a four-point-oh every semester, right? And what did you get on your SAT? A twenty-three sixty?"

Walker blushed. "Twenty-three forty," he said.

"Nerd," she teased.

"Like you're Miss Slacker," he said back to her. "Didn't you get awards in math at your last school in the city?"

"That was a fluke," she said. It was kind of annoying that Walker knew so much about her past.

"Hey, man," Remington said, coming over to them. "Thanks for coming!"

"You bet," said Walker. "You sure it's okay that I'm here?"

"Of course. Come over and meet the CEO of Time Warner."

As Remington led him away, Walker looked back at Emma. "See you," he said. For a moment it looked as if he didn't want to leave her. And then the two of them disappeared.

Emma stood there holding the flowers, until it occurred to her to give them to one of the waiters. *Walker thinks I'm smart*, she thought. *So why was I trying so hard to tell him he was wrong?*

Suddenly there was the chiming of a fork against a glass, and Emma turned to see her father trying to get everyone's attention.

"So, before I bend everyone's ear," he said, speaking above the noise of the crowd, "I would just like to thank you all for coming here on such short notice."

The guests immediately stopped talking, and stepped back a few feet to give her father a stage.

"This is a very exciting time for me, and for my family," he said, "and we wanted you all to be the first few people to hear about what we've got planned. And of course a few bucks to get us started wouldn't hurt, either."

The guests laughed. Emma had to admit that he had very good comedic timing.

"And I also want to thank my lovely wife, Carolyn," he continued, "who very graciously decided to host this event at the last minute, before I go back down to Washington."

Her mom came to stand next to her dad. She looked different with her hair swept up in a topknot, and with eye shadow and mascara on. "After twenty years, I think I'm used to my husband being spontaneous," she quipped, eliciting some chuckles.

"And I'd also like you all to meet my children," her dad said. "First is my son, Remington, who's standing over there."

Her brother waved from his spot next to the piano.

"He studied History and English at Cambridge this summer, and now he's in his senior year at the Chadwick School, where he captains the swim team and the speech and debate team."

Impressed *ooh*s and *aah*s rose up from the crowd. Emma felt a distinct urge to flee.

"And *this*," her dad said, pointing at her, "is my daughter, Emma."

The guests turned around to look at her.

"She just turned fifteen," he said.

The guests seemed to wait a moment for something a little more impressive, and then they tepidly clapped their hands.

Emma stared at the carpet, feeling her cheeks burn. So that was her defining accomplishment? She'd turned fifteen?

"As you know," her dad went on, "it's our children whom we always have in mind at election season — how to leave them a better world, how to ensure and safeguard their future. So I've asked each of them to say a few words to you about what they want, and what their generation wants. Remington?" her father asked. "Want to come up here and say a few words?"

The man standing next to Remington slapped him hard on the back, as if they were old friends. Remington took a few steps forward.

"Thanks, Dad," he said, walking to the front of the room. "I guess it's true. I've been doing a lot of thinking. About what's waiting for me, for everyone my age, in twenty years." He faced the crowd. "Global warming. Trillions of dollars of debt. An endless war in Afghanistan. A rising divide between the haves and the have-nots of America. But before I get too depressed," her brother said with a smile, "I remember that I'm lucky. Lucky enough to know that right now, down in Washington, there's someone who's fighting for us." He turned to look at Adam. "For me. For my generation. To make this country safer. To make sure that people my age won't look back on their youth as the good old days. Thank you."

There was a moment of silence, and then the room erupted into applause.

"Bravo!" someone shouted.

"Is your son going to be your running mate?" someone else yelled.

"Thank you, Remington," her father said, practically bursting with pride. "Now I'd like my youngest to speak. Emma? Would you come up here and say a few words?"

Emma felt her stomach begin a slow slide down to her ankles as she walked over to him.

"So tell us *your* concerns, Emma," her father said. "What are your worries? What keeps you up at night?"

Emma turned to face the room, struggling to think of something to say. Her brother had covered every possible worry she and "her generation" could ever have. The environment. The war on terrorism. Economic inequality, for God's sake.

"Emma?" her father prompted. "Anything at all?"

She turned and saw Tom Beckett standing by the door. He was looking at her with the same smirk he'd had on his face at the Boathouse. As if he were just humoring her—the unwanted, embarrassing, inappropriate Conway.

"Well, you know, Dad," she suddenly said. "There's only one thing that keeps me up at night. Will Jen and Brad ever get back together?"

People traded uncomfortable glances. Nobody spoke. Her father froze.

"Dinner is served!" her mom said, breaking the sudden silence. "Now, if everyone just wants to move this way!"

The guests snapped out of their collective coma and began to move toward the dining room. Emma stood by herself for a moment, trying to gather her thoughts. It had felt great to say that, she had to admit. But she also had the distinct, bitter aftertaste in her mouth of having done something foolish.

"What the hell was that?" Remington looked furious as he walked up to her. "Was that supposed to be a joke?"

"Uh, yeah," she said. "Take it easy, Rem."

"Why would you do that?" His green eyes blazed. "Are you crazy? How could you do that to him? You just basically gave all the people in there the finger."

She rolled her eyes. "It was a joke, Rem."

"Do you think I like having to be the responsible one all the time? Do you think I like having a sister who's a total goof-off?"

His words cut right through her. "I'm sorry, Rem —"

"Forget it." He stormed out of the living room and across the foyer toward the dining room, where Walker waited for him by the French doors. From the slightly revolted look on his face she could tell that Walker had seen everything — and possibly heard everything, too.

Slowly she walked back to her room, shut the door, and lay down on her bed. She felt like she'd just been punched in the face. She'd never expected that kind of outburst from her brother. She'd actually thought he'd find her joke funny.

But instead he'd ripped her apart. That horrible loneliness swept over her. She realized that it didn't matter what her parents thought of her, but Remington — he mattered. If he'd finally had it with her, then she would have nobody in this family. She'd never get through the next year on her own.

She reached over to the floor and picked up her laptop, which she'd covered with Radiohead stickers. After she'd put on "Down by the Water" by PJ Harvey at top volume, she clicked on her Internet browser. There was one thing she could do to turn this around, one thing she could do to show Remington that she cared. In the search bar on Google she typed three words: *Vanessa image consultant*. It couldn't be too hard to find her.

chapter 10

Monday morning Emma sat at the center table in the library, trying to concentrate on her Spanish homework. Lizzie and Todd had gone to get bagels from the deli on Madison, and as she waited for them she started to feel like she might jump out of her skin. Nothing had been the same since Saturday night. Remington was still mad at her. Earlier that morning he'd left for school while she was still in the shower. And then there was Walker, who probably thought she was a moron. When she glimpsed him in the hall before homeroom he'd only given her a feeble smile.

She'd tried to apologize to her parents as soon as the party was over. But when she saw her dad heading into his office, he just held up his hand to ward her off.

"Don't bother," he said. Then he and Tom — who Emma could swear still had that smirk on his face — walked into his office and shut the door.

Then Emma went straight to the kitchen to find her mom. "Mom?" she said. "Can I talk to you?"

"Save it, Emma," her mother said, keeping her back to her as she placed Saran Wrap over a plate of uneaten mini-quiches. "It's kind of pointless to explain."

"But what was I supposed to say?" she argued. "I didn't know we had to give a speech. Nobody told me that."

Carolyn turned around. Her eye makeup was starting to run a little, and it made her eyes look fuzzy. "I guess we all learned our lesson tonight about that," she said.

Emma stayed in her room the next day, doing homework and feeling pathetic. Her dad had gone to the steak fry in Iowa and that night, on her laptop, she watched coverage of it on the news. He looked tan and fit as he walked the line and shook people's hands.

"Over three thousand people showed up to hear Conway speak," said the newscaster, as the camera showed a sea of waving, applauding people in the middle of a green field. "A record number for the annual Democratic event."

In the news clip of his speech, her dad stood in front of a gigantic American flag, looking out over the crowd. "China is not our personal bank," he said to overwhelming cheers. "America *must* get back on its feet."

It was a little surreal. He almost looked like the president already. *This might actually happen,* Emma thought.

She decided to dial the number she'd gotten from Google. Vanessa's voice-mail greeting was brisk and calm at the same time.

"Hi, Vanessa," she said shakily. "This is Emma. I think I'd like to see you. Call me back." She hung up, feeling ridiculous. It was probably hopeless. There was likely nothing Vanessa could do to help her at this point.

Now, as she turned the page in her Spanish book, she wished that she'd never made that dumb crack at the party. But it had all felt like a trap. Of course she wouldn't be able to compete with Remington's speech. Of course her parents would wind up disappointed in her, no matter what she said.

Suddenly she felt her cell phone buzz in her bag. She grabbed her backpack and walked out of the library. She had a feeling it was Vanessa, returning her call, and she didn't want to have to let it go to voice mail.

In the deserted hallway behind the theater she finally pulled the phone out of her bag. "Hello?" she said quietly.

"Emma?" said a familiar newscaster-like voice. "It's Vanessa. I got your message. You can come in this afternoon at four, if that works for you," she said.

Emma toed the ground. This would mean trusting a woman who wore coral eye shadow. But she didn't have much choice. "Okay," she said.

"I'm very happy you called me," Vanessa said.

"Okay, I'll see you then," she said, and clicked off. She couldn't do this alone, she thought. She needed someone to go with her. Lizzie. She hurried down the hall, walked past the door to the library, and ran down the steps to the lobby.

It was cooler outside than it had been over the weekend, but it was still sunny, and the sky was a deep, cloudless blue. The streets were clear of students, but the Upper East Side moms had come out in full force. A group of them in running gear pushed their exercise strollers onto the curb, and as Emma waited for them to pass she walked over to the newsstand on the corner of Madison. A collection of tabloids faced out to the street, and one headline in particular leaped out at her: PIEDMONT PIRATE, it read in big block letters, and at the bottom of the page a smaller headline read $$$ OBSESSED CEO GOES ON TRIAL TODAY. A picture of a rakish-looking, dark-haired guy with Todd's large, deerlike eyes was splashed next to it. It had to be Todd's dad. *Ugh*, Emma thought. *Poor Todd.*

"Hey! We were just on our way back."

Emma turned to see Lizzie and Todd approaching, eating their bagels. She wanted to fling herself in front of the newsstand to try to keep Todd from seeing the headlines, but she couldn't move. "Hey, guys," she said. "What's up?"

Todd's gaze drifted past Emma to the newsstand, and then his face darkened. "How original," he said. "What happened to innocent until proven guilty?"

"Excuse me," Emma said, going up to the man behind the newsstand. "I'd like all the *New York Post*s, please."

The newsstand man looked up from the lotto ticket he was scratching. "All of them?"

"Emma, what are you doing?" Lizzie asked.

Emma reached around into her backpack and pulled out her wallet. "Sir? Did you hear me? I'd like every *New York Post* you still have. How much do you think that will be?"

The man still looked confused. "They're not all for sale."

"Will this do the trick?" Emma asked, laying down a couple of twenties.

The man shrugged and took the money. "Go for it."

She grabbed as many of the newspapers as she could. "You guys, give me a hand," she said to Lizzie and Todd.

"Sure," Lizzie said, leaning down to help.

Todd was the last to pitch in. Finally they staggered away with their arms full.

"You didn't have to do that," Lizzie murmured.

"Like everyone at Chadwick needs to see that?" Emma asked, turning up the block toward school. "I don't think so."

They dumped the newspapers in a trash can on the way back to school. Maybe just this once it was okay not to recycle, Emma thought.

In the ladies room, she and Lizzie washed the newsprint off their hands and arms.

"That was amazing of you," Lizzie said. "Todd's been pretty upset all day."

"It was the least I could do. But I need to ask you something. You know that image consultant I told you about? Well, I think I need to see her after all."

Emma told her the story of Saturday night in painstaking detail. When she was finished, Lizzie stood against the bathroom wall with her arms folded, the paper towels balled in her hand. "*I* couldn't have come up with something to say off the top of my head," she said. "No way. At least you made a joke out of it."

"Except now my brother's pretending I don't exist," she said. *And Walker has completely written me off,* she wanted to add. "So I made an appointment with her. For today at four. Will you go with me?"

"Do you really think that an image consultant is the answer?" Lizzie asked, arching one of her thick eyebrows.

"I have no idea," Emma said. "But at this point I'll try anything. So you'll go with me?"

Lizzie smiled. "No problem," she said.

The rest of the day Emma sat through class wondering just what to expect from her first image consultation. During lunch she googled pictures of the Gore daughters, marveling at their straight hair and beautiful white teeth. She didn't have perfect teeth. She didn't have blond hair. She hoped Vanessa wouldn't tell her that she had to be like them, because then this was all going to be a waste of time.

After school she and Lizzie walked down Fifth Avenue until they came to a massive Beaux Arts–style town house with an impressive glass canopy. "This is it?" Emma asked when she located the brass plaque that read DREESEN AND SAWYER, LLC. She looked over her shoulder at the Met across the street, its steps crawling with tourists. "These people must be making *bank*."

"You don't have to do this if you don't want to, you know," Lizzie said, hitching her book bag farther up her shoulder.

"I know," Emma said, ringing the doorbell. "But I just have to see what this place looks like inside. And I want you to see this woman. She wears so much hair spray, if you lit a match twenty feet away from her she'd burst into flames."

There was a click behind the iron-gated glass doors, and Emma pushed them open. Once inside they passed through a small marble-floored anteroom and into a lobby, where a female receptionist wearing a Bluetooth sat in front of a sweeping stone staircase.

"Dreesen and Associates," she said, staring straight ahead.

"Yes, just one minute." She pressed a button on her phone. "Yes?" she asked them.

"I'm here to see Vanessa," she said.

"Your name?"

"Emma Conway. I made an appointment this morning."

The woman looked Emma over carefully, her gaze coming to rest on Emma's mustard-stained kilt. "I'll let her know you're here," she said stiffly, gesturing to a row of plush chairs off to the side.

Emma and Lizzie surveyed the magazines piled on the coffee table: *Vogue, The Economist, Foreign Affairs,* and *Martha Stewart Living.* "Random," Lizzie said. "Is this place about politics or personal style?"

"I don't know," Emma said, perching herself on the edge of a chair. "But I think I'm out of both categories."

Lizzie's cell phone chimed with a text.

"Who's that?" Emma asked.

"Todd," Lizzie said. "He wants me to stop by his place when we're done." Lizzie typed a message back to him and then slipped the phone into the book bag at her feet. "He really appreciated what you did today."

"I'll keep doing it if I have to," Emma said.

"Well, this trial's going on for a while. We're not going to be able to buy every tabloid at that newsstand."

Emma heard the *clip-clop* of heels coming toward them, and then Vanessa walked into the lobby. "Emma!" she said, holding out her hand. "It's so good to see you." Vanessa's suit was pastel blue, and her clunky jewelry was silver instead of gold, but her frosted blond hair was as firm as ever around her face.

"This is my friend Lizzie Summers," Emma said. "I asked her to come with me."

"Very pleased to meet you, Lizzie," Vanessa said, politely offering her hand.

Lizzie shot to her feet and shook hands with Vanessa.

"Please, let's go into the conference room."

As they walked behind her, Emma glanced at Lizzie. *What did I tell you?* she mouthed, pointing to Vanessa's back.

Aqua Net, Lizzie mouthed.

They entered a small conference room, and Lizzie and Emma took seats next to each other at the oval table. A TV hung on the wall at one end, while at the other was a tastefully painted beach landscape. The track lighting was dim, and Emma immediately felt herself get sleepy.

"So," Vanessa said, sliding into a chair behind a sleek gray laptop. "You changed your mind about seeing me."

"Well…yes," Emma said. "I mean, that's okay, right?"

"Of course," Vanessa said. "I'm thrilled that you're here."

"Wait, first, can someone tell me what an image consultant actually does?" Lizzie asked.

"Any public person nowadays — including a presidential candidate — has to package himself. Everyone has to have a brand. Obama's was hope, for example. That was his catchphrase, the way people knew who he was and what they would get if they voted for him. This is your father's," Vanessa said, touching a key on her laptop.

On the TV flashed a screen that showed her father's face. Underneath it were the words *A New Beginning.*

"'A New Beginning'?" Emma asked. "That's the best you guys can do?"

Vanessa frowned. "It's not set in stone yet," she said. "But it's the one we all like the best."

"So what's Emma's brand?" Lizzie asked.

Vanessa smiled. "Well, it's not quite the same thing. But for the child of a candidate, there is a certain standard. Let's look at some other daughters." She touched another key. "Caroline Kennedy," Vanessa said as a black-and-white image of the teenage Caroline came up on the TV screen. "True, she didn't exactly grow up in the White House, but she always shined in the public eye. Quiet, dignified, intelligent. Fiercely private."

Emma looked at the photo of Caroline walking with her mother and brother down Fifth Avenue. She looked mysterious, unknowable, reserved. Emma couldn't relate to that at all.

"Then there was Tricia Nixon," Vanessa went on as a photo of a beautiful, doll-like blond girl in a wedding dress came up on the screen. "Maybe not as elegant as Caroline, but still a force to be reckoned with."

Emma and Lizzie traded a look but didn't say anything.

Vanessa went to the next photo. "Chelsea Clinton," she said as an image of the adult Chelsea with straightened hair and wearing a twinset and pearls appeared on the screen. "In the White House for eight years, until she was twenty. Look at that. True elegance."

Emma started to fidget in her seat.

"And then, of course, there were the Bush twins," Vanessa began as a photo of Barbara and Jenna appeared on the screen. "First there was Barbara, who I like to call —"

"But what about me?" Emma asked suddenly. "I came here for you to help *me*, not hear about how great all these other girls were."

"Okay," Vanessa said. "Here." She touched a key and another photo flashed on the TV screen. It was of Emma, walking up Fifth Avenue with her parents.

"Where'd you get this?" Emma asked.

"We found it," Vanessa said breezily.

"What's up with your bangs?" Lizzie asked Emma. "Why are they in a zigzag?"

"I'd just cut them with kitchen scissors," Emma said. "I guess they didn't turn out so well."

Emma looked at herself in the shot. It had been taken two years ago at the Columbus Day parade. She'd wanted to spend the day off from school playing Rock Band with Mary-Louise Banning, and instead her parents had made her walk with them in a parade for twenty blocks. In protest she'd worn jeans, Doc Martens, and a scowl.

"This is what I like to call Before Emma," Vanessa said. "Angry. Raw. A rebel. Now, here's New Emma."

Another photo appeared. At first Emma thought it was the same picture, but then she noticed that her clothes were different. In this shot she wore a pencil skirt, high-heeled boots, and a chic white coat with oversized black buttons. Her bangs had grown out and were swept back from her face with a barrette at the back of her head. And instead of a scowl she gave the camera a wide, dazzling smile.

"You Photoshopped this?" Emma said.

"It's our own software," Vanessa explained. "This is the Emma

I know you can be. This is After Emma. Happy. Confident. Stylish."

Emma looked at the photo. After Emma *did* look pretty good. She wanted to ask Vanessa where she could find those boots.

"This is the Emma I think we can find *together*," Vanessa said. "A little more polished, a little more confident."

"A little more J. Crew," Emma said sarcastically. "And a little more Crest Whitestrips."

"If that's what that means to you," Vanessa said. "Politics is perception, Emma. There's no doubt about that."

The photo disappeared and Vanessa shut the laptop. "But aside from changing your look and teaching you how to smile at the camera, there's very little about you that I would change."

"Really?" Emma asked. She was fairly sure she hadn't heard Vanessa correctly.

"You have something that those other girls didn't: Spunk. Energy. Presence," she said. "And all of those qualities could actually help your dad's campaign. You could reach young people in a way that no other candidate's daughter ever has."

It was so quiet in the room that Emma could hear the *whoosh* of the central air-conditioning. Emma looked at Lizzie out of the corner of her eye, but Lizzie was nodding as if Vanessa had said exactly what she'd been thinking.

"I'm serious," Vanessa said. "I think you could be a tremendous asset."

"Then I wish you could have been at my house Saturday night," Emma said. "My dad had this party for all these rich people to donate to his campaign. And he made my brother and me get up and talk. And of course my brother — the speech and debate master — gets up there and kills. And then it's my turn." She kicked the table leg. "So I made a joke. And everyone freaked. Now my brother won't talk to me. My dad thinks I'm an idiot. And you think I'm an asset?"

Vanessa took a deep, thoughtful breath. "You said your brother's the speech and debate master?" she said.

Emma nodded.

"What if *you* took speech and debate?" she asked. "What then?"

"Uh, *what*?" Emma asked.

"What if you could do what your brother does?" she said. "You don't seem to have a shyness problem. I think you'd probably be great at it. So why not?"

"Because my brother's the *captain*?" Emma offered.

"So you're not allowed?" Vanessa asked.

Emma snapped forward in her chair. "It's not that I'm not allowed. It's that it's his thing." She shook her head. "There's no way."

"You should do it," said Vanessa. "If only so that the next time you're in that situation, you won't have to panic."

Emma snorted. "I don't think there will be a next time," she said. "Tom Beckett's probably out right now looking for a muzzle for me to wear."

For a moment Vanessa seemed to flinch, as if she were offended. But then she smoothed a piece of poker-straight hair and said, "All I'm saying is that you could actually help your dad on this campaign. *Because* you're different. But you can't do that until you're a little more confident. Which is where the speech class comes in."

Emma looked at Lizzie. "I think you'd be great at it," Lizzie pointed out.

Emma turned back to Vanessa. "So that's your advice? Muscle in on one of the two teams that my brother is captain of?"

"You don't have to join," Vanessa said, tapping her French-manicured nails on the conference table. "Just go to a couple of practices. Try it out." She leaned forward. "You need to believe in yourself, Emma. If you don't, no one else will."

Emma glanced at Lizzie, ready to break into giggles, but Lizzie looked back at her with a straight face — apparently she agreed with Vanessa. "Well, thanks for the advice," Emma said, pushing herself back from the table. She picked up her book bag. "I'll give it a go."

"Check in with me next week to let me know how it goes," said Vanessa. She stood up and shook Emma's and Lizzie's hands once more. "It was a pleasure to meet you, Lizzie."

"You, too," Lizzie said.

Emma nodded and stepped back toward the door. "See you later," she mumbled, and soon she and Lizzie were out in the lobby, walking past the receptionist.

"So what'd you think?" Lizzie asked.

Emma pushed open the heavy glass door. "Total waste of time. Join my brother's speech and debate team? Is she serious?"

"I think you'd be really good," Lizzie said as they stepped out onto Fifth Avenue. "She was right. People pay attention to you. I don't know if it's your voice or the way you say things, but I've seen it. Even the teachers pay attention."

"Not like the way they pay attention to Remington," Emma said.

"But whatever about Remington," Lizzie said. "You're *you*, Emma." The wind lifted the ends of Lizzie's curls and blew them up around her face as she looked down Fifth. "You and Carina are so brave. I wish I could be like that sometimes."

"You *are* brave. You got suspended for modeling."

"It's not the same thing," Lizzie said. "You're, like, fearless."

Emma thought about Lizzie's words. In the past two months, she'd gotten expelled, started a new school, and embarrassed herself in front of the wealthiest people in America. Maybe she *was* brave.

"Oh. Hold on." Lizzie pulled out her cell phone. "Todd just texted me again. I think I should probably go."

"Tell him I said... well, tell him I said hi," Emma said.

Lizzie smiled and shook her curls out of her face. "I will," she said. "And hey. Never underestimate the power of being underestimated."

"What?" Emma asked, laughing.

"I don't know. I got it in a fortune cookie once," she said, smiling. "It always sounded kind of cool."

"Yeah, it kind of is," Emma said, thinking about it. "Bye, Lizzie."

"Bye, Em."

Emma watched Lizzie set off down Fifth Avenue. Across the street the silken exhibition banners attached to the front of the Met made a faint snapping sound, and then, lost in thought, Emma turned back uptown.

chapter 11

That night, Emma picked at her kung pao chicken and snow peas as Remington sat across from her in silence, flicking through a brochure for Georgetown. Emma looked down at the same page of *The Scarlet Letter* that she'd been reading for half an hour. Her brother was still giving her the silent treatment, two full days after the party.

"When did Mom say she was going to be home?" she asked.

"Around nine," he said, turning a page.

"I didn't know that you were applying to Georgetown," she said, spearing one of her snow peas.

"It's my safety," he replied, not looking up.

His safety, she thought. *Of course it is.*

"You know we're going down to D.C. in a couple weeks for Dad's birthday, right?" he asked.

"No," she said. "I'm not exactly getting family bulletins these days."

"Well, we are." He finally looked up at her, and she could see a weariness in his eyes. She wondered if this was a new thing, or if he'd been like this last year while she was gone.

"Look, Rem, I'm sorry," she said. "Please don't be mad."

"I'm not mad," he muttered.

"You haven't talked to me in over two days," she said. "I'm counting."

"Sorry, it's just..." His voice trailed off as he put his head in his hands. "Maybe it's all these AP classes and the applications, plus the swim team and speech team, but it's all just a grind."

"Speaking of the speech team...I was wondering if I could sit in on a practice."

He looked up at her. "O-*kay*," he said, digging into his rice. "Why?"

"I need an extracurricular."

He gave her a searching look, as if he didn't quite buy her story. "Well, it's tomorrow at four. In the library."

"You don't mind or anything?" she asked.

"Why would I mind?"

"Because it's sort of your thing," she said.

Remington shrugged his broad shoulders. "It's not just *my* thing," he said. "And Walker asked you to join last week, anyway."

"Is he mad at me, too?" she asked.

Remington looked at her over his glass of soda. "Since when do you care if other people are mad at you?" he asked.

"I don't," she said, burying her face in her Hawthorne.

*   *   *

106

The next morning at the diner near school Emma slipped into a booth across from Lizzie. "So, I'm gonna sit in on speech practice today," she said.

"Awesome!" Lizzie said, putting away her math homework.

"You know, why not? I don't think it's going to change my life, but it's a good idea."

"What's a good idea?" Carina asked, sliding into the booth. They'd all decided to do a weekly breakfast together before school. Carina had gotten her hair cut to just below her jawbone, and it looked incredibly chic and very blond.

"Wow, you look gorgeous," said Lizzie.

"Oh, thanks," Carina said, running her hand over her new 'do. "Alex doesn't love it, but I do. And I'm thinking of running a story on short haircuts in the next issue of *Princess*. If Barb is into it." She wrinkled her nose. "Is it bizarre that I'm really starting to like working with her?"

"No, I saw this coming a mile away," said Lizzie. She turned to Emma. "Carina's dad owns *Princess,* and a bunch of other magazines."

"And he's sort of gotten me interested in working there," Carina said, opening her menu.

"Yeah, *Princess* has gotten a lot cooler lately," said Emma.

"You can thank Alex's sister for that," Carina said. "She's got the best style of anyone I know. Except for Hudson," she said, glancing at the door.

"Hey, everyone," Hudson said as she dropped her book bag and climbed into the booth next to Emma. "What are we talking about?"

"Your amazing style," Lizzie said. "Like right now." She gestured to Hudson's fake-fur vest and headband dotted with faux diamonds. "What's going on with the album?"

"The photo shoot for the cover came out really well," Hudson said. "The label wants it to be just me, but I'm fighting hard to get the rest of the band on it, too."

"And what's going on with you and Ben?" Carina asked.

Hudson blushed and bit her pouty bottom lip. "Nothing," she said.

"Who's Ben?" asked Emma.

"He's the guitarist," Hudson explained. "And I *think* there's chemistry there, but —"

"Someone's too scared to do anything about it," Carina interrupted.

"What am I supposed to do? Jump him?" Hudson asked, pulling at the cluster of silver coins dangling from her ear.

"Why don't you just tell him how you feel?" Emma asked. "What's the worst that can happen?"

"Um...he could say that he's not interested and then feel weird around me for the rest of his life?" Hudson offered.

"But at least you'll know, right?" Emma asked. "That's got to be better than constantly wondering."

"So you've done that with a guy?" Hudson asked. "You've told him how you felt?"

Emma rolled her eyes. "Guys are never into me enough for me to do that with them."

"What?" Hudson asked. "Do you see the way guys look at you at this school? Are you blind?"

"What? No," Emma scoffed.

"I've seen it, too," Carina said.

"Yeah, especially one guy," Lizzie said. "Walker Lloyd."

"*What?*" Emma exclaimed.

"Yup," Carina said. "Every time he passes you in the hall, he totally checks you out."

He does? Emma wanted to squeal, but she didn't say anything.

"I know!" said Hudson. "I've seen that!"

"Don't get too excited, you guys. He's my brother's best friend. He, like, grew up at my house. He was around when I had clear braces and no boobs."

"So what? He obviously doesn't think you're awkward anymore," Carina said.

"And even if he was maybe a little into me, somehow," Emma said, "he definitely isn't now."

Just then the diner's only good-looking waiter stopped at their table. "Ready to order?" he asked, peering at them from under his tousled hair.

"We'll have four OJs and two fried-egg sandwiches," said Emma. "And on another note, I'd love to cut your hair sometime. I'm really good at it. And I wouldn't charge you a lot."

The waiter looked like he wasn't sure he'd completely understood her. "Uh, okay," he said. "Be right back with your drinks."

The four of them giggled as he walked away. "You are insane, you know that?" Carina asked with a devilish grin.

Emma shrugged. "Just trying to help someone in need," she said, chuckling.

"Okay, so why wouldn't Walker be into you anymore?" asked Hudson, her sea-green eyes full of concern.

Emma poked at the piece of lemon in her water glass with a fork. She was going to have to tell Hudson and Carina everything after all. "I need to tell you guys something," she said, knitting her brow. "It's sort of a secret."

"Go ahead," said Carina.

Emma paused. "My dad is going to be running for president."

"Holy *shnit*!" Carina yelled at the top of her lungs.

"Carina," Lizzie said under her breath.

"I can't believe it!" She slammed her palm down on the table and the silverware jumped. "*Oh* my God!"

"Wow," Hudson said softly, twisting an opal ring on her finger.

"C, you have to calm down," Lizzie added.

"I already told Lizzie this past weekend, when we went shopping," Emma said. "But I had to tell you guys. It felt weird that you didn't know."

"So are you gonna get Secret Service guards?" Carina asked breathlessly. "Are you gonna have to go on the campaign trail? Are you going to get free clothes?"

"I have no idea," said Emma, trying not to laugh.

"When are they going to announce it?" asked Hudson.

"January, February? I'm not sure."

"We won't tell anyone," said Carina. "Not a soul. They'd have to kill me first."

Hudson shook her head solemnly. "But what does this have to do with Walker not liking you anymore? Sorry, I'm still confused."

Emma had almost forgotten what they were talking about. "Last weekend my dad had a party for these rich people he knows — hoping to get them to give him money for the campaign. And Walker was there with my brother. And my dad wanted Rem and me to go up and give some speech about the plight of teenagers today or something."

"Oh, no," Carina muttered sympathetically. "I would die."

"And I just made a dumb joke about hoping Jen and Brad get back together," she said. "It was kind of a huge deal. My brother freaked out on me."

Her friends looked somber as they considered this.

"Well, *I* would have laughed," offered Carina.

"Thanks, C," said Emma. "Anyway, ever since then Walker has kind of... well, I can only imagine what he thinks. Which is where the image consultant comes in."

"I've heard of those," Hudson said. "A lot of people use them when they're trying to make a comeback or something."

"Or when they're running for president and they think their daughter's a freak," Emma explained.

"So did you actually see one?" Carina said.

"Yep," Emma answered.

"What was she like?" Carina asked.

"Kind of a cross between a shrink and a woman who does the weather on channel five," Emma said.

"Right," Hudson nodded.

"So she suggested that I sit in on a speech team meeting. So I don't totally embarrass myself when my dad asks me to speak in front of a crowd."

"I can kind of relate," Hudson said thoughtfully. "I got stage fright last year. I thought I'd never get past it."

"Believe me, you'd be the best thing to happen to the White House if your dad got in there," Carina said. "And we could come visit, right?"

"Absolutely," she said. "But it's still a little too early to talk about that."

The waiter brought them their fried-egg sandwiches, still unable to look at them.

"Sir? I'm sorry if I offended you," Emma said to him. "I actually think your hair looks fine just the way it is."

The waiter put down the plates and hurried away. Carina kicked her under the table, and they burst into giggles again.

chapter 12

Later that day, Emma made her way down to the library after her last class. For a moment she was tempted to just go home — her motivation to show up at speech team practice had waned a little after lunch — but when she saw Walker at one of the library tables, unpacking his book bag in the empty room, she changed her mind.

"Hey," she said, walking into the room. "Guess who changed her mind about speech team?"

He looked over his shoulder. "Hey," he said. For just an instant his eyes seemed to light up. "What's up?"

"Not much. Still thinking about Jen and Brad." She put her book bag on the seat next to his as he gave her a skeptical look. "I'm kidding."

"Yeah, what was that about?" he asked, taking out a thick binder.

"I had, like, five minutes' notice," she said. "And you saw who I had to follow. Sorry if I couldn't come up with anything better."

He shrugged. "Hey, I know you were on the spot, but you could have said something. Remington's a good speaker, but you still have stuff worth saying. You could have rocked it up there."

Then why didn't you throw out a topic? she wanted to ask as she played with the edge of her notebook. "Okay," she said. "Thanks?"

"Sorry," he said. "Forget it. I'm sure you were under a lot of pressure."

Her arm brushed up against his as she opened her notebook. Her heart did a somersault. "Whatever," she said. "Live and learn, right?"

He turned to a blank page in his notebook and started scribbling. She wasn't quite sure what he thought of her anymore. All she knew was that she wanted him to touch her arm again, but the moment was over.

As people started to trickle into the room, Emma recognized a few of them, particularly one junior girl named Laetitia with long blond hair and jaded blue eyes. Another girl marched in wearing a square pink and blue backpack strapped to both shoulders. She had an intensely focused expression, as if she were mentally rehearsing the State of the Union address she was going to give later that night. Her Chadwick kilt hung well below her knees, and her legs were painfully pale.

"This seat taken?" she asked Emma as she pulled out the chair on Emma's other side.

"Nope," Emma said, slightly intimidated.

The girl sat down and plunked her backpack on the table. "I'm Hillary Crumple," she said, offering her tiny hand.

Emma submitted to a bone-crushing handshake.

"I've got plenty of index cards and highlighters," she said, all business. "Just ask."

"Thanks, I will."

Out of the corner of her eye Emma noticed Ava Elting sashay into the room on her kitten heels. She sat across from Emma and threw a look of disdain at Hillary. "Are you joining us?" she asked.

"I just thought I'd sit in," Emma said.

"Oh, good," Ava said distractedly.

Emma turned to see her brother walk into the library.

Ava arched one of her perfectly tweezed eyebrows. "Hey, Rem," she called out in an unmistakably saccharine voice.

"Hey, Ava," he said, barely acknowledging her, much to Emma's relief. He carried his blazer over his arm and his tie was loosened. He looked tired, but it was probably because he'd gotten up at dawn for his daily run around the reservoir.

He waved to Emma and took a seat at the end of the table. Not next to Walker, Emma noticed.

"All right, let's get started!" said a familiar, strident voice, and Emma turned to see Mrs. Bateman walking into the room in her orthopedic shoes. "We've got a lot of ground to cover, and we're already behind on our research assignments," she said, dragging out a whiteboard on wheels from the corner.

Emma eyed the door. Maybe it wasn't too late to leave. Mrs. Bateman was the coach!

"But first let's do a little exercise." Mrs. Bateman lurched around the table, passing out some xeroxed pages. "Miss Conway," she said when she reached Emma's seat. "What are you doing here?"

"I'm just sitting in," Emma said, eyeing her brother for support.

"Oh, well, lucky us," she said, dropping what appeared to be a photocopied *New York Times* article in front of her and the rest of the people at the table. "You all have five minutes to read, and then we're going to do some quick two-minute speeches summarizing the issue and its pros and cons." She looked down at her thin gold watch. "Go."

Emma started the article. *Amidst growing convertorsy...* *controversy...*As she read, certain words refused to unscramble themselves, and then there were other words that she knew weren't scrambled, but which she couldn't understand just the same.

"All right, that's time," Mrs. Bateman said from where she leaned against the window. The late afternoon sunlight glinted on her red hair. "Who wants to go first?"

Remington raised his hand.

"All right, Remington," she said. "You have two minutes. Summarize the issue and present a pro or con position."

Every girl in the room stared at Remington as he got up. Emma suddenly wondered why she'd decided to come. The last thing she felt like doing was watching her brother give another perfect speech, this time surrounded by fans.

"The recent leaks of several State Department cables have raised the question of whether releasing certain classified information is harmful to American interests," he began. "But in fact these leaks are a perfect example of democracy in action. The entire point of a democracy is that the American public has the right to know what's being done in its name. Without being held account-able to its citizens, our government is allowed to act within its own moral code. These leaks are actually working to enforce our First Amendment rights of free speech."

Emma began to feel herself zone out. She'd already seen enough of Remington's oratorical skills to last her a lifetime.

"And in conclusion —"

"Time," Mrs. Bateman called, her eyes on her watch. "Very good, but you went a little too long. And you were reaching a bit with the constitutional argument. Still, excellent work, Remington."

The other team members clapped as Remington sat down. Emma joined in just before the applause ended.

"Now, who would like to present the opposing opinion?" Mrs. Bateman's beady eyes traveled around the table until they landed on her. "Miss Conway?"

"Oh, thanks, but that's okay," she said. "I'm just sitting in."

"Go ahead," Mrs. Bateman said, gesturing to the whiteboard. "You must have had some interest in actually doing this if you're here."

Emma eyed her brother furiously across the table. He could have warned her that this might happen.

"We're waiting," Mrs. Bateman added.

Emma felt Hillary give her a nudge. With an annoyed look in Hillary's direction she got up and approached the whiteboard.

"So, Miss Conway," Mrs. Bateman said, folding her arms, "why shouldn't classified information about diplomatic relations be leaked?"

Emma tried to block out the twelve blank faces staring at her from around the library table. "Well," she said, "I guess it can actually cause more trouble than it's worth."

"Your reasoning?" asked Mrs. Bateman.

"Well, it sort of reminds me of what happened with these girls at my last school," she began. "This one girl, Jessica, was writing notes about these other two girls, who were supposed to be her friends. But they were really mean notes. Like, saying how they had mustaches and back fat."

Remington began to flip his pen in a circle between his fingers, the way he always did when he was nervous.

"So this other girl, Phoebe, who was friends with Jessica, decided that the girls needed to know what Jessica was saying about them. So she found the notes and put them up on the bulletin board next to the student lounge so everyone could read them. And the girls went ballistic, obviously, and Jessica was furious, and Phoebe made out like she was a hero. But then everybody was mad at Phoebe, because posting someone else's notes to a wall — well, that's pretty mean. Especially when they're supposed to be your friend, right? And everybody was mad at Jessica, because she'd written these really mean things. And the school was totally annoyed because it had been trying to deal with its clique problem. So at the end of the day, I believe telling other people's secrets really just isn't worth it."

"That's time," Mrs. Bateman said, sounding distinctly nonplussed. "You can sit down, Emma."

Emma walked quickly back to her seat. Nobody at the table was looking at her.

"Miss Conway," Mrs. Bateman said, walking slowly toward

the front of the room, "there will come a moment — at someone's wedding, or a birthday party — where you may be called upon to enlighten an audience with a hilarious or touching true story. But for *persuasive speaking*," she said, karate-chopping the air, "we want to hear *facts*. We want to hear *statistics*. We want to hear an argument based on the evidence, not on things that have happened to you."

Emma felt her face burn. *But I was just sitting in,* she wanted to say. *Don't I at least get points for trying?*

"Now, let's move on to this week's assignment. I'd like to call up someone else to give you an example of what persuasive speaking actually is. Mr. Lloyd? Do you have something prepared on standardized tests?" she asked.

"Yes," Walker said as he slid out of his chair and walked purposefully to the front of the room. Emma was almost too embarrassed to look at him after the verbal smackdown from Mrs. Bateman.

"Last year, more than eight hundred music classes had to be dropped from public school curriculums," Walker began in a full, rich voice. "Four hundred science classes had to be dropped, too. And last year the average school lunch period was cut down from half an hour to twenty minutes. This is directly the result of standardized tests, which are singlehandedly destroying our educational system."

Emma noticed that everyone in the room was giving Walker their rapt attention — maybe even more attention than they had given Remington.

"There are many arguments for why standardized tests like the

119

Regents Exam and the SAT should be banned, but here are the three most important reasons," he went on. "Standardized tests can be biased against women and minorities; they encourage schools to teach only the subjects covered on the test; and they have been shown to be an inaccurate predictor of college success."

Walker was an even better speaker than her brother, Emma realized. He'd finally beaten him at something. She suddenly flashed back to a memory of the day Walker and Remington had gotten into a fight, when they were about thirteen. They'd been playing Xbox, and Walker, who normally never got mad at Remington, and who let him be in charge of what they were going to do, play, and eat whenever they were at the lake house, said Remington was cheating. Remington denied it. Emma watched it get more and more heated until Remington and Walker were in the middle of the living room floor, pounding each other with their fists. Emma threw her glass of lemonade all over them to get them to stop. It worked, but then her mom was furious that she'd ruined the new carpet.

"In conclusion, our students deserve more than a biased, unimaginative form of testing that is predetermining the curriculum," he said. "Standardized testing should be eliminated as part of the college application process. Doing so would return autonomy to our schools and give more heft to the No Child Left Behind Act. Thank you," he said, walking back to his chair.

Emma clapped longer and louder than anyone else at the table.

"Excellent," Mrs. Bateman said, going to the board. "Does everyone know why that worked?" She picked up a black erasable marker and began to scrawl on the board. "First, a perfect introduction with *statistics,*" she said, writing the word *statistics* on the board.

To Emma, the word looked like *caustics.*

"He gave three main points," she went on, writing *three main points* on the board. "Which were all backed up with research."

Everyone scribbled in their notebooks. But Emma was too interested in looking at Walker's profile.

"And then the conclusion restated those three points. Emma Conway!" Mrs. Bateman shouted.

Emma jumped in her seat. "Yes?"

"Was there any personal experience in that speech?"

"Um…" she answered.

"Did Mr. Lloyd tell a story about something that happened to him?" she asked, glaring at her.

"No," she replied.

"Exactly. So for next time, I want you to give a speech on standardized tests," Mrs. Bateman said to her. "Taking the pro position. Everyone else will start doing their research for their final project. But you, Miss Conway, will deliver your speech using Mr. Lloyd's sterling example. And some actual research."

"That's really okay," Emma said. "This was just a onetime thing. And I'm not really on the team."

Mrs. Bateman narrowed her eyes. "I'm asking you to join," she said, as if Emma was a little slow on the uptake.

Emma looked around the table. Almost everyone seemed engrossed in reading, taking notes, or checking their cell phones, but Walker gave her a quick thumbs-up sign. *Do it,* he mouthed.

"Okay, thanks," she said. "Sounds good." So maybe her speech hadn't been *too* terrible, she thought. And maybe Walker would help her.

"Hey, good job," he said, when they stood to pack up their bags. "Mrs. Bateman would never invite just anyone onto the team. Especially when you weren't even trying out."

"Well, the last time someone asked me to be on a team was for kickball in the third grade. So I guess I'm flattered. And *you* are amazing at this. Really. I had no idea."

"It was pretty rough when I first started. And I definitely didn't have your presence."

"My 'presence'? Is that good or bad?" she joked.

"It's good," he said, smiling at her. His eyes seemed to look right through her. He began to gather up his things.

"Do you think you might be able to share some of your genius?" she asked. "Just for a few minutes? To sort of help me get off on the right foot?"

Walker glanced across the room, to where Remington and Mrs. Bateman were talking. "But what about Remington?" he asked.

Emma wasn't sure what to say to this. "What do you mean?"

"Wouldn't you want him to help you?" he said, unbuttoning the cuffs of his shirt and pushing the sleeves up to his elbows. His forearms looked ropy with muscles.

"Not really," she said.

He seemed to consider the implications of this for a moment, and then shook his head. "How about we just have lunch tomorrow? Would that work? I'm at twelve thirty."

"Me, too," she said.

"Cool. I'll meet you in the lobby."

Remington walked up, carrying his book bag. "Good job," he said to Emma. "And you, too, man," he said to Walker.

"You, too," Walker said briskly, shoving his binder into his book bag. "See ya later," he said to Emma, and left.

It seemed strange for Walker to leave so quickly, but Remington didn't seem to notice. "So, uh, congratulations, Em," he said. "Sounds like you're on the team."

"Thanks," she said, unable to resist feeling a little smug.

"But do you *want* to be on the team?" he asked, slipping on his Chadwick blazer. "It's kind of a big commitment. And we don't want to take someone on and start training them unless they're seriously into it."

Emma felt a flicker of anger deep down in her stomach. "Yes, I'm into it," she said, hitching her book bag up her shoulder. "Why wouldn't I be into it?"

"I'm just asking, Emma," he said. "Don't be mad."

"Whatever," she muttered, turning to leave. She walked out fuming but with her head held high. *Never underestimate the power of being underestimated,* she thought. It was the best advice she'd ever heard.

chapter 13

Emma lay on her bed, listening to Magnet's cover of "Lay Lady Lay" on her headphones. On a legal pad she wrote out a list of speeches that she suddenly wanted to give for speech team:

Why Uniforms Suck
Why Cell Phones Should Be Allowed in School
Why Being Grounded Doesn't Work
Why Schools Should Do Away with Grades

She was putting an asterisk next to the last one when a knock on her door made her jump. She pulled off her headphones. "Yeah?" she called out.

"Come into the office!" her mom called. "CNN's doing a piece on Dad!"

Emma swung her feet off her bed. Lately her mom had been calling her into the office almost every night to see something about her dad on the news. It was kind of exciting, as much as she didn't want to admit it.

She padded into her parents' office. Her mom sat behind her desk in the corner, while Remington lay on the couch in a T-shirt and his Chadwick sweatpants, a textbook on political philosophy in his hand. She'd said little to him over dinner. She knew that he hadn't meant to be rude about her joining the team, but his words had stung anyway.

"Where is this?" she asked, looking at her dad on the flat-screen. He was speaking in front of another large crowd outside under a crisp blue sky.

"Ohio," Remington said.

"As Americans, we deserve better than a country that clings to two extremes," her dad was saying. "What about a third option? What about an administration that will keep its promises?"

The camera cut to the crowd, cheering and waving. Home-made signs that read CONWAY FOR AMERICA and CONWAY FOR PRESIDENT bobbed up and down in the crowd.

"What about an administration that won't suddenly flip-flop on the promises it made to the American people?" he called out, getting the crowd riled up even further. "That won't just pay lip service to the idea of change?"

The clip ended and a female newscaster with short blond hair and a hawkish face came on the screen. "The more than fifteen hundred people who showed up today for Senator Conway's last-minute speech are just further proof that this hotly contested state might have already chosen its Democratic front-runner," she said.

"Holy shit, did you hear that?" Remington said, almost jumping out of his seat.

"Remington," Carolyn warned. "Language."

"Sorry," he said. "But fifteen hundred people?"

Carolyn sighed and furrowed her brow. "That's what she said."

The cordless phone rang.

"Hello?" Carolyn answered. "Yes, we're watching it now."

Emma turned back to the TV. The newscaster turned to three panelists. "So, Mark, what can we make of this early show of support for Conway, before he's even announced his candidacy?"

"This is amazing," Remington said, his eyes still glued to the TV. "Do you get how amazing this is? CNN's already covering his every move. And it hasn't even started yet."

"But aren't these shows always making a big deal about stuff?" Emma asked. "Does this really mean anything?"

Her brother's face fell. "Brimming with support as usual, Em," he said.

Her mom hung up the phone. Her cheeks were flushed a bright pink and her eyes were bright. "Well, that was Dad. They just hit a million dollars."

"Already?" Remington asked.

"And Dad wants you to say a few words at his birthday party next week," her mom said to Remington. "Something like what you said here the other night. About your generation, its fears, its problems —"

The phone rang again.

"So Dad is going to announce that he's running at the party?" Emma asked.

"Not yet," her mom said. "Hello? Yes, we just saw it. I haven't watched all of the panelists yet."

Remington pushed himself up from the sofa, and Emma followed him out of the office. "Is Dad coming home again before we go to D.C.?" she asked.

"I don't think so," Remington said, running a hand through his chestnut hair. "According to the schedule, they've got him working every weekend until then."

"What schedule?" she asked.

"Dad's schedule. Tom sends it to me a few times a week."

"Wow," she muttered. "I guess I'll just direct my questions to you now."

"You can ask to be on the list, too, Emma," he said, as he came to a stop in front of his door. "It's not that big a deal."

"That's okay," she said.

Remington shook his head. "Why don't you care about this? Do you know how important this is?"

"Just because I'm not Tom Beckett's e-mail buddy doesn't mean I don't care."

"Whatever, Em."

"What's your problem?" she asked.

Her brother answered by walking into his room and closing the door. "Hey, what's your problem?" she yelled again. Emma raised her fist to pound on it and then stopped.

It wouldn't make any difference. *Let him think what he wants to,* she thought. There was nothing she could do about it anyway.

The next morning, Emma sifted through a stack of research on standardized tests that she'd printed out in the computer lab. She didn't want to sound like a complete idiot when she met up with

Walker. But the articles were so dense. Just reading the first one would probably take her all morning in between classes.

Lizzie walked in and claimed the seat next to her. "Cool color," said Lizzie, leaning over to check out Emma's nails. "What's it called?"

"Frog Prince," Emma said, admiring the dark green hue. "But guess what? I made the speech team."

"You did?" Lizzie cried, dumping her book bag on the ground. "That's great! Good for you!"

Todd walked into homeroom and Emma almost did a double take. His eyes looked red and raw from lack of sleep, and the color had been leached from his face. It was now the third day of his dad's trial, and from the few headlines Emma had seen online, she gathered that some damaging evidence had already been leveled against Jack Piedmont. Todd was probably going through hell, Emma thought. It definitely looked that way.

"Hey, Todd," she said, as brightly as she could. "What's up?"

"Not much," he said, trying to smile as he sat down next to them.

Lizzie took his hand. "Are you feeling okay?" she asked. "You look a little sick."

"I'm fine," he said, pulling his hand away.

Emma gave Lizzie an encouraging shrug. But Lizzie barely smiled back. She just looked down at her History homework and let her red curls fall over her face. Emma didn't know Lizzie very well yet, but she figured that this meant that Lizzie wanted a little privacy.

At lunch Emma walked down to the lobby to wait for Walker.

She'd checked herself in the mirror before coming downstairs, and even pulled her dark-brown hair back into a ponytail, but now she was sure that a large zit was starting to pop out of her forehead. But what did it really matter? she thought. Walker had seen her with plenty of zits before. So many that there was probably no way that he was into her.

"Tell your brother I tried that power shake he told me about," said Dori, the receptionist, from behind the desk. "So far I've lost three pounds!"

"I will," Emma said, feigning a smile.

"He's always got the best nutrition advice," Dori said adoringly.

Emma said nothing.

Suddenly the front door opened and Hillary Crumple trudged into the lobby. "Um, excuse me," Hillary announced. "But there are photographers out there." She pointed to the street. "Just thought you guys should know."

The security guard ran to the door and slipped past Hillary, out onto the sidewalk.

"Did they say anything to you?" Dori asked, picking up the phone. "What did they want?"

"I think they're looking for Todd Piedmont," Hillary said.

Emma whipped out her phone and sent Lizzie a text:

Photogs out front. Looking for Todd. Don't leave the bldg.

The security guard stomped back in through the doors. "Call the police," he said to Dori. "They're not gonna budge."

"What a shame," Dori said, picking up the phone. "He's such a nice boy." She dialed. "Yes, I'm calling from the Chadwick School," she said into the phone. "We have a situation here."

Just then Walker came down the stairs. "What's going on?" he asked, seeing the commotion in the lobby.

"Paparazzi are out front," Hillary informed him. "They're looking for Todd."

"Who?" Walker asked, confused. "Oh, right, the guy with the dad on trial."

"Let's go give them dirty looks." Emma grabbed Walker's hand and led him out of the lobby. Outside it was a soft, mild, late-summer day, spoiled only by the sight of a cluster of burly men with cargo vests and shorts across the street, aiming their zoom lenses at Chadwick's doors. "You guys should really get a life!" Emma called out to them.

"Shhh!" Walker said, pulling her down the block. "What are you doing?"

"Telling them what I think," she said.

"Well, what do you want them to do? Come after us?"

"So what?" she said. "I'd love for them to."

"Right," he said, laughing. "Like you'd really teach them a lesson."

"I just don't think it's fair what they're doing," she said. "Why are they stalking Todd Piedmont? It's totally lame. What does he have to do with any of it?"

"That's just the way the world works," he said. "Todd can probably handle it. You can't save everyone, Emma."

"At least I tried."

They walked into the crowded diner and grabbed a table near the back. Fortunately nobody in her class was there. Emma knew that it looked a little strange for her to be having lunch with a senior boy, even though Walker was practically her brother.

"So," she asked, when they were settled, "you're going to have to share all of your speech secrets. How did you learn to speak like that? It couldn't have been from Mrs. Bateman. Every time she opens her mouth it's like hearing a machine gun."

"Years and years of practice," Walker said. "And you know I have an older brother, right?"

"Oh, yeah. Wesley, right?" Emma suddenly remembered that she'd never met Walker's much-older brother.

"Yeah. He was the captain of the debate team at Chadwick years ago. I used to watch him practice when I was a kid. I think I wanted to be him so badly that I picked some of it up."

A busboy came by with two glasses of water and menus.

"What did he end up doing with it?" she asked, taking a sip of water.

"He's a lawyer at Skadden," said Walker. "But in law school he was on the moot court team. Argued in front of the seventh circuit once. He's a genius," he said, shaking his head.

Emma noted the resigned way he said this, as if he didn't want to admit it. "So you know how it feels, then, to have a perfect brother," she ventured.

"Yeah, I do," he said, with a rueful smile. "But I think I like it. If I hadn't had a brother like that, I would have turned out very different."

"How would you have turned out?" she teased. "Like me?"

"Emma," he said. "Stop. You're smart, okay? As much as you try to play it off."

"Play it off?" she asked, startled.

"Yeah. I've seen it since you were ten. You're really bright. You could memorize anything. I think you once memorized half of the M volume of *Encyclopedia Britannica*." He opened his menu. "I just don't get why you have to hide it all the time."

"I'm not hiding it," she said. "You know I have dyslexia."

"So because of that you can't be yourself?"

"What is it with you and the left-handed compliments?" Emma groused, opening her menu. "And if I hide it all the time, then how do you know I'm so bright?"

"Because I just do," he said, in a way that made a knot form in the back of her throat. Suddenly the floppy-haired waiter she'd teased the day before stopped at the table to take their order.

Emma discreetly looked away. "I'll have a grilled cheese," she said to the wall.

"Two grilled cheeses," Walker said, and the waiter grabbed their menus and left.

"Okay, I have all this research I printed out," she said, leaning down to pull the articles out of her backpack. "And I know I'm supposed to take the pro side of things. And have a three-part shape?"

Walker blinked for a moment, as if he was surprised that she wanted to change the subject so fast. She noticed for the first time how long his eyelashes were. "Okay, you start with an introduction," he said. "That's where you summarize the issue — like with standardized tests, you mention that there's some controversy over whether they're good or bad. Then you say which argument

132

you're going to make, and you give three points that support that argument. Then, in the body of the speech, you explain each point and give a reason why it's valid, with some facts based on your research. And in the conclusion, you basically repeat what you've just said in a very quick way." He shrugged as if this were a piece of cake. "That's it."

"That's *it*?" Emma asked. "I'm supposed to know how to do that by next week?"

"Since I can't help you with the speech you have to give," he said, pushing up his sleeves, "let's just figure out a different speech together. Pick a topic."

Emma smiled. "Should my dad run for president?" she asked with a grin.

"Okay," he said, not missing a beat. "I'm assuming you'd take the pro position on that?"

Emma hesitated, then nodded.

"So...what do you think are the three best reasons for him to run?"

The waiter brought their sandwiches and placed them on the table. The long spear of pickle that came with everything at the diner looked unbelievably gross.

"Emma? You there?" Walker asked. His brown eyes searched her face.

"I'm thinking," she said. "Hold on."

"I can think of a few reasons," he said. "First, his record in Congress shows that he can work successfully with Republicans," he said, counting on his fingers. "Second, he's committed to finally pulling troops out of Afghanistan. And third, his youth and

133

optimism are what the Democratic party needs to recapture voters under forty-five."

"That's what *you* would say," she said. "That's not what *I* would say."

"So, spill it," Walker said, reaching for a napkin. "What would you say?"

"He really cares about doing the right thing," she said, picking off a piece of crust. "Even when it's not the popular thing. Or the thing that you'd want to do. Like, in fourth grade, there was a girl in my class who was really mean to me. She had a big party for her birthday at Dylan's Candy Bar and didn't invite me. And then when it was my birthday, I wasn't going to invite her at all. But my dad made me. He even gave her the biggest slice of cake and let her sit at the head of the table."

Walker nodded as he chewed. "Sounds like your dad."

"He's always been like that," she said. "It's not just a turn-the-other-cheek kind of thing. It's a make-sure-and-be-super-nice-and-understanding-to-people-even-when-they're-jerks kind of thing." She took a bite. "And he's the smartest person I've ever met. And he doesn't go to extremes about things. And he's fair. And he always expects a lot from people." *Which is why I'm always disappointing him,* she wanted to say.

"Those all sound like pretty good reasons," Walker agreed.

"But those are all personal, right?" she asked, smiling.

"Yup," he said. "But I think in this case you're allowed," he told her, crinkling his napkin. "Too bad your speech won't be about that. You'd probably nail it."

"And too bad I don't really want him to run," she said.

Walker stopped chewing. "What?"

She put her sandwich down. "Would you be excited about something that was going to change your entire life? About being trailed by Secret Service and being this weird freak when you went to college? About never being able to get in trouble again?"

Walker frowned. "Huh?"

"What if you knew that you'd have to be perfect all the time because your *dad* was supposed to be perfect all the time?" she said. "What if you were supposed to be this straight arrow who never wore green nail polish or got a tattoo and people were always watching you? And don't tell me that I'm totally selfish and shouldn't be thinking about myself. That's what Remington lays on me all the time, and it's really annoying."

"You really think this isn't going to let you be yourself?"

She nodded. "Wouldn't you be freaked out?"

He thought for a moment. "You know, maybe you won't have to change as much as you think. Yeah, it's going to be invasive and a little annoying, and maybe it's going to cramp your personal style once in a while. But this is really important, Emma. Your dad could change the world. Have you thought about that?"

She traced a finger around her water glass. "Sure I have."

"And do you really think it's going to change *you*, Emma Conway? I don't think so." His large brown eyes zeroed in on her face. "I mean, I hope it doesn't."

She felt herself blush. She reached for her water glass and knocked over the saltshaker by mistake. Salt spilled all over the table. "Oops," she said.

"You okay?" he asked.

"Uh-huh," she said, aware of her heart starting to pound. "So, is that bad luck?"

"I think we're supposed to do this," he said, pinching some salt between his fingers and throwing it over his shoulder. "Right?"

"Um, I don't know, but I like how serious you look when you do that."

He laughed. "Are you all set? Or do you want to meet again?" he asked.

She was tempted to say yes, but instead she just said, "No, I think I'm good."

He stood up and repacked his book bag. "Just remember, it's all about threes," he said. "The introduction, the body, and the conclusion. And three main points. That's it. Once you have that, you're golden." He grabbed his wallet and pulled out a couple of bills.

"Here, let me split it with you," she said.

He shook his head. "My treat."

"You sure?"

"Glad I could help," he said as they walked out. "And why didn't you want to have your brother help you with this, again?"

"You know why—he's my brother and he thinks he knows everything." They stepped out onto the street, and for a moment her shoulder touched his arm. "You know what I was just thinking of the other day? That day you and Rem had a fight. When I threw the lemonade all over you? I was secretly rooting for you, by the way."

"You were?" he asked, suddenly serious.

"Oh, sure. 'Cause I think sometimes I wanted to do the same thing to him. But I guess you guys grew out of all that, huh?"

"I don't know," he mumbled. He suddenly came to a stop, as if he'd forgotten something.

"What's wrong?"

"Actually, I need to run to the deli for a second." He looked over his shoulder. "But I'll see you at practice. 'Kay?"

Without a word he turned around and left, weaving his way past a group of juniors walking back to school. Emma watched him go, wondering if she'd suddenly gotten bad breath from the grilled cheese. But something told her that it was the lake house story that had made Walker do a literal about-face. She kept her eyes on the back of his blazer as he walked down Madison and into the deli. Something was up between him and Remington, she thought. Something that had made him scurry out of the library the day before as soon as Remington had approached them.

When she walked back up the block the photographers were gone. And so was Todd, Emma learned, when she got back to the Upper School. He'd gone home.

"But is everything okay?" Emma asked.

"With me or with Todd?" Lizzie looked off into the distance at the lockers, her hazel eyes seemingly far away.

"With both of you."

Lizzie blew a curl out of her face. "He doesn't want me to come over tonight," she said. "That's all I know."

"Don't worry, he's just going through a hard time," Emma offered.

Lizzie shrugged but Emma could see a lost look in her eyes. "I hope you're right," she said.

chapter 14

Over the next few days, whenever Emma passed Remington in the halls, she noticed Walker wasn't with him. Instead, her brother now seemed to be spending lots of time with two senior guys she barely knew — Steven Hall and Chris Flagg. Steven and Chris were swimmers and straight-A students, just like Remington, but there was something about them that she didn't like. One day she heard Steven whispering numbers to Chris as certain girls walked by them in the hallway. And whenever she walked past them when her brother wasn't around they leered at her.

She understood why Walker wouldn't want to be around them. He was way too classy for that kind of stuff. But she wondered why Remington did, even if it was just during school. He'd never been into hanging out with people like that. He didn't drink, he didn't party, and he was the last guy to call out numbers as girls walked by. The only thing she could figure was that they'd gotten to be friends during

Remington's preseason swim team training and on runs around the reservoir. She made a mental note to say something to Remington about this. Preferably the next time he did something to annoy her.

But when she wasn't picking apart her brother's choice of friends, Emma concentrated on her speech. She finally read through all the articles she'd printed and picked out her three main points. She tried to remember what Walker had said about the introduction, the body, and the conclusion, and spent the weekend writing it all out. Over and over, she practiced speaking it out loud to Archie in his tank, trying to make it shorter each time. Mrs. Bateman hadn't given her a time limit, but Emma was guessing that she liked things on the shorter side.

On Sunday night, the night before speech team practice, Emma was delivering her speech to Archie, who was quietly slithering around on her bedspread, when there was a knock on her door. "Honey?" her mom called out. "Can I come in?"

"Yeah."

The door opened and Emma's mom walked in carrying a zip-up clothing bag over her arm. "Honey, do you mind if I get your opinion on a couple things?" she asked. "These are some dresses that I might wear to Dad's birthday party this weekend in D.C." She laid the bag on Emma's bed.

"Mom, watch out for Archie!" Emma said, snatching him up out of harm's way and depositing him in his tank.

"Oh, honey," Carolyn said with a sigh. "I always forget you have that thing." She laid the bag down again and unzipped it. "So, there are three choices," she said, and Emma saw silk ruffles and sequined hems spilling out of the bag. "I don't know if any of them are me, but there's going to be press there...Of course." She pulled out the first dress, which was a midnight blue sheath with only one sleeve and a ruffled hem. "What do you think?"

"Definitely not," Emma decided.

"Okay," Carolyn said, tossing it. "Tell me how you really feel. What about this one?" She pulled out a fire-engine red sleeveless dress with a deep V-neck.

"Oh, God, no." Emma pulled out the last one, a teal green dress with a dramatic petal-shape pouf at the neck and sleeves. "Who picked these out? None of these look like you."

"These are the dresses that Tom sent me. He has very definite opinions, it turns out. And don't even get me started on what he said about my Kelly bag. He thinks I should lock them all in my closet." She sat on the edge of her bed and clutched her stomach. "Eighteen years of practicing law and I've never felt this much anxiety."

"Mom," Emma said, touching her mom's shoulder. There was no cushion — only bone. "Don't listen to Tom. What does he know about fashion? Nothing. Just wear something that you already have and that you know looks good on you."

Carolyn smoothed her black hair and attempted to smile. "I know," she said, standing up. "I'm just trying to listen to these people. Even though they've got your poor father running around this country as if he were already in the middle of a campaign."

"So what should *I* wear to this? And is there going to be a kids' table? Please tell me there isn't."

"Wear the black Betsey Johnson. *Not* the tight one," she added.

She zipped up the clothing bag. "And I don't know yet about the kids' table. I'm not going to know much about the seating until we get down there on Friday. Believe me, I'm just getting through this day by day." Her mom noticed the pile of articles on standardized tests next to the laptop on her bed. "Honey, why don't you work at your desk? Do you have any light to read by?"

"I'm fine, Mom," she said. "I think I'll make it."

"Okay." Her mom pulled the bag off her bed. "Thanks for your input." She leaned over and gave her a kiss on the cheek. "And thanks for the advice."

From the office, Emma could hear the shrill ring of the cordless phone, which sent her mom scurrying out the door.

The next day she kept her eye on the clock, waiting for four o'clock and speech team practice. The idea of getting up in front of that table again was terrifying, but she also couldn't wait to do it. Her speech on why standardized tests were the best yardstick of a student's academic success clocked in at exactly two minutes, and it had three distinct points. No matter what, she was sure it was going to kill.

When she got to the library a few people were already around the table, including Walker. Ava Elting was already seated, marking an article with a pink highlighter. Emma picked the chair farthest from her.

"Okay, let's get started!" Mrs. Bateman called out in her usual irritated tone, as she sauntered in. She dragged the blackboard over to the corner and said, "Miss Conway, let's start with you! You're delivering a speech on standardized tests, right?"

"Correct," Emma said, clearing her throat. She saw Walker

smile at her across the table as she got up and walked to the front of the room. Her speech was rolled up in her hands, but by now she knew it so well that she didn't even have to look at it.

She cleared her throat and started talking. "The SAT is the four-hour exam that all juniors and seniors must take to get into college," she began, speaking extra slowly. "And the score one receives on this exam is what college application officers use to determine who may enter their universities."

Everyone at the table was looking at her as if they were truly interested. Even Mrs. Bateman seemed to be on board.

"It is a three-part exam made up of a writing sample and multiple-choice questions. Students are tested not only on their verbal and mathematical abilities, but on their time-management skills. These abilities and skills are supposed to predict future academic success in the college environment. Recently, controversy over whether or not these exams are accurate predictors have —"

"Okay, stop," Mrs. Bateman called out. "Why do you sound like a robot?"

Emma blinked. "A robot?"

"Yes, you sound like somebody programmed you," she said. *"Students are tested not only on their verbal and mathematical abilities but on their time-management skills,"* she said. "It's flat and robotic. It's not a speech. It's like you're reciting a script."

Emma looked past Mrs. Bateman to see Ava laughing into her palm. Her brother kept his head down, staring at his notebook. Walker was looking at her with visible pity.

"You are not a robot," Mrs. Bateman said. "You are someone

142

who is trying to persuade me of your argument, as dry and as toothless as it may be." She rocked on her feet. "That is one of the cardinal sins of speech-giving: Being boring. And you, my dear, just committed it in the third degree."

Emma felt her face get hot. "But last time you told me to make it less personal."

"I didn't say to turn it into a monotone," Mrs. Bateman said, checking her watch. "Now, let's start from the top." She walked closer, her orthopedic shoes making a slight squeaking sound.

"But...this isn't fair," Emma said. "You told me I had to make it drier. You told me I had to make it less personal. Now I have. It's not fair."

"If you can't take criticism, Miss Conway," Mrs. Bateman said, "then you're never going to get better. So start again."

"No," Emma said. She crumpled the speech into a ball in her fist. "Forget it." She walked over to her bag. The tears in her eyes were making it hard to see, but she was aware of faces watching her closely. Breathing fast, she pulled her bag onto her arm.

"So you're leaving us?" Mrs. Bateman asked.

"What do you think?" she blurted out, much louder than she'd expected to. On the way to the library door she listened for footsteps — her brother, maybe Walker, running after her trying to convince her to stay, to tell her that Mrs. Bateman was mean and not to take it seriously, that she had talent and was good. But there were no steps running after her. Nobody was following her.

She ran down the steps, through the lobby, past Dori answering phones behind her desk, and out onto the street. Seconds later she was on Fifth Avenue, walking quickly toward the Guggenheim in the late afternoon breeze.

Of course this had been a mistake. Of course she wasn't good enough to do this. It had been a joke to think that she would change, she thought, tears burning her eyes. Nobody ever did.

chapter 15

The Acela Express had a funny smell sometimes, and it was even more intense on Friday afternoons, when the train was packed with business travelers headed back to D.C. from New York for the weekend. Emma slouched in her seat, listening to PJ Harvey on her iPod, and tried to figure out the smell. Sweat, stale chips, and aftershave, she thought. Or a hundred different kinds of aftershave, all mixed together. Whatever it was, it was almost comforting. It felt good to be out of New York. Going to Mrs. Bateman's class every day that week had been unbearable. She'd spent most of every period studying the faint pink lines on her loose-leaf paper and avoiding eye contact. And every time she saw Walker in the hall she gave him a vague smile, looked past him, and kept walking. He never tried to speak to her or get her attention. She knew she'd lost his respect.

But her brother, to his credit, had somehow restrained himself from delivering one of his "I told you so" lectures. He sat in front of her, next to her mom. As usual, Emma had opted for the seat by herself.

Suddenly a bag of Famous Amos chocolate-chip cookies came over the top of the seat in front of her and hovered in front of her face. She grabbed the bag and tipped a few cookies into her hands.

"Hey, don't take the whole thing," her brother said, getting up and coming around to where she sat.

"I didn't," she said. "Here." She held the package out to him, but instead he moved the massive carry-on from the seat beside her and sat down. Emma noticed a woman across the aisle gawking at him. Sometimes she forgot how good-looking her brother was.

"So are we going to talk about what happened last week?" he asked. "Or are we just going to forget about it?"

"Guess there's no such thing as a free cookie," she said, chewing.

"I admit that Mrs. B went a little overboard," he said, popping one of the cookies in his mouth, "but was it worth quitting over?"

"It was to me," she said.

"You have talent, Em. Maybe I wasn't all in your face about it, but that's what I think."

"Well, you could have let me know at the time," she muttered.

"What? So it's my fault that you walked out?"

Emma sighed. "No," she said. "It's over. I tried it and it didn't work."

They sat in silence for a moment as the train swayed left and right on the track. Emma felt the usual golf ball of shame beginning to form in her throat, and she pushed it down. "So...you're going to Georgetown tomorrow?" she asked.

"Yeah," he said. "I have my interview at eleven. And then I'm going to a football game. Chris is gonna be there. His cousin is a sophomore."

"Chris Flagg? You mean that Neanderthal you're friends with?"

Remington frowned. "He's not a Neanderthal. He got a twenty-three hundred on his SATs."

Emma snorted. "Wow. Did he cheat?"

Remington gave her a look.

"So why aren't you friends with Walker anymore?"

Her brother crumpled the empty bag of cookies. "We're friends," he said with the slightest hint of irritation. "Why do you think we're not?"

"I just never see you guys in the hall together."

"That's because this whole semester he's been a shut-in with all of his work. I guess he really wants to get into Stanford." He stood up. "I gotta go to the bathroom. I must have had three bottles of water." As he strode up the aisle, Emma knew that her brother wasn't telling the truth — at least, not all of it. But she had a feeling that this was as much information as she was going to get.

They pulled into Union Station just after sunset. After walking through the station they stepped out onto the curb into thick, humid air. Emma peeled off her jacket. A white SUV drove up and behind the wheel Emma recognized the blond crew cut and thick neck of Randall, one of her dad's aides. They piled into the car.

"Hello, Mrs. Conway," Randall said.

"Randall, how are you? How's your wife?"

"She's wonderful," he answered. "Due any day now. Hi, Remington, Emma."

"Hey," Remington said. "So he's in Orlando tonight, right? I think that's what the schedule said."

"Wait. Dad's not even *in town*?" Emma asked.

"He's coming back tonight," her mom said, annoyed.

"Actually, he's coming back tomorrow," said Randall. "After Orlando he's flying to Birmingham."

They were quiet for a moment as they drove. Even her mom seemed disappointed to hear this news.

They glided down First Street, and Emma saw the Supreme Court, its pillars lit from behind, and the Capitol, its majestic dome glowing ivory white against the sky.

"I love how it looks at night," her brother said. "It never gets old, you know?"

Emma thought of the first time she ever saw the Capitol, on a trip to D.C. right after her dad became a senator. It was after Thanksgiving and the wind was bitterly cold, but her dad's hand was warm as he led her around the grounds. For some reason it had been just the two of them, and she'd been thrilled to have his undivided attention, especially after months of sharing him with seemingly every citizen of New York State. Finally they went into the rotunda that connected the House and the Senate.

"See that, Em?" he'd said, pointing to the fresco painting at the very top, as the voices of tourists echoed against the walls. "It's called *The Apotheosis of Washington*. A man who painted the Vatican also painted that. You know what the Vatican is, don't you? It's where the Pope lives."

She looked up at the painting. It was impossible to see clearly, because it was a circle, and because it was so high. She circled around and around, trying to take it in, until she got so dizzy she couldn't walk anymore. Her dad grabbed her hand and steadied her.

"Slow down there, tiger," he said. "You always go so fast. Just like I used to. You're just like your dad, you know that?"

Thinking of that now, she felt a pang in her chest. She couldn't imagine her dad saying that to her anymore.

Randall pulled into the driveway of their hotel, a corporate-looking glass structure just down the street from the Capitol. "I've already checked you in," he said, handing Carolyn the key cards in their envelopes. "You and the senator are in the presidential suite, while Emma and Remington are next door to each other on the fourth floor."

"Thank you, Randall," said her mom.

"I'll make sure the senator calls you as soon as he's off the stage tonight."

"Thank you," her mom said. "Any idea what time he will arrive tomorrow?"

"Not yet," Randall said, "but I'll let you know as soon as I do."

As they walked to the elevator, Emma heard her phone chime inside her bag. It was a text from Lizzie:

How is it so far?
Awkward and lonely, Emma wrote back.
Have fun! Lizzie wrote.
Miss u guys, she texted. *And don't worry. I won't.*

"I still don't get why we're at a hotel," she said, as they walked into the elevator. "Dad's apartment's big enough for all of us."

"It's his fiftieth birthday," her mom said. "Let's live a little."

But judging from the tension in the elevator, Emma didn't feel like any of this was going to be a good time. They'd come all this way, and her dad wasn't even here. It gave her a pit in her stomach.

Emma and Remington got off at the fourth floor and walked to their adjacent rooms.

"This feels really weird," Emma said, trying to fit her keycard into the door lock. "Do you know what I mean? Like Dad's just going to swoop into town for his own birthday party, and then leave again."

"This is the reality of it, Em," Remington said. "It's not Dad's fault." He slipped his card into the door and turned the knob. "I think I'm gonna do room service tonight," he said. "Tell Mom I'll see her tomorrow." He closed the door.

The next morning the three of them ate breakfast together in the café in the lobby. "So Dad should be back around four," her mom said, digging into a grapefruit.

"*Four?*" Emma asked.

Under the table, she felt her brother's foot come down hard on her toes.

"So, who wants to spend the day with me?" she asked. "I hear there's a fantastic show at the Smithsonian."

"I have my interview," her brother said, tearing into a scone.

"Emma?" Her mom dug her spoon into a grapefruit. "What about you?"

"Sure," Emma said, knowing she had no choice. "I'd love to."

"Rem, tonight we're meeting in the lobby at six," she said. "Six *sharp*. Randall's going to be taking us to the dinner in his car."

"No prob'm," he said.

"You have your speech ready, right?" she asked.

"Yup," he said, eating the rest of the scone.

"And it's about what we talked about, right?"

"Mom, I sort of have this Georgetown interview on my mind, okay?" He stood up so quickly that he almost collided with a waiter behind him. "I'll see you tonight."

"Sure, sweetie," Carolyn said, trying to sound nice. "Good luck. You know where to grab a cab, right?"

As Remington nodded and walked away, Carolyn raised her eyebrows. "What's wrong with him?" she asked.

"He's probably just nervous." Emma ate a slice of bacon and looked over her shoulder at Remington leaving the room. He definitely didn't seem like himself.

After their trip to the Smithsonian, an interminable walk around the Mall, and a last-minute trip to Saks to help her mom look for shoes for the party, Emma staggered back to her room. She watched only a few minutes of *Keeping Up with the Kardashians* before her eyes closed. After what felt like five minutes, she snapped awake. The digital clock near her bed read five-forty-two. She'd been asleep for two hours. She raced to the shower.

Dripping wet, with a towel wrapped around her, she reached for the dinky hair dryer attached to the wall and turned it on. Nothing happened. She made sure it was plugged in and tried again. Nothing.

She threw on one of the hotel bathrobes and stepped out into the hall. "Rem!" she called, rapping on his door. "My hair dryer's broken! Can I use yours?"

The door stayed shut. She wrapped the belt of the bathrobe tighter around herself.

"Rem!" she yelled. "Come on, help me!"

Just then the door opened a crack. Her brother looked terrible. His eyes were puffy and his face had a weird greenish tint, and a strange, sickly smell hit her nostrils. "Jeez, Rem," she said. "What happened to you?"

"I don't feel that well," he said in a raspy voice. "I think it's something I ate. Can you just tell Mom and Dad that I can't go tonight?"

"What? You're not going? What about the speech?"

"Just tell them I can't do it," he said. "Tell them I'm sorry."

"But…do you need a doctor? Do you think it's food poisoning?"

The door shut in her face.

"Rem? Rem? You all right?" She put her ear to the door and heard the faint sound of Remington getting sick. *Yikes,* she thought. Her brother definitely hadn't been kidding. She didn't want to have to be Housekeeping tomorrow.

This still left the dilemma of the hair dryer, though. She went back to her room, dug out the non-offensive Betsey Johnson dress from the duffel bag she'd brought but hadn't unpacked, and slipped it on with her heels. She quickly put on some eyeliner and lipstick. Then she rode up to the penthouse and marched down the hall to the presidential suite.

Her mom answered the door wearing the fire-engine red dress that Emma thought they'd both vetoed. "Honey?" her mom asked. "Why do you have a wet head?"

"A couple of things," Emma said, walking into her parents' room. "Can I use your hair dryer? And Remington can't come tonight. He's really sick."

Her mother frowned. "He's sick?"

"I knocked on the door and he was in the middle of throwing up. All over the place. Wait," she said, looking past her mom into the suite. "What's going on in here?"

The living room of her parents' suite held a grand sitting area with two couches, a twelve-seat dining table, a baby grand piano, and another sitting area with a giant flat-screen television. And crammed into every nook and cranny were people she'd never seen before. Most of them looked like aides — they were young, clean-cut, and dressed in jeans and ties or classic twinsets and skirts. They slumped in chairs and huddled together on the couches, talking on their cell phones, typing on laptops propped on their thighs. Stacks of memos were piled high on every surface. And not one of them had noticed that she'd come in.

"Your father just got back," her mom said quietly. "And some people decided to come back with him to the hotel."

"But where's Dad?"

"He was just here a minute ago..." She sighed. "Wait here. I brought a hair dryer you can borrow."

As Emma stood alone, her hair dripping on the marble floor of the foyer, the slim, tall figure of her dad walked into the living room. Emma almost didn't recognize him. In the past three weeks since he'd been gone, his hair had gone almost completely gray at the temples. Bags hung under his eyes. He looked like he hadn't slept in weeks.

"Hey, Dad," she called out.

He waved at her and walked over. "Hi, honey," he said. He threw his arms around her and squeezed her tight. "How's my little girl?"

"I'm good."

Her dad didn't seem to notice that her hair was dripping wet, but this wasn't surprising. "Where's Remington?"

"He's really sick," Emma said. "I think it's food poisoning. He said to say he was sorry but he probably can't give that speech tonight."

"Does he need a doctor?" he asked, as Tom Beckett approached them. Unlike her dad, Tom looked exactly the same. *Then again, pure evil probably doesn't age,* Emma thought.

"If I were you, I'd just let him throw up for a few hours," she told her dad.

"What is it?" Tom asked, just barely acknowledging Emma with a glance.

"Remington's sick," her father said. "Sounds like he's got food poisoning. He can't make the speech."

Tom Beckett rubbed the back of his neck. "Anyone you can think of to replace him?"

"Is that necessary?" asked her dad.

"Well, we did invite Maria from the *Post* and Helen from the

154

Times. Remington's remarks were supposed to kick-start the college-demo campaign."

"So I'm supposed to find a teen speaker in the next ten minutes?" her dad asked.

"Let me look into a few options," Tom said to Adam. "Shanks!"

Shanks lumbered toward them. His gray mop of hair fell halfway over his eyes and he seemed to walk with his belly leading the way.

"Remington's sick," her father said. "Tom thinks we need a replacement."

"Okay," Shanks said calmly. "Like who?"

"Like someone *young*," Tom said, annoyed. "Remington was supposed to reach out to the college demo."

"Well, what about Emma?" Shanks asked, his eyes twinkling.

"Emma?" her dad repeated.

Carolyn walked over with her hair dryer. "What are we talking about?" she asked.

"We're trying to come up with a replacement for Remington," Tom explained.

"And Shanks just suggested Emma," her dad said. "No, I don't think that would be a great idea. Emma, I hope you don't take that personally."

"Not at all," she said, even though it was hard not to feel a little bit offended.

Her father sighed. "When does this damn thing start?" he asked his wife.

"Well, we're supposed to leave in ten minutes," her mother

said. She handed Emma the hair dryer. "Honey, hurry up. I don't want you getting a cold."

"Senator?" one of the campaign people yelled. "I've got Senator Reid on the phone."

"Be right there!" he yelled. "Okay. Someone should give Remington a call," he said distractedly. "See if he's okay."

"I will," said Carolyn. Emma noticed that her dad didn't volunteer to do it himself. Emma's mom turned to her. "We'll meet you in the lobby in ten minutes. And honey, please take off some of that eyeliner."

Emma scurried to the door. She didn't have much time.

chapter 16

"So, are you into World of Warcraft?"

Emma prodded the bundle of baby green beans with her fork and tried to think of a polite way to discourage the Senate majority leader's creepy son from talking to her. "No, Mark, I'm not," she said.

"It's really cool," he replied, staring at her with heavy-lidded eyes.

Under the table, she checked her watch for the hundredth time. She'd guessed correctly about the kids' table. At least they were almost to dessert.

"I'm working on my own role-playing game," he said. "Some of my buddies and I are writing the code for it."

"That's awesome," she said.

"Right now there aren't any girls in it," he said, "but I could base one on you. If you wanted me to." He stared at her, breathing heavily through his nose.

"That's really okay."

"Oh, hey, my dad's about to speak," he said, as the almost-eighty-year-old Senator O'Halloran tottered across the stage. Emma looked across the enormous gold and cream ballroom of the Dupont Hotel, its banquet tables lit with candles and laid with gold linen. She wasn't quite sure where her parents had been seated, but if she found their table she planned to make a beeline for it, just to get away from Mark.

"All right, all right, I promise not to take up too much of your time," the elderly senator said in a crotchety voice, "but I do want to say a few words about the man of the hour, Adam Conway."

A photographer leaped up and started taking his picture.

"Adam first came to visit me in my office right after he was sworn in," Senator O'Halloran said. "To pay his respects, I thought. But no. I think he wanted to know when I was planning to retire."

There was an outbreak of laughter throughout the room.

"Yes, he's ambitious. Yes, he's confident. But I've never met a man who was more able to support that ambition and confidence. And after what he managed to do last spring with the health-care bill...I don't know that I'll ever see anyone pull off that kind of politics again."

Emma noticed that the waiters were busy handing out champagne to all the guests. A toast was about to happen.

"He reminds me a lot of how I was at his age. Hardworking, good-looking, and cocky as hell."

More laughter rippled through the room.

"So let's have a toast: To Adam Conway, the luckiest guy in Washington."

An aide scuttled onstage and handed the senator a glass of champagne, just in time for him to hold it up as everyone in the room shouted, "Hear, hear."

The senator took a sip of his champagne, then said, "And now I've been told that his brilliant son, Remington, would like to say a few words." He swiveled his head toward the kids' table. "Remington? You ready, son?"

Apparently Senator O'Halloran hadn't heard the news that Remington was sick. Emma felt her pulse quicken as people craned their heads, looking for her brother.

The same aide walked hastily across the stage and whispered into the senator's ear.

"What do you mean, he's sick?" the senator asked. "He's too sick to come up and say something for his father's fiftieth birthday?"

Nervous laughter floated through the room.

"Maybe we can have *my* son get up here and say a few words!" he exclaimed.

That was all Emma needed to hear. She scrambled to her feet. "I can speak!" she yelled. Making sure not to trip on her heels, she started to make her way to the stage.

"I see we have someone coming over here," the senator said, squinting hard to make out the someone. "I think it's his daughter, Erma."

"*Em*ma," she clarified as she took the stairs up to the stage two at a time, disregarding the pain from her high heels. She shook the senator's hand and stepped in front of the mic. "Yes, I do have something to say," she said. Below her she could see her parents at their table, shocked into complete silence. "I know my brother

159

wishes that he could be here tonight, but I think I have a pretty good idea of what he would have said," she began. "Actually, I don't really know what he would have said, but I know what *I* want to say. And that's that my generation — whatever that means — needs someone to look up to. And not someone who's on reality TV or has an awesome Twitter feed, but a *real person*. To tell us that we're gonna be okay. And make sure that we're going to be okay. Who's going to let me and my friends know that we're gonna be able to pay off our college loans and get jobs and live in a world that isn't going to be melting away in twenty years." She paused. "Who's going to tell us that we have a future, instead of just debt and disease and despair. Because sometimes that's what it feels like, you know?"

She looked over at Senator O'Halloran, whose eyebrows were arched so high they almost touched his fake hairline.

"And I don't mean to pass the buck or anything, but it doesn't help that wherever you look, someone's trying to sell us something or promise us something and tell us who to be and how to be and how much we're supposed to weigh and how many kids we're supposed to have. When we're all supposed to be figuring that out for ourselves."

Nobody moved out in the crowd. Even Mark O'Halloran seemed attentive. *Maybe this is going well*, she thought.

"So I guess what I'm trying to say is, we all need a hero right now. Someone who's not an actor, and not a reality star, and not some made-up character in an online role-playing game. We need a real person who we can trust." She paused and looked right at her dad. "Which is why I'm glad that my dad is running for president."

The words were out of her mouth before she could stop them. *Oh my God,* she thought. *I did not just say that.*

There was an audible gasp. She looked down at her father's table. He looked stricken. Tom Beckett and Shanks closed in around him, hiding him from sight. Emma looked at her mom, hoping for some assurance that this wasn't as bad as it seemed. But her mom only gripped the stem of her wineglass and stared straight ahead.

But then somebody started to clap. Soon the applause picked up across the room, building in a wave until everyone, it seemed, was applauding. One by one, people rose to their feet. They were giving her dad a standing ovation, even though he hadn't said anything.

Finally her dad stood up. Shaky at first, and then gaining more confidence, he lifted his hand and waved. His gleaming white smile was almost triumphant, as if he'd already won the nomination. *He's playing along,* Emma thought. *He's letting them think that I did this on purpose.*

But just as she started to clap, too, she noticed Tom Beckett, standing right below the stage. He was staring at her. His bright blue eyes glittered with anger, and with the side of his hand, he mimed slicing his own throat over and over. He wanted her to get off the stage, and quick. It didn't matter that her dad was handling this perfectly. She was in massive trouble. Again.

chapter 17

"I didn't mean it! I swear to *God* I didn't mean it," she said as the elevator carried them swiftly up to the penthouse floor.

Her dad sighed loudly. Her mom patted her gently on the back but shook her head, her eyes on the floor. Shanks studied the buttons as they lit up one by one.

"This is a disaster," Tom murmured, pacing around the elevator. "A disaster."

"Tom, calm down, it's all okay. He covered well," Shanks said as the elevator doors opened.

"But it's too soon," Tom said as they headed down the hall. "We were going to wait until we had everything in place. We don't even have a budget set up yet. Now we're doomed before we've even gotten out of the gate."

"We're *not* doomed," Shanks said, sliding the keycard into the door of the presidential suite. "Let's keep this in perspective."

The several aides still inside the suite sat up at attention as they walked in. From the worried looks on their faces Emma could tell they knew already. One girl grimaced sympathetically as Emma sat down on the couch.

"I think we all have to take a deep breath and look at this rationally," Shanks said, as her parents sat down on the couch opposite Emma. "What's done is done. Now we just have to figure out how to spin this."

"There is no spinning this!" Tom blurted out. "Who the hell announces they're running for president *this* early? Nobody! How are we going to afford a campaign for the next twenty-six months?"

Randall put down his cell phone. "The *New York Times* wants to know if what Emma said was a mistake or not."

"Christ," Tom groaned.

"It was a mistake," her father said.

"No," Shanks said, holding up a beefy hand. "If we're trying to get the young voters, maybe we shouldn't be so quick to shoot it down."

"What do you mean?" Tom asked.

"I mean, the way we've been talking about branding the senator is through his relatively young age. The way he appeals to young voters. And if he has a teenage daughter who can boil it all down and speak from the heart like that, then let's go with it."

Emma glanced at her dad. His fingers rubbed his cleft chin, and his green eyes had a distant look. "Maybe you're right," he mused.

"So, nothing?" Randall asked.

Tom shook his head. "We don't confirm or deny. We say that his daughter spoke from the heart. I want to know the second anyone has the story up," he said. "And that includes the blogs."

Randall went back to the phone.

"I think I'll go to bed," Emma said, standing up. "If that's okay with everyone."

"No, don't go," her father said, also getting to his feet. "Hold on. I want to talk to you for a second." Emma and Carolyn followed him into the bedroom and he closed the door.

"So, Emma," her father said. "*What* were you thinking?"

"I was just trying to help," she said. "Remington was gone, and trust me, you *really* didn't want Mark O'Halloran up there, so I just did it. And I knew you didn't think I could do it —"

"So you wanted to prove me wrong," he said with a smile. Her father picked up a bottle of water from the bedside table and twisted off the cap.

"Not just that. I guess I...I guess I've changed my mind about all this."

Carolyn sat on the bed and gently took off her shoes. "Adam, do you think those people might be able to go home soon?" she asked.

"Story's up!" they heard Tom yell from the other room.

They ran into the living room. Everyone was huddled in front of someone's laptop. Emma hung back while her parents elbowed their way to the screen. She was terrified to know what it said.

"Conway's kin announces presidential run," Tom Beckett read aloud. "Senator Adam Conway's teenage daughter reportedly stunned friends and colleagues tonight when she announced his plans for a presidential run in the next election. Fourteen-year-old Emma spoke about her generation's fears for the future, explaining her relief and pride that her own father would be seeking the Democratic presidential nomination, concluding with the words, 'This is why I'm glad my dad is running for president.'" Tom cleared his throat. "Guests at the Dupont Hotel greeted the news with shock, and then something close to hysteria. Senator Conway confirmed the announcement himself by waving to the crowd. Even though announcing his run this many months in advance could be a liability, many see this stealth announcement as a brilliant publicity move. 'If I were going to announce my candidacy this far in advance, then I'd have this girl do it for me,' said Senator Frawley, a guest at tonight's event. 'This girl has all the charisma of her father, and then some.'"

Shanks looked at Emma and held up his bear paw of a hand. "High five, little lady," he said.

"The *Post*'s up!" The girl who'd given Emma the sympathetic smile carried her laptop to the dining room table. "They're calling it a genius move," she said as everyone flocked to her screen. "And Emma's speech 'winning.'"

Her father scanned the screens of both computers. "Wow. They really do think we planned it this way."

"Emma Conway's announcement of her father's campaign is a historical first," Shanks read. He turned to Adam. "Congratulations, Senator," said Shanks. "You're officially running for president."

"I am, aren't I?" Adam said, finally looking relaxed. He slapped his chief of staff on the back. "Let's have some champagne!"

Randall produced a bottle of Krug and two glasses from a gift basket on the coffee table and popped the cork. Her father filled a glass and gave it to Carolyn, then filled another for himself. "To breaking the rules," he said, "and to our secret weapon." He raised his glass to Emma and smiled. "Good job, Emma."

"Hear, hear!" everyone yelled, even if they didn't have a glass. Randall handed her a 7Up and clinked glasses with her. Someone else clicked on CNN, and plastered across the bottom of the screen were the words CONWAY RUNNING FOR PRESIDENT. Just seeing those words made Emma feel giddy. This was actually happening, and she'd been the one to kick it off.

The only person who wasn't smiling or drinking was Tom Beckett. He was already in a corner, typing furiously on his laptop, on to managing the next crisis.

By the time Emma left the room she had two texts from Carina.

Holy SHNIT, read one.
Double *Holy SHNIT,* read the next.

And there was a third text, from Lizzie:

Do u know what u've started here???

Emma laughed out loud for the first time that night. Then she sent a reply:

Absolutely not.

chapter 18

The next morning Emma stepped into the shower and stood under the hot stream of water. She'd slept only two hours, but she felt wide awake, so awake that she sang a little tune as she lathered up her hair. She assumed that by now the news had traveled to every media outlet in the country, and the announcement was probably on all the news crawls, in all capital letters: CONWAY RUNNING FOR PRESIDENT. *Here we go,* she thought. *Let's rock this thing.*

When she'd dried off she pulled on the jeans, ripped T-shirt, and long black cardigan she'd worn on the train and stuffed her Betsey Johnson dress back into her duffel. It was tempting to turn on CNN and get a peek at the news, but watching a bunch of people yelling about her dad's decision — either for it or against it — would be too weird right now.

Down in the lobby she spotted her brother in one of the leather armchairs, reading the *New York Times.* His hair was still wet from the shower and he wore a crisp-looking white button-down shirt.

Yesterday's green tint had left his face. "Hey," she said, letting her book bag—stuffed with schoolbooks she hadn't yet opened— drop to the floor at her feet. "You look a lot better."

"Yeah, I am," he said, looking at her with clear eyes. "Guess I just needed to ride it out. So. Looks like I missed a big night last night." He folded the *Times* over and held it up to show her the headline: CONWAY ANNOUNCES CANDIDACY VIA DAUGHTER. A picture of her dad waving outside the Dupont Hotel accompanied the piece.

"Oh my God," she said. "It's the cover of the *New York Times*?"

He gave her the newspaper. "Did you and Dad plan that, or was it a mistake?"

"What do *you* think?" she asked, scanning the article.

"I'm going with mistake?" he said, cracking a smile.

"Kind of. They didn't know you were sick so I kind of rushed up to the stage."

"Well, pretty impressive," he said.

Emma thought he sounded a little hurt, but she was too busy scanning the article for her name. "Oh my God," she said. "They're saying I'm fourteen. How annoying." She looked over at him, and saw that he was giving her a funny look. "How was Georgetown?"

"Fine," he said, as if she'd just asked him how he'd slept.

"Just fine?"

"Yeah. Fine. Let's go to the café."

As he got up, she got the same feeling she'd gotten on the train the other day, when she'd asked about Walker, as if Remington wasn't giving her the whole story. But she shrugged it off as they walked into the hotel café to meet their parents for breakfast.

"Let me just tell you, it was phenomenal," her father said once they'd ordered, as a waiter poured him coffee. "I couldn't believe she got up and spoke. And then, listening to what she had to say ... I couldn't believe it. No offense, Emma, but compared to the last time I saw you speak in front of a crowd —"

"I got it," she said, spreading some butter on her toast.

"But then when you said —"

"'I'm glad my dad is running for president,'" her mom interrupted. She stirred her coffee, smiling. "My heart stopped. I'll admit it. But then it was just perfect."

Emma studied her orange juice. She wasn't sure why she felt so embarrassed, but suddenly she couldn't look at her brother.

"So when are you going to announce this formally?" Remington asked, sounding oddly uncomfortable.

"Next week or the week after, at the latest," Adam said, wolfing down his eggs. "Tom thinks any later than that and we're going to lose momentum."

"Honey, are you feeling okay?" Carolyn asked Remington. "Maybe you should just have dry toast."

Remington looked down at his barely touched Denver omelet. "Oh. Yeah. I think I'm fine." He took another bite. "Where are you going to make the announcement?"

"New York," Adam said. "Tom's working on the best location."

"What about at the nine-eleven memorial?" her brother said.

"Too political," Adam said.

"Or the Statue of Liberty?" Remington asked.

Adam shook his head. "Not easy enough to get to."

"What about the Great Lawn in Central Park?" Emma suggested. "It'll look really pretty with all the leaves changing. Plus, you'll have the shot of the skyline in the background."

"Great idea." Adam fished his BlackBerry out of his pocket and typed with his thumbs. "But you kids would need to be there, too, you know. All of us, as a family." His BlackBerry chimed and he looked at the screen. "Tom loves the Central Park angle," he said.

Remington drank his orange juice, a smile stretched tightly across his face.

Emma fiddled with a crust of toast. As nice as it was to finally be taken seriously in this family, it also felt bizarre.

For most of the train ride back to New York Emma ignored her homework and stared out the window. It had been just twenty hours since her speech, and already everything felt different. She almost wished she had her brother beside her to discuss it, but instead he sat in front of her with a pair of Bose headphones clamped around his head, almost as if he didn't want to be bothered. Maybe he still felt sick, she thought. Or maybe he was a little annoyed that she'd suddenly moved into his Perfect Child territory.

When the train finally pulled in to Penn Station Emma lugged her bags up the aisle, still listening to her iPod. Her mom and Remington waited for her on the platform.

"Get some work done?" her mom asked her, with a glance at her backpack.

"A little," she said.

They walked up the stairs to the terminal among a sea of exiting passengers. She couldn't wait to be back in her own room.

"Carolyn! Carolyn!"

Emma looked up. At first all she saw were camera flashes.

"Emma! Look over here! Emma!"

The passengers parted and Emma froze. A thick crowd of paparazzi formed a wall in the center of the Amtrak terminal and were shooting so fast she could barely blink.

"Carolyn! Over here!"

"Emma! Emma! Look this way!"

Carolyn grabbed Emma's arm. "Let's go!" she said, pulling Emma and Remington past them.

"Emma! When did you decide to announce your father's campaign?" a voice shouted.

"Did you write the speech yourself?" another one called out.

"Whose idea was it? Did your dad put you up to it?"

Emma felt her mother pull her forward, and suddenly they were running quickly toward the stairs up to the street. The photographers ran after them, shouting all the way.

Somehow they reached the stairs up to Eighth Avenue, and they ran out onto the street. A driver with a sign that read CONWAY stood outside a town car.

"Hey!" Remington called out to him. "Hey, we're here!"

The driver opened the door to the backseat just in time. The three of them jumped inside, still carrying their bags.

"Emma! Carolyn!" The photographers circled the car, blocking it, until the driver almost hit one of them trying to pull away from the curb.

"Oh my God," Carolyn said, panting heavily with her coat on her lap. "I had no idea."

"You okay?" Remington asked.

"Yeah, I'm fine," said Carolyn. "Emma? You okay?"

"I'm okay. So are we celebrities now or something?" she asked.

"It seems like you are," her mother said.

Her brother didn't say anything, but it was the loudest silence Emma had ever heard.

"One twenty-two East Eighty-ninth Street," Carolyn said to the driver.

Rem? You okay? she wanted to ask. But she knew that she wouldn't get an honest answer.

chapter 19

"Emma!"

Emma stopped on her way into the lobby of Chadwick, half expecting to see another photographer. But it was just Dori, the receptionist.

"I just wanted to say congratulations! What an exciting turn of events! I'm so happy for you!"

Emma unbuttoned her coat. "Uh, thanks, Dori. How was your weekend?"

"Who cares how my weekend was? It was fine, just fine!" She waved her off. "Now you go and have a good day!"

Okay, that was weird, she thought. She and Dori had never exchanged more than a few words, and now she was a getting a hero's welcome.

Emma went straight up the limestone stairs, keeping an eye out for Lizzie, Carina, and Hudson. She still hadn't spoken to any of them about this. The only person she really wanted to talk to was her brother, but he'd left for school by the time Emma emerged from her room that morning.

She pulled open the door to the Upper School and came face-to-face with Hillary Crumple, who stopped in her tracks and held up her hands.

"Oh my God!" Hillary said. "Can I get a photo with you?" she asked, taking out a disposable camera. "Hey!" she yelled at a girl walking by. "Could you take my picture with her, please?"

"Uh... sure," Emma said.

The girl snapped the photo.

"Oh my God!" Hillary yelled. "This is amazing! You are awesome, you know that?"

"Thanks," Emma said, edging away down the hall. She found Lizzie at the lockers by herself.

"Hey!" she said, taking Emma by the arm. "Are you handling this okay? This wasn't planned, was it?"

"Please," Emma said. "I was just talking off the top of my head. And now everyone thinks I'm, like, the mastermind behind my dad's campaign."

"Just stay calm and know that it'll all blow over in the next couple days. As soon as your dad makes his formal announcement they'll forget all about this."

"I just hope he makes it soon," Emma said.

Carina and Hudson rushed over and took turns hugging her. Carina pushed her blond hair out of her eyes and said, "So, was that planned? My dad said that it was a brillz PR move."

"No, it wasn't at all," Emma said. "I wasn't even supposed

to make a speech, but Remington couldn't do it because he was sick."

"It looked like you did a great job," Hudson said.

"Thanks, but I kind of wish I hadn't said a word."

On her way into homeroom she heard a familiar voice say, "It was awesome, dude — you should have seen him!" She looked over and saw Chris and Steven standing with Remington at the lockers. Chris was talking to Steven but Remington was focused on his books. "He was a total maniac," Chris went on. "They almost pulled him from the stands. It was ridiculous."

"No way, really, man?" Steven asked. "They had to *pull* you?"

Emma wanted to hear more but she followed her friends into homeroom. Mr. Weatherly beamed at Emma as she sat down. "Everyone?" he said, standing up to his full six-foot-five height. "Your classmate Emma Conway did something truly historic this weekend. She became the first daughter of a presidential candidate to announce her father's run."

Most of the class just continued passing notes to one another and whispering, but Mr. Weatherly wasn't deterred. "Well done, Emma. What was going through your mind as you made this announcement? Can you share with us?"

"Um, nothing was going through my head, really," Emma said, playing with her rope bracelets.

"What about before you did it?" he asked, sitting on the edge of his desk. "How did you decide this? Did you talk with your dad? His team?"

"No," she said, shaking her head. "Not at all."

Mr. Weatherly's smile faded. "Huh," he said. "Well, in any event, congratulations."

Emma got the distinct feeling she'd disappointed Mr. Weatherly, but she wasn't sure how.

After homeroom she was on her way to Mrs. Bateman's class when Mr. Barlow came up to her. "So?" he said. "First you spill coffee, then you spill the news of your father's campaign to the world? Is this carelessness or genius?"

Emma had to smile. "I couldn't have done it without you, Mr. Barlow."

But Mrs. Bateman had a decidedly less enthusiastic reaction to Emma's news. She barely flicked her eyes in Emma's direction, behaving just as she had the week before. "So, let's talk about the filibuster," she said, already sounding annoyed. "Who wants to demonstrate to me how little they know about it?"

Emma knew all about the filibuster — her dad had explained how a senator could hold up voting on legislation by basically talking about nothing for hours. But she stayed quiet. She wasn't going to say anything in Mrs. Bateman's class, ever again.

At the end of class, she was packing her bag when Mrs. Bateman said, "Emma? Could I speak to you, please?"

Emma walked over to her. "Yes?"

Mrs. Bateman blinked her beady eyes. "I heard about what happened this weekend. With your father. Congratulations."

"Well, my speech didn't have any supporting research," said Emma. "And it was all based on personal anecdotes. You probably would have given me an F."

"Precisely," Mrs. Bateman replied with a tight smile.

"And you still thought it was good?"

"Good enough to ask you to rejoin the team."

Emma paused. "If I'm going to come back, I want to be able to be myself doing this. At least just a little bit."

Mrs. Bateman didn't say a word. "Practice is today at three thirty," she said. "Here's the topic everyone prepared." She pulled out a stapled handout and gave it to Emma.

Emma took the handout. She could see that this was as good an agreement as she was going to strike with Mrs. Bateman. "Okay."

Mrs. Bateman gave a curt nod. "Good," she said. "And if you ever have an outburst like the one a couple weeks ago, that's the end of your speech career at this school."

"Fine," Emma said. She walked away feeling scolded. But she also felt a flush of triumph. Mrs. Bateman hadn't written her off yet. She'd been impressed with her speech, despite all its flaws. Maybe Emma was better at this than she thought. Even when she was being personal.

At three thirty Emma headed to the library, where she found Walker unpacking his book bag. "So, I changed my mind," she said.

"Good," he said and smiled. "And I see you got some real-life experience this weekend."

"I did," she said. "Even though I kind of forgot about the rule of three."

"You did a great job anyway," he said. "One that even Mrs. Hateman would be proud of."

Just then her brother walked into the library.

"Hey," he said to Walker. "What's up?"

"Not much," Walker said, looking down. Emma could tell that he was uncomfortable.

She turned to her brother. "I'm back, Rem. I changed my mind."

"Yeah, I heard," he said coolly. He sat down and didn't say anything more.

"Well, *I* think it's cool you're back," Walker whispered to her, giving her a smile that made her stomach turn to jelly.

She smiled at him and got out her speech binder. *He likes me,* she thought. *He definitely likes me.* But she wondered if he was ever going to do anything about it. And if whatever had happened between him and her brother was the reason he never would.

chapter 20

Emma had never seen so many people camped out on the Great Lawn before. The crowd for her dad's formal announcement speech seemed to stretch as wide as the park itself, and almost as far back as Belvedere Castle.

"How many people do you think are here?" Carina asked her as they followed an armada of security guards toward the makeshift greenroom behind the stage.

"Ten thousand," Emma said. "Maybe more."

"I think it's twenty," Lizzie said.

"It's twenty for sure," Hudson said. Emma realized that Hudson probably had experience sizing up that kind of crowd from her mom's shows.

"Maybe even more than that," Todd said, shading his eyes with his hand. Todd had come back to school only a few days earlier, and Emma still thought he looked pale.

They passed by row upon row of people sitting on towels and

blankets. Almost everyone had some kind of sign or banner, a cooler, and, occasionally, a sun umbrella. Even though it was the first week in October, it was unusually warm. The sun beat down on them as they walked and Emma squinted in the brightness. As usual, she'd forgotten to wear her sunglasses. Carolyn and Remington had come earlier, in an SUV that practically drove them up to the stage from behind, but Emma had wanted to walk in with her friends.

"Are they selling T-shirts yet?" Hudson asked, slipping on her gold-framed aviator shades.

"I don't think they've figured that out yet. Wait — I take it back," Emma said as she passed by what looked like fifty college students, all wearing navy blue T-shirts emblazoned with the words CONWAY FOR AMERICA. "I guess they *have* figured it out."

"This is crazy," Lizzie said, her red curls blowing in front of her eyes as she looked over her shoulder. "Can you believe this? All these people are here for your dad! How weird is that?"

"It's like they're all here for a huge concert," Carina said.

They reached the front of the crowd and a wall of police horses. "You kids all have bracelets?" the head security guard asked as they came to a cordoned-off area near the front of the stage.

They nodded and held up their right wrists to show him.

"Then go on in through here," he said, handing them off to another burly guard, who walked them out of the sun and behind the stage. Staffers, most of them in their twenties, scurried around with big laminated IDs that read TEAM CONWAY strung around their necks. Her dad's staff appeared to have doubled in size.

"Look at all these people," she said to Lizzie. "There are so many of them."

180

"It's only gonna get bigger," Lizzie said. "At least, that's what my dad says."

They walked into an air-conditioned tented area and grabbed bottles of water from the ice-packed coolers set up on folding tables. "You guys hang here; I'm gonna go try to find my mom and my brother," Emma said.

"Where do you think they are?" Carina asked as they claimed an empty circular table.

Emma craned her head to scan the room. "I have no idea," she said. "I'll be right back." She elbowed her way through the crowd to another room. She wondered if anyone here knew that she was Adam Conway's daughter. She still felt fairly anonymous, but that probably wasn't going to last.

"Hi there," she said to a security guard. "I'm Emma Conway. I'm looking for my dad?"

The security guard waved her into another tented room, where she spotted her mom talking to Shanks. Remington stood off by himself, drinking iced tea. Her mom looked pretty in a peach-colored silk sundress, but her heavy foundation, eyeliner, and lipstick made her look like a child playing dress-up. And the gold chandelier earrings she wore also looked strange.

"Hey," she said to her brother.

"You're wearing that?" Remington asked.

Emma looked down at her purple jeggings, black studded T-shirt, and Doc Martens. "Yeah. So?"

"You know we have to be onstage, right?" he asked. She could tell that he was sweating under his gray-and-blue-striped button-down and tie.

"It's just going to be for two seconds, though."

"Let's ask Shanks," Remington said.

By the time they walked up to their mom, a woman with short, curly hair and a clipboard had joined them. "How's everyone doing?" Shanks asked benevolently. "You guys staying cool?"

"How is he?" Carolyn asked. "I hope you're not talking him to death over there. He does best when he doesn't overthink everything."

"He's just fine, Carolyn," Shanks said. "Don't worry. This here is Marcy. She's the stage manager. She's going to tell you where to be for when you go out onstage with him."

The girl named Marcy checked the clipboard in her hand. "So, at approximately minute twenty-two, Carolyn's going to go out, as soon as he's done speaking, and both Adam and Carolyn will wave for a few minutes, then we'll send out Remington and Emma after that for a quick wave to the crowd," she said.

"All right, that sounds fine," Carolyn said. "When does he go on?"

"In about four minutes," Marcy said, checking her clipboard again.

"Where's Dad?" Emma asked.

"Over there." Carolyn pointed to Adam and Tom, who were in close conversation. A PA hovered over her dad, helping to put the clear plastic earpiece in his ear. Someone had sponged his face with orange pancake makeup, which made him look a little alien. Suddenly, music came from the stage.

"Would you like to watch the speech in here, on the closed-circuit TV?" Marcy asked. "Or in the wings, so you can see the crowd?"

"In the wings," her mother said. "No, wait. If I do that I'll get nervous. Maybe just back here."

"I want to watch it in the wings," said Emma. "Let me get my friends. They want to see the crowd, too."

On the way back to her friends she stopped at her dad's chair and inserted herself between him and the PA.

"I just wanted to wish you luck," she said. "I'm really proud of you."

"Thanks, honey," he said, squeezing her hand. "How've you been? School good?"

"It's okay." She shrugged. She knew that now wasn't the time to have a heart-to-heart with her dad about her life.

"Listen, Tom and I just had a thought." He turned to Tom. "Tell Emma the idea."

Emma noticed that Tom's forehead shone with sweat, and for the first time she got a look at his flabby, lily-white arms, exposed by a dark green polo shirt.

"We want you to go out there with your dad alone," Tom said. "Just at the very beginning. Just go out and wave to the crowd."

"So, before my mom and brother?" she asked, glancing over at Carolyn, who was being powdered by the makeup woman.

"I'm going to talk for a minute about what happened in Washington," her father said, grinning. His orange face made his eyes look strange. "It's just for a laugh. Sound good to you?"

"Uh…okay," she said.

"It's just going to be a quick wave," Tom said. "Marcy'll tell you when to walk out. You got it?"

So I guess that night at the Boathouse is just a faint memory, she wanted to say, but instead she just nodded and said, "No problem."

183

A male campaign staffer wearing a laminated ID appeared at her father's side. "Senator, you've got one minute. I can take you to the spot."

Her dad handed him the speech. "Teleprompter's turned on, right?" he joked with a wink. He patted Emma's shoulder. "See you out there," he said, getting up.

"Good luck, Dad." She watched him slip on his suit jacket and wave to her mother and brother as he followed the staffer to the stage. She couldn't believe this. She was about to walk out there by herself, in front of twenty thousand people. It didn't seem real.

When she walked into the other tent, Lizzie, Carina, Todd, and Hudson were milling around, taking pictures with their iPhones.

"Hey! He's about to go on!" she called to them. "We have a spot where we can watch from the wings."

They followed her through the tent and into the VIP area. By now the music had gotten louder, and outside the crowd sent up a roar. It only grew in volume as Marcy led them closer to the stage.

"Oh my God, they're so loud," Lizzie said.

"It feels like the stage is gonna fall down," Carina said. "It's shaking."

Marcy led them up a short flight of iron stairs to a small landing. Emma grabbed the railing — Carina was right. The stage was actually shaking from all the applause.

"Stand over here," she said, pointing her friends to a small spot where they'd have a good a view of the crowd.

There was a clear shot of the Great Lawn through the flaps of the tent, and Emma peeked out at the crowd. It was a sea of banners and flags. From where she stood it looked like every person in New York City was waving something with her last name on it. It was so strange. She wished that she were with her brother to watch this. But he'd seemed like he was in a terrible mood, which didn't make any sense.

When her dad walked out onto the stage, the crowd roared and applauded so loudly that the four girls held one another to steady themselves.

"Even my *mom* doesn't get this!" Hudson yelled in Emma's ear over the noise.

Emma's dad came to stand behind a podium draped with a navy blue banner that read ADAM CONWAY FOR A NEW AMERICA. The sun shone directly over him, as if it were his own personal spotlight. Three teleprompters stood like tall sentries over the crowd, reflecting the words of his speech in their screens. But the crowd refused to quiet down. He had to wave them down several times before they would let him start speaking.

"Thank you, everyone, for coming out here today, though I understand this might be old news to some of you." He paused for what seemed like laughter, but the crowd was so large it just felt like a big rumble. "About two weeks ago my fifteen-year-old daughter told a crowd of my colleagues and friends of my decision to run. Some of you may have heard of it. Today I'd like to tell you all myself. But first, let's bring my daughter out here to say hi to all of you." He called to her offstage. "Emma, honey? Would you please come out here and just say hello to the crowd?"

Suddenly she felt someone grab her arm, and a moment later a staffer was pulling her toward the stage.

"What do I do?" she said.

"Go!" he yelled, almost pushing her onto the iron catwalk.

When she reached the stage the crowd roared so loudly that her heart almost stopped.

"My daughter told a crowd of senators and congressmen that she needed someone to look up to," he said. "She told them that her generation is scared, that they're tired of bad news, that they need a reason to look forward to the future."

Emma stood there, not knowing quite what to do. She looked out at one of the banners being held aloft in the crowd; it read WE NEED YOU ADAM.

"And I, for one, think she's right. America needs a future for our children, and for our grandchildren. We need an end to the patterns of foreign debt and useless war that have plagued this country for the past decade. We need to give my daughter a reason to hope."

The crowd roared again.

"My fifteen-year-old daughter represents all of you out there," her father went on, his voice ringing through the park. "And I'm running for president so I can ensure that all of you have a future!"

The applause came at them in waves, over and over. "Okay," her dad whispered. "You can say something if you want to." He stepped aside and gestured for her to take his place behind the podium.

Really? she mouthed.

He nodded.

For a split second she was scared, but then the same sense of duty she'd felt that night in Washington propelled her to move. She slipped behind the podium and leaned into the mic.

"How many of you out there are scared?" she yelled.

There was a howl from the crowd.

"How many of you out there feel confused?" she yelled.

The crowd roared in agreement.

"How many of you need someone to look up to?" she asked.

The crowd waved its banners and stomped its feet.

"I'm just as confused and scared and freaked out as all of you," she said into the mic. "But knowing my dad is entering this race is giving me hope! And it will give you hope, too!"

As the crowd screamed and roared and clapped in agreement, her dad squeezed her shoulder. He was happy, she knew. He was proud of her.

"Thank you, everyone!" she yelled, and then she stepped back from the podium, waving her arm in long, sweeping movements as she made her way off the stage.

She walked into the wings, shaking from the adrenaline. The first person to reach her was Lizzie. "Oh my God," she whispered, hugging her. "Emma, that was incredible. *You* were incredible."

"I have to sit down," she said, her legs starting to buckle.

They led her down the rickety iron steps to the VIP room in back. Her mother and brother stood watching the closed-circuit monitor, but as soon as they saw her come in, they were by her side in an instant.

"Oh, honey, you were fantastic," her mom said, throwing her arms around her. "You were just fantastic."

"Thanks," she said.

But her brother didn't move. He just stood there looking at her. She could tell from his eyes that he was dazed by what had just happened, and maybe just a little annoyed.

Her father was still giving his speech so they quickly turned their attention back to the screen. Emma could barely listen to it. *I just spoke to twenty thousand people,* she thought. *Off the top of my head.* It was surreal. She couldn't believe it. It didn't make any sense. She'd had no warning, no preparation. And yet, the entire Great Lawn had gone crazy for her words.

When Adam's speech was coming to a close, Marcy came by their table and led them out to the stage again. This time Emma made sure that she was the last one to walk out, and as they gathered on the stage around her dad, she stepped partially behind her brother's shoulder. The same U2 song started again, drowning out the crowd's roars and screams and making the stage jump with the bass. After waving for what felt like an eternity, they again made their way backstage. She'd never been so adrenalized, so full of emotion before. It was as if she'd just parachuted or bungee-jumped, and she was still tumbling through midair, her heart racing as she neared the ground.

When they reached backstage Tom and Shanks cheered.

"I think that went okay, right?" her father joked.

"That was amazing!" Remington said, shaking his head. "Dad, that was amazing!"

Adam hugged Remington, but quickly broke loose to turn toward Emma. "There you are!" he said, scooping her up in his arms. "You were terrific!" He spun her around and around in his arms as all of the staff gathered to watch. "She's a better politician than I am!" He put her down, and everyone patted her on the back and gave her hugs.

"I think we should have her go to the event next weekend," Tom said.

"What's next weekend?" Emma asked.

"He's giving a speech at SUNY Binghamton," said Shanks.

"Emma could introduce him," Tom said. "It makes sense for the college audience, especially considering how this crowd connected with her."

"Let's do it," her father said, still out of breath. "Honey, that okay with you?" he asked Carolyn.

"If Emma wants to do it," her mom said, pride shining in her face.

"I'll be right back," her father said as a staffer pulled him away by the arm to talk to the press.

"So, what do you think, honey?" her mom asked. "Do you want to introduce him next weekend?"

Emma's mind reeled. She looked at her mom, the staff, and her friends waiting to talk to her a few feet away. "Of course!" Emma said.

"Great! We'll prepare something for you to say," Tom said. "It won't be much. Just a few words. It'll be a big audience, though. And it's going to be televised."

Suddenly Emma was aware of Remington standing next to her, studying the ground. He hadn't said a word. In fact, he was being so quiet that she'd almost forgotten that he was standing nearby. "What about Remington?" she asked. "Can he say something, too?"

"Well, I don't know if there'll be enough time on the schedule,"

Shanks said, glancing at Tom. "But sure, if you want to, pal, that would be great."

"That's okay," Remington said. "Don't worry about it." He walked away toward the iced tea.

"Looks like your friends want to talk to you," Tom said, pointing to Carina, Lizzie, Todd, and Hudson waiting nearby. "Who's the boy? He looks familiar."

"That's Todd Piedmont."

"Jack Piedmont's son? The one whose picture I just saw in the paper?"

"Yeah. Why?"

Emma thought she saw a frown pass over Tom's face, but then it was gone. "We'll be in touch with you this week," he said, slapping her on the back. "Good job."

As her friends circled her, Emma started telling them all that had just happened. But all the while, only one thought kept going through her mind: *Finally, I'm a Conway after all.*

chapter 21

"Emma? You look over your speech? You good to go?"

Emma looked up from her laptop to see Shanks standing over her with a Styrofoam cup of what she knew was terrible coffee. Behind him she could see a row of blue lockers and a poster listing the SUNY Binghamton hockey team's last few championships. She would never have guessed how much time presidential candidates spent in college locker rooms before.

"Actually, I'm wondering if I can change a few things," she said, pointing to the screen with her pen. "Like when I say that my dad is a hero for a new time. Could I say that he's a hero for *our* time? You know, connect with the audience a little bit more?" It had been easier for her to memorize the speech, instead of taking her chances with the teleprompter and possibly having a dyslexia moment.

Shanks scratched his thatch of scruffy gray hair. "Okay," he said. "Just tell Gary, so he can put in the change."

"I will," she said. There were many other changes that she'd made and memorized, but she figured it was best to keep quiet about them.

"And you're okay with the teleprompter?" he asked. "There'll be three of them, so wherever you look, you'll see your speech on the screen."

"That's okay," she said. "I have it memorized."

"But you don't need to do that," Shanks said gently.

"Yeah, I do. I have dyslexia."

"Oh." Shanks looked surprised. "Okay."

"And is this really going to be streamed live to CNN?"

Shanks nodded. "It'll air pretty much all over the world."

Emma felt her stomach turn over. "Great. That's all I wanted to know."

He lumbered off, drinking his coffee, and she quickly dropped the speech into her e-mail. "Gary? I'm sending this to you!" she yelled, pressing Send on her laptop screen.

Her dad's head speechwriter — a twenty-three-year-old Columbia grad with amazing arms — waved at her. "Got it!"

She grabbed her bag and headed to the bathroom, past the table of campaign staffers double-checking her dad's speech on a series of laptops. Her eyes felt gritty, and she stifled a yawn. She'd woken at five that morning for the four-hour bus trip up to Binghamton, and already it felt like it was midnight instead of noon.

In the bathroom she reapplied her purple kohl eyeliner, her extra-black mascara, and her light pink lip-gloss. Amazingly, nobody had commented on the streak of blue she'd painted into her hair the night before with some Manic Panic. Nor had they commented on her makeup, her Doc Martens, or her toothpick jeans with the distressed knees. It was as if she finally had a free pass to be herself, especially at home. Ever since her dad's announcement speech, she could do no wrong. Her mom finally stopped asking her if she was really wearing what she was wearing. She didn't comment when she played her music too loud. And she could do no wrong with the media, either. The blogs and cable news networks talked about her "spontaneous stumping" for her dad for days. "Emma Conway" had been trending on Twitter for two days, and her Facebook page was so flooded with friend requests that she had to shut it down. People were calling her the "freshest face to come into politics in years," and the clip of her addressing the crowd in Central Park was getting all kinds of repeat airplay. She would overhear her mom on the phone with her friends at night, proudly telling them how much Emma had taken them all by surprise.

And if she'd thought her teachers had made a big deal about her speech in Washington, then their reaction to her speech in Central Park had stunned her. Everyone congratulated her on Monday morning (especially Dori). Chadwick built an assembly around it — Mr. Weatherly aired the clip and then brought Emma up in front of the entire Upper School to ask her some questions. Kids who'd never spoken to her before, like that cute guy Carter McLean, were inviting her to parties and asking her to go to the diner — not that she was about to ditch her real friends, but still, it was pretty exciting.

When she walked back into the locker room, her dad had returned from makeup and was getting some last-minute prepping from Tom and Shanks on the couch. This time she walked right over to him, sat down, and quietly listened.

"So remember," Tom told him, "even though this is a college, kids are still worried about getting jobs when they graduate."

"And Afghanistan," Shanks chimed in. "Some of these kids could have older sibs or parents serving."

"And don't forget the riff on a new brand of politics," Tom said. "*Brand* is a big word. These kids'll respond to that."

"Do you think so?" Emma interjected.

Tom and Shanks just stared at her. "What do you mean, Emma?" her father asked.

"I just think they'll catch on to that," she said. "Young people are sick of hearing about brands."

"You're probably right," said her dad. "Scratch that, Tom."

Emma caught Tom and Shanks exchanging a peeved look.

"Okay, we're on in about five," Marcy said, coming up to them. "Emma, I'm going to bring you back first. Remember, you have just a minute to speak. Does the prompter have the speech?"

Emma gave her a thumbs-up and stood.

"Good luck, honey," her father said.

"You, too," she said back to him.

He gave her a high five, the kind that she'd only ever seen him give to Remington, when he'd gotten straight A's or scored another victory in the pool. She followed Marcy out to the stage, beaming. She wished that her mom and Remington were here. She wanted them to see her like this — in control, useful, needed. But she was also happy Remington wasn't there. He'd been so moody lately. He stayed in his room at night, and came home from school only right before dinner. Swim practice had started, which ate up a lot of his time, but she still got the distinct feeling that he was avoiding her.

Now, as they walked toward the stage, she could hear the echoes of people in the bleachers. "How many people are here again?" she asked.

"About five thousand," Marcy replied.

Emma shook out the cricks in her neck and cracked her knuckles. A Journey song came over the loudspeaker to fire up the crowd. Finally they walked out of a hall and into the basketball stadium and Emma gulped. Red, white, and blue bunting had been draped over the stage, along with a gigantic sign that read CONWAY FOR AMERICA. A press pen crammed with photographers and cameramen faced the stage. And on all sides were bleachers of people, rising up above the stage.

"Okay, I'm going to give you your cue in a few seconds," Marcy said as soon as she'd led Emma to a backstage area. "You ready?"

Emma nodded. A makeup woman came out of nowhere and dotted her face with a powder puff.

"Remember, you only have a minute," Marcy said. "And address the crowd, but keep an eye on the prompter. And there'll be a clock counting you down. *Don't* go over time."

"I won't," Emma said, feeling the blood start to beat in her ears.

"Okay, ten seconds," Marcy said, holding a headset to her ear. "And five, four, three, two…"

A booming voice that sounded a little like Mr. Barlow's came over the loudspeaker. "And now to introduce Senator Conway," it rang out, "please welcome his daughter, Emma Conway!"

The crowd cheered, but it was a slightly less enthusiastic reaction than she remembered from Central Park. She strode out onto the stage, feeling incredibly tiny surrounded by so many bodies under one roof. At the last minute, she remembered to wave.

She went to the podium and found the mic. In front of her was the teleprompter, hovering over the crowd. The words of her speech were illuminated against the glass, but looking at them made her anxious. She didn't need them, anyway.

"Hello," she said. "I'm here today because my dad has decided to run for president." Her voice echoed around the stadium, distracting her for a moment. "But I want to be honest about something," she went on. "I didn't want him to run. I really didn't."

These weren't the words that had been written for her, but she didn't care. And she knew that nobody could really stop her now. She looked down at the fleet of cameras in the pit below the stage and tried to stay focused.

"For as long as I can remember, I've had to share my dad with this country," she continued. "And sometimes it's not that easy. He's so passionate about his job that sometimes, well...I get kind of jealous. So when my dad told me that he was going to run in this next election," she said, "I was less than thrilled. But then I realized that I needed to get my head out of my butt and stop being selfish. Because if I truly wanted change, if I truly wanted to stop being scared about my future, if I wanted to have someone to look up to, then I would need to think of what was best for everyone else. And I would do everything I could to support a man who has always taught me right from wrong, to turn the other cheek, to think of people less fortunate than me, and to never stop trying to be better."

She remembered to keep turning to face different sections of the stadium.

"So here he is, everyone. Let's give him a big hand. My dad. Adam Conway."

She looked over and saw Marcy waving for her to walk off. And behind her, waiting to go on, stood her father, looking slightly startled, and then pleased, by the thunderous applause shaking the stadium.

A staffer led him past her to the stage.

"Thanks, honey," he said as he passed by.

Then he was up on the stage and the noise was so loud she thought the roof might cave in.

She walked over to where Marcy stood with a few staffers. "How'd that go?" she asked.

"What was that?" Marcy said, her brow furrowed. "Did you write that yourself?"

Emma nodded.

"You've got guts, kid." Marcy pressed her earpiece farther into her ear and listened for a moment. "Okay. They want you to go back out at the end, with your dad. Stay here." She gave Emma a rueful look. "You're lucky. Normally they would have freaked. But I guess they liked it."

Emma gave the air beside her leg a discreet fist pump. The speech had been a risk, she knew. But it had worked. She was actually doing something right.

chapter 22

It was almost eleven o'clock when she staggered through the front door of her apartment. The drive back to the city had taken almost seven hours, thanks to all the New Yorkers who'd driven upstate to pick apples and look at fall foliage, and she'd fallen into a sound sleep for the last hour. She dumped her bag on the floor and felt her stomach gurgle. She was starving.

"Honey! I'm in here!" her mom called from the kitchen.

Emma found her mom seated at the kitchen table amid a sea of legal briefs. "Hi, Mom," she said.

Her mom stood up and threw her arms around her. "Did you see MSNBC?" she asked excitedly. Her face was devoid of makeup, and to Emma she finally looked normal again.

"No, I haven't seen anything. I've been in a car."

"They couldn't stop talking about it," her mom said, pulling out a plate of chicken breast and roasted potatoes from the refrigerator. "I taped it for you. They had a panel on, talking about how your speech upended all the rules, and then CNN spent about ten minutes talking about your 'refreshing honesty.' Even Fox News said that you were a role model for other teens." She put the plate in the microwave and shut the door.

"Are you kidding?" Emma asked. "I'm a role model?"

"I spoke to Dad," she said, tucking a strand of black hair behind her ear. "He was a little surprised. They didn't know you'd changed the speech. Or done *this*," she said, touching the blue-painted lock of Emma's hair. "But he was very impressed all the same. And so was I."

Before Emma could answer, the front door opened and shut.

"Remington?" her mom called out. "Emma's home!"

There was no reply. Emma listened to her brother's footsteps in the hall.

"Remington?" her mom called out again. "Come in here!"

"Just a second," he yelled back, and then they heard his bedroom door close.

"Is everything okay with him?" Emma asked.

Her mother took her plate out of the microwave. "I think so. Why?"

"Just…he's been acting a little weird to me," she said. She didn't want to say any more; it was an understood rule that she and her brother didn't complain about each other to their parents.

"He seems fine to me," her mom said, putting the plate down on the table in front of her.

"Be right back," Emma said. She walked to Remington's bedroom. "Hey," she said through the door. "Can I come in?

Remington?" After waiting a moment and not getting an answer, she finally opened the door.

He sat at his desk, playing Red Dead Redemption on his desktop computer.

"What are you doing?" she asked.

"Working on my Harvard application," he said, not taking his eyes off the screen. "What does it look like?"

Emma couldn't tell for sure, but his words sounded slightly slurred. And there was a familiar smell wafting through the room, the same odor she'd smelled coming out of his room that night in Washington. She couldn't quite place it.

"Where were you tonight?" she asked carefully.

"Out," he said, keeping his eyes on the screen.

"With who?"

"What are you, Mom?" he asked, pausing the game and swiveling in his chair to face her. "Just focus on your new political career, okay?"

"Don't be a jerk," she said.

"Just get out, okay?" he yelled.

"Fine!" She left his room without closing the door. A moment later she heard it slam so loud that the walls shook. Remington never slammed doors.

"What was that?" her mom called from the kitchen.

"Nothing!" she yelled out. She stood in the hall, perfectly still, and felt a solitary, angry tear well up and fall down her cheek.

He's jealous, she thought. She'd always wondered what that would feel like. But it felt nothing like what she'd imagined. It only made her feel lonely.

In the kitchen, her mom was back at the table and absorbed in her work. "Is everything okay?" she asked.

"Everything's fine," she said, and sat back down to her dinner. But when she picked up her fork, she found that she'd lost her appetite.

chapter 23

"So, can we talk about the fact that you're a nationwide sensation?" Lizzie asked Emma on Monday morning as they walked up the block to Chadwick. It was the first cold morning of the fall, and the steel-gray sky seemed to threaten rain. Lizzie wore an adorable black fedora and a vintage-looking olive-green suede coat. Emma wondered if she'd ever be able to pull off a hat. She'd tried many times, but they always looked contrived on her.

"I'm so *not* a sensation," Emma said, pulling her black vinyl motorcycle jacket tighter around her.

"My dad wants to write about you in his column for the *Times,* okay?" Lizzie said. "That equals sensation. And Manic Panic Shocking Blue is sold out at the Ricky's on Seventy-second and Columbus," Lizzie said, touching Emma's blue-painted strands. "I'm just saying."

"I'm just trying to help out my dad. And be honest at the same time."

"Maybe you'll inspire everyone else," Lizzie said. "If you can make a political speech and be yourself, then there's hope for adults."

They walked into the lobby, where Dori the receptionist launched herself out of her chair. "Oh, Emma!" she cried, throwing down her headset. "I saw the clip on CNN. You were just spectacular!"

"Thanks, Dori," Emma said as she and Lizzie quickly mounted the stairs. "This is starting to get a little embarrassing," she said to Lizzie under her breath.

"Just enjoy it," Lizzie said.

They climbed the stairs to the Upper School and walked to the lockers, where Todd was getting out his books.

"Hey, stranger," Lizzie said, leaning in to kiss him on the cheek. "Where were you last night? I called you. And texted."

"Oh," Todd said, looking vaguely guilty, Emma thought. His floppy brown hair was long over the back of his collar and needed a cut. His blue eyes looked puffy. "I was downtown with my brother." He fumbled with his lock.

"Well, how is he? How's everyone?"

"I'm fine," he said hurriedly, darting a glance at Emma. "Can you guys save me a seat? I'll be there in a sec." He slung his book bag over his shoulder and took off toward the bathroom.

"What's with him?" Emma asked.

Lizzie sighed as she dialed her combination. "It's gotten worse. The prosecution found all these receipts from a hotel in Grand Cayman." She lowered her voice. "Turns out Todd's dad took over the top floor to throw his girlfriend a party. And charged it to the company. It's all so mortifying for everyone."

"But he's being weird with *you*?" Emma asked.

"I wish I knew what to do. Leave him alone? Give him space? Be a shoulder to cry on? I have no idea." She pulled off her patchwork-style scarf and stuffed it into her locker.

"Huh," Emma said. "I don't know. This really isn't my area of expertise."

"Hey, guys," Carina said, walking up to them. "Okay. What's going on?" She looked from one to the other of them. "I'm sensing drama."

"Todd is being weird," Emma said.

"Oh," Carina said. "What else is new?"

"Hey!" Lizzie said, playfully giving her a jab on the shoulder.

"No, he's *really* being weird," Emma supplied. "We think it's the trial. It has to be, Lizzie."

Just then Remington walked past them. Emma gave him a wave but her brother only glowered at her.

"Yikes," Lizzie said. "I thought Todd was being weird."

"He just has something up his butt, as usual," Emma said. "Forget it."

"Actually, I heard kind of a weird story about him just now," Carina said.

Emma felt the hairs on her arm suddenly stand up. "What do you mean?"

"Well, I didn't want to say anything, but I'd rather you hear it from me than from some other kid." Carina cast her eyes down. "He supposedly got kind of wasted at a Brearley party Saturday night. With Steven and Chris. The three of them were totally out of control. Some of the other guys there had to ask them to leave."

Emma felt a knot form in the center of her chest. "Are you sure?"

"Positive," Carina said. "At least, that's what I heard."

"Wow," Lizzie said. "He's always been, like, the model student."

"He *is* a model student," Emma said. "He's going to get into Harvard early. I don't know what that's about." But she remembered the weird smell in his room Saturday night. And how he couldn't look her in the eye.

"Well, it probably has more to do with the Cro-Magnon twins than it does with your brother," Carina said, waving it off.

Emma let it drop as they walked into homeroom, but the story gnawed at her for the rest of the day. It made her think of other things that didn't quite make sense: That night in Washington, when Remington got so ill, for no real reason... Seeing Steven and Chris the following Monday, and hearing Chris talking about someone being a "maniac" at Georgetown... How Remington's words had sounded slurred in his room the other night. Maybe there was some truth to the Brearley party story. But how could there be? Remington had never gotten in trouble for anything, ever. He'd never even gotten detention. And now he was getting thrown out of parties? How?

There was only one person who could possibly help her figure this all out. When she walked down to the library for speech team, she saw him standing at one of the seemingly always broken vending machines.

"Hi," Walker said, banging the side of the machine. "How's the campaign trail?"

"There's always room for improvement," she said, coming to stand next to him.

"I'm starting to think you don't need much," he said, hitting the machine again. "You're doing great. Really. I'm impressed."

"Thanks," she said, letting the compliment sink in.

He smiled at her for a moment, and then he turned back to the vending machine. "Is this thing ever not broken? Jeez." He banged it again and a granola bar dropped into the tray. "Finally." He reached down to grab it.

"Hey, can I ask you something?" she said. "Why aren't you friends with my brother anymore?"

Walker carefully unwrapped the bar. "Why do you ask that?"

"Because it's obvious you're not. You're never around each other anymore. Did you guys have a fight about something?"

Walker frowned. "No."

"Well, what was it? Can you tell me?"

"Sometimes people just stop being friends," he said. "There doesn't have to be a reason."

"Come on. Was it something about school? Or speech team?"

"Emma, it's between me and him. Sorry, but it is." They began to walk toward the library.

"So there was something that happened," she observed.

"Why do you care?" he asked.

"Because he seems to be acting kind of weird, and I heard this bizarre story today. I don't know. You were his best friend for so long. You're the only other person who knows him like I do."

Walker sighed and studied the ground. "Look, your brother's

in a different scene now. And it's just not one that I really want to be part of."

Before he could speak there were footsteps behind them. She turned to see Remington coming toward them. "What are you guys doing?" His blue-green eyes darted from her to Walker and back again. His voice was friendly, but there was a ripple of tension underneath it. *He heard,* Emma thought. *He totally heard us.*

"Nothing," she said, as innocently as she could muster.

"Hey, Walker," Rem said, in a way that was a little too friendly.

"Hi, Rem," Walker replied.

"You guys going to the library?" Remington asked.

"Where else?" Walker answered.

The three of them walked silently into the room, the air so thick with tension that Emma couldn't speak. It was obvious now that the two of them were in a fight. But she didn't know whose side of the fight she was on.

"So you want to come over for dinner tomorrow night?" her brother asked him.

Emma stayed quiet but watched Walker for a reaction.

"I really can't," Walker said. "I have some applications to work on."

"That's what you said last week," Remington said. "What did I do to you, man? You can be friends with my sister, but not with me? What the hell?"

"Relax," Walker said. "Don't be an idiot."

"Do you think I'm being an idiot?" Remington erupted. "Is that what you think? That I'm being an *idiot*?"

Emma watched her brother step toward Walker in a threatening way. It looked like they might actually have a fight, and then Walker pushed past Remington into the library.

Remington stared at Walker, obviously fuming.

As more people trickled into the room behind her, Emma took a deep breath and sat down. They seemed to have avoided a fight. But whatever had happened between Remington and Walker, it seemed about to boil over.

chapter 24

"How're you doing, Emma?" said a male campaign staffer with blond hair wearing a CONWAY FOR AMERICA T-shirt. "I'm Jeff, your point person. If you need anything, just let me know. I think we're probably gonna start in about forty-five minutes."

"Thanks," Emma said, reaching for the bottle of water she'd gotten out of the cooler and turning back to her laptop.

As Jeff walked away, Lizzie nudged Emma in the side and said, "These campaign aides are kind of cute, I have to say."

"Uh-huh," Emma said, putting the finishing touches on her speech. "Will you read this for me? Tell me what you think?" She handed her laptop to Lizzie.

"You really like Radiohead, huh?" Lizzie said, checking out the stickers on the top.

"Just read it," Emma said. "We don't have a lot of time."

"So you wrote this all by yourself?" Lizzie asked, placing the laptop on her knees.

"They let me," Emma said, getting to her feet and stretching. "I know. I couldn't believe it, either." This time, she'd left out the stuff about not wanting her dad to run — she'd gathered from Shanks that that part had made them all a little nervous, despite the positive press reaction. Instead, she'd focused more on why she considered him a hero, and why kids her age desperately needed one. All the stuff that she'd said that day in Central Park. Shanks and Beckett had approved it in an e-mail, and by now she'd committed it to memory.

As she waited for Lizzie to finish, Emma walked back to the cooler to get another bottle of water. There was a palpable excitement in the backstage area of the main theater at the University of Pennsylvania. Conway mania had been steadily building in the press, and when Emma got the invitation to speak again from Shanks she jumped at the chance. This time her entire family was here, and she'd brought Lizzie for moral support. Tom and Shanks stayed close to her dad, prepping him in the corner as a makeup artist sponged makeup on him. Her mom and Remington hung out with Marcy, the stage manager, near the big closed-circuit television monitor. She stepped in front of one of the makeup mirrors and checked out her outfit: black-and-white-striped miniskirt, ankle-high Doc Martens, black tights, and a silk purple top with plenty of silver chains around her neck. She'd also replaced the blue Manic Panic dye with hot pink. To her amazement, nobody had said a word. True, it wasn't much — just a few strands — but it had definitely been enough to get her grounded in the past. The pink was meant to get her in the mood for Halloween; later that night, she was going to go to Alex's party as Gwen Stefani from her *Return of Saturn* days.

"I think this looks great," Lizzie said, closing the laptop.

"Really? You sure? I mean, they all approved it already, but still…"

"I love that part about needing something besides the advertising on TV and on Google. You're really good at this, you know that?"

"Who would have thought, right?" Emma said as she watched Tom Beckett coming toward her. His hairline seemed to have receded a bit since the beginning of the campaign, and his dark suits looked looser. But he still emanated a fidgety intensity. "Emma," he said, "can you hold on a second?"

"Okay."

"We just made a few changes to your speech. Here's the new one." He handed her the pages.

"The *new* one?"

"This is what we'd like you to say instead," he said. "We just got it written."

"But…you already approved my speech," she said. "Why do I need this one?"

"A new poll came in last night," Tom said. "Turns out that some people weren't so bowled over by your last appearance. This is just to put everyone's mind at ease."

"Put their mind at ease," she repeated. "About what?"

Tom twisted the band of his silver watch. "Some people were concerned about your outspokenness," he said. "They thought what you said last time wasn't as…supportive as it could have been. Now, people love the fact that Adam has a daughter who's got stage presence and a good voice, and it's something new. But

211

your particular brand of honesty... Well, it's rubbing some people the wrong way."

Emma and Lizzie traded a suspicious glance. *You mean it's rubbing* you *the wrong way,* she was tempted to say. And maybe a few weeks ago, she would have said it. But now things were different. She was officially part of Team Conway, and she had to at least try to toe the party line.

She looked down and skimmed the speech. As usual, some of the words were jumbled, but enough of it was clear.

"'Today's out-of-control and disconnected youth need someone to look up to'?" she read. "What is this?"

"Well, it's what you've been saying all along. That teens are scared and confused and need a hero, right?"

"But you're putting the blame on teens," she said. "That's not what I said. I wasn't criticizing people my age."

"Look, just trust us on this," he said, smirking a little. "Also, we have something else for you to wear."

"W-what?" she sputtered.

"Something a little more conservative," Tom added.

"Are you kidding?" Emma eyed Lizzie again. "Where's my dad?"

"He's with us on this," Beckett said coolly. "Now, just look that over. And I'll get you a new dress. Also, Todd Piedmont: We'd appreciate it if he didn't come with you to any more campaign functions. We can't afford to have your father associated with criminals." He walked away before she could say anything more.

"Oh my God," Emma said. "Lizzie, I'm so sorry. I have no idea what that's about."

Lizzie had gone pale. "Where did that come from?" she asked. "What does Todd have to do with any of this?"

"He saw Todd at Central Park," she said. "I don't know what's going on. Hold on, let me just think," she said, trying to read the speech through her fury.

It was even worse than she thought. *Today's teens are in desperate need of some real substance in their lives,* read one line. *Glutted on reality television, obsessed with the latest labels, we need a leader who can make us appreciate something honest and true,* read another.

She couldn't go out there and give this speech. Her friends would never speak to her again. Nobody would.

Out of the corner of her eye she saw Remington, off by himself, reading a campaign memo. He would know what to do. "I'll be right back," she said to Lizzie, who had gone oddly quiet.

"Fine," Lizzie murmured.

Emma rushed over to Remington, almost bumping into a coffee urn on the way. "Rem?" she asked. "Can I talk to you about something?"

From the way he looked up from his memo she could tell he was in no mood to give advice. "What?" he asked, looking at her coolly.

"Look at this," she said. "They just gave me this. It's terrible. It's nothing that I would ever say in real life. Or even that Dad would say." She handed it to him. "Read it," she said.

He scanned it quietly. "I don't really see what the big deal is," he said when he finished.

"But look at what it says. This isn't me. I would *never* say this," she argued.

213

Remington sighed. "You've been pretty lucky so far," he said. "Going out last weekend and giving a speech that you changed without anyone's permission? About how much you *didn't* want Dad to run? What did you think was going to happen?"

"But it went okay. People liked it."

"The *press* liked it. The *people* didn't. And Dad can't afford to alienate potential voters," Remington said.

"But this is ridiculous," she said. "They like me because I'm outspoken, because I say what I think. Now they want me to change?"

"Welcome to politics, Emma." He handed the speech back to her. "Sorry."

"Then I'm going to go find Dad."

"What do you think Dad's going to do? He can't go out there and just say whatever he wants. He has to listen to them, too. It's called being part of a presidential campaign."

"Right. I forgot you know everything," she spat.

"About this? Yeah. I do."

"Look, you're the one who totally blew it in Washington, okay? Ever since this all started for me you've been a total jerk."

She stormed off but Tom intercepted her, holding a plastic dry-cleaning bag, containing what looked like a plain navy dress on a hanger.

"What's this?" she asked.

"What we'd like you to wear," he said, giving her the plastic-covered dress. "It should be your size."

She looked in horror at the dress. It was shapeless, with darts in the bust and princess-style cap sleeves.

"And shoes are in here," he said, grabbing a shopping bag from beside the sofa. "You should probably get changed."

"I'm not doing this."

Tom gave her the same eerie, fake smile she'd seen at the Boathouse that night all those weeks ago. "Then you don't have to speak, Emma," he said. "The choice is yours." He held out the shopping bag.

She stared at him, unwilling to believe this. But she took the shopping bag.

"And you might want to tone down that eyeliner, too," he said. "You know, try the fresh-faced look. That's what America wants to see." He patted her shoulder. "Oh, and your hair…" He waved the makeup artist over. "Is there any way we can hide this?" he said, pointing to the colored strands.

The makeup artist tugged at her heavily pierced earlobes. "I think if we just pull it all back," she said, taking Emma's hair and pulling it into a severe bun.

"Perfect," Tom said approvingly, as the woman twisted an elastic around Emma's hair.

"That's enough," Emma said, stepping away. She was so angry that she was practically trembling.

"Emma?" Marcy said, coming up to her, her laminated ID bouncing. "Are you getting dressed? You're running out of time."

Emma went to the bathroom and shut the door. She was so angry that her vision was blurry. She grabbed a paper towel and put it under the faucet to wet it, then dabbed at her eyeliner until most of it was gone. With another paper towel she wiped off her lipstick. The dress slipped on easily, but when she zipped it up she realized that it was at least a size too big. Then she pulled the shoes out of her shopping bag: horribly clunky black heels. They fit, but she would much rather have gone barefoot.

Then she looked in the mirror. With her makeup gone, her hair pulled back into a Quaker-style bun, and her body obscured by this navy blue tent, she looked like a stranger.

When she walked out of the bathroom she found Lizzie in the hall, waiting for her. "Oh, Emma," she said, with a stricken face. "Do you really want to do this?"

"I can't say no," she said. "I have to do it."

"Why?" Lizzie asked, taking her arm.

Just then Emma saw her mother look over at her from where she sat in front of the monitor. She expected her mom to smile approvingly, to finally be happy at this kind of transformation. But instead she looked slightly appalled.

"Emma! It's time!" Marcy called, trudging over to them. "Let's go!" She grabbed Emma's arm, wrenching her away from Lizzie.

"Bye," Lizzie said.

Emma walked through the backstage area, feeling everyone's eyes on her. If it was this embarrassing to be dressed like this in front of the campaign staff, then Emma could only imagine how she was going to feel onstage. And in front of the cameras.

This isn't me, she thought as she walked to the stage. *But there's nothing I can do about it now.*

chapter 25

On Monday morning, Emma knew things were off when Dori didn't leap up from her chair in greeting.

"Hi, Emma," Dori said, waving at her. Then she answered a call. "The Chadwick School," she said brightly into the phone.

Emma walked up the stairs, unable to shake the bad feeling that had stayed with her since Saturday afternoon. The speech had technically gone fine — she hadn't flubbed any of the words, and she'd been able to get the crowd sufficiently riled up for her dad. But afterward she'd sunk into a funk that hadn't yet lifted. Lizzie had offered her a tepid smile when she came offstage and said "You did great!" Her mom had gently hugged her and mumbled that she was proud. Carina and Hudson had both texted her vague messages like *"Good job!"* and *"Amazing!"* but nothing else. Remington, naturally, had said nothing.

The only person who seemed truly happy with what she'd said had been her dad, who apologized for switching the speech on her at the last moment.

Lizzie had said little on the drive back to the city. Emma couldn't figure out what was bothering her more: the comment Tom had made about Todd, or the way Emma had completely failed to protect her own dignity.

At dinner that night, Emma didn't say much at the table. Remington and Carolyn chatted about Iowa precinct captains and campaign finance reform as Emma picked at her food. When it came time to get ready for Alex's party, she felt so depressed that she decided not to go.

She went to bed early, and then tossed and turned, punching her pillow over and over. Anger bubbled up inside her, keeping her awake. But when she tried to put a face to the anger, the only one she could see was her own.

The next day she'd typed her name into the Google search bar. Seven thousand news articles came up. She clicked on the first one.

CONWAY KID HITS WRONG NOTE, read the headline. The piece accused her dad of "blatantly pandering" to the swing voters and trying to "muzzle" his "controversial, blue-haired" daughter. "Seems like Conway wants to have his cake and eat it too," the writer said. "He uses his kid to get young people's attention, and then wants to apologize for it at the same time."

Emma shut her laptop. She put on "Cities in Dust" by Siouxsie and the Banshees and took Archie out of his terrarium and let him slither around on the floor, trying to lose herself in the music. *That's not me,* she thought. *I'm not really the girl who said those things.*

So now, as she walked down the Upper School hallway and saw Hudson waiting for her at the lockers, she was relieved. Of her three friends, Hudson always seemed the least judgmental.

"Hey," she said, forcing herself to smile. "Sorry I didn't text you back yesterday. I was kind of sick."

"That's okay," Hudson said sweetly. "I just wanted to tell you how great you did. I saw a little bit of it on CNN."

"Just so you know, that wasn't the speech I wrote," she said quietly. "They switched it at the last minute. It was kind of annoying."

"So you *don't* think that the Internet is ruining the fabric of American teenage life?" Hudson kidded.

"Uh, no," Emma joked. "Definitely not." She shut the locker and leaned her forehead against it. "I'm so embarrassed."

"Don't be," Hudson said. "It wasn't that bad. I mean, you really sold it up there. Technically, you were perfect. Even my mom was impressed. She actually watched a little bit of it with me. I couldn't believe it."

"I don't know what to do, H," Emma said, using Hudson's nickname for the first time. "My brother went off on me, saying that this isn't about me, that even my dad can't say what he wants, blah, blah, blah, but it just doesn't feel right. It's not what I believe. So I shouldn't keep doing it, right?"

Hudson untangled the cluster of silver charm necklaces at her throat as she thought. "I don't know, Emma. Maybe you should just take a break for a while. It's been kind of a whirlwind. And you've done a lot for your dad, you really have. More than most kids could or would."

Emma thought about this as they walked into homeroom. Maybe it was time to stop.

Carina and Lizzie had already sat down in the back. Lizzie looked even paler than usual, and she and Carina seemed to be in deep conversation.

"Hey guys, what's going on?" Emma asked as they slid into their seats.

Lizzie flinched at the question. Carina looked somber. "Todd and I are taking a break," Lizzie said quietly.

"Oh my God," said Hudson.

"We talked about it last night. It just seemed the right thing to do. With everything that's going on." She paused. "It looks like his dad isn't going to win this. And if he gets convicted, then they're definitely going to send him to jail."

"Oh my God, Lizbutt, I'm so sorry," said Hudson. "That's terrible. For both of you."

"But you did the right thing," Carina counseled in her best no-nonsense tone. "You've been dealing with his weirdness for forever. If Alex pulled all that stuff on me I would have totally moved on by now."

"Where is he?" Hudson asked, looking around.

"He's not going to be in this week. The case is probably going to the jury tomorrow. And if his dad gets convicted, then he's going to want to just be with family."

"I'm so sorry, Lizzie," Emma said.

But Lizzie didn't look at her. She just stared straight ahead as if Emma hadn't said anything at all, curling a strand of hair around her finger.

"Lizzie? I'm sorry."

"Thanks," Lizzie said in an icy tone, as Mr. Weatherly began to call roll.

Yikes, Emma thought. Lizzie was mad at her. It only compounded the dread that she was already feeling.

Her pariah status continued for the rest of the day. Mr. Barlow barely noticed Emma in the hall, and at speech practice that afternoon, Walker kept his head down almost the entire time, except for when he had to deliver a killer monologue on why cell phones should be allowed in schools. During the entire speech, he didn't make eye contact with her once.

After practice, as people trudged out of the library, she forced herself to approach him. "Great job," she said, as he began packing up his book bag. "That was, like, your best one yet."

"Thanks," he said, shoving his books into the bag.

"How've you been?" she persisted. "How was your weekend?"

"Fine," he replied. He seemed to be in a gigantic hurry. The zipper on his bag stuck and he had to literally force it to keep moving.

"Is something wrong?" she asked.

He finally stopped his frantic movements and looked at her. "Actually, yeah. How could you give that ridiculous speech?"

"Excuse me?" she asked.

"I'm serious," he said, scratching his head. "That was terrible. That wasn't you at all."

"I'm sorry you didn't approve," she finally said.

"You were doing so well, Emma," he said. "You were really becoming...I don't know...the best version of you," he said. "And then, last weekend, I had no idea who that person was onstage. It didn't even look like you."

"Why don't you tell me how you really feel?" she muttered.

"I *am* telling you how I feel," he said. "It was a mistake. You're better than that."

"Okay, I got it, all right?" she snapped. "Do you think that's

221

what I wanted to do? No. They made me. They changed it on me at the last minute."

"You could have said no." Walker threw his book bag over his shoulder. "Your dad's the one running for president. Not you. You could have said no."

"Well, what's it to you, anyway?" she yelled. "What do you care what I say? Do you want me to tell you what I think of you?"

She couldn't stop herself, even though Walker's expression had turned stony.

"I think you couldn't handle being my brother's friend anymore," she said. "I think you just couldn't take the competition and you decided to never speak to him again. I think you're a terrible, terrible friend. And I think you hold grudges, too. He asked you over for dinner that night, and you didn't even have the decency to say yes."

Walker's jaw muscle began to pop up and down.

"So that's what I think of you," she said. "Mr. Four-Point-Oh. So you can just stop judging everyone else."

She brushed past him and walked to the door. Her heart beat so rapidly that she almost tripped on the stairs, and when she got to the lobby she ran through the doors without giving Dori even the smallest glance.

She turned uptown on Madison and walked a few blocks, until she was well out of the private-school zone. On East Ninety-fourth Street, she turned toward Fifth, and found her favorite spot to be alone: the deep, curved stoop in front of the Russian Consulate. She sat down on the edge, out of the sight of passersby, and let herself cry.

chapter 26

"So what's after Toledo?" her mom asked as she put a basket of rolls on the dining table.

"Cincinnati, Detroit, Iowa City, and then down in Orlando for a bit," said her father, helping himself to some roasted chicken. "They're expecting Senator Gibbons to make his announcement any day now, so they're really ramping things up."

Emma took a bite of her salad. When she'd finally made it home that afternoon, half-drenched from the rain, she'd heard her dad's voice in the office and seen his battered luggage in the foyer. She knew that she was supposed to be happy that her dad had surprised them with a quick pit stop at home for the night, but his timing couldn't have been worse.

"So I finished my Harvard application," Remington said. "I'm turning it in tomorrow."

"Good for you," her mom said.

"What about Yale? You finished with that one?" Adam asked.

"Not yet. But I will be," he said. "I'm going up there in a few weeks."

"You are?" their dad said, eating some green beans.

"I have an interview, and I know some people up there," her brother said. "They said I can spend the night in the dorm. Get a real feel for the school." He took a sip of water. "You think I could borrow the car to go up there? It's only a two-hour drive."

"You can also take the train," Carolyn said. "It might be easier."

"Let him take the car," Adam said. "That's fine. And what about Columbia?"

"Application is in," Remington said.

Emma poked at her rice with her fork. It was almost like she wasn't there.

"So, Karl Jurgensen's throwing me a fund-raiser," Adam announced. "At the Temple of Dendur at the Met."

"Really?" her mom asked. "When were you going to tell me this?"

"It just happened," Adam said, his eyes gleaming. He turned to Emma. "You're friends with his daughter, aren't you?"

She nodded, uncertain where this was going.

"Well, how would you like to speak with me there? It's only fitting, since all your friends will probably be there."

She struggled to think of the right response. "I don't know if that's such a good idea."

"What do you mean?" her dad said. "You've been doing a great job."

She put down her fork. "The last one didn't seem to go over so well."

"It didn't? I thought you did perfectly."

Emma watched him devour his chicken breast. "Dad, can I ask you something? Are you still embarrassed by me?"

Her father looked up from his chicken. "What on earth are you talking about?"

"Why did you let them change my speech like that?"

Her father patted the corners of his mouth with a napkin. "First off, I'm never embarrassed by you," he said. "You're my daughter. But those polls came back and people were upset, and Tom and Shanks thought we could use a slight change."

"I thought you liked me being myself out there," she said. "I thought that was what got you guys so much attention. Or am I wrong about that?"

"Emma, a campaign is always honing its message. That's part of it. You can't take this all so personally. You've done a wonderful job. And you really ran with things the other day. You're a team player."

"But did you see the blogs?" she asked. "Did you see some of the stuff they said about me? And *you*?"

"If I read every blog…" her father said, giving her mother a smile.

"You don't believe that all of the teenagers in America are brainwashed idiots. I mean, come *on*."

"Emma," her mom said, in her best mediator's voice, "you did a wonderful job the other day. And your father wouldn't have let you make that speech if he thought it was going to harm him in any way."

"But what about *me*?" she asked. "What about harming me? Did you see the way they made me dress? The way I had to look?"

Her father dropped his fork. "Do you think that I can go out there and say whatever I want to?" he asked. "Do you think you're the only one who's being told what to say? Or how to look? Or how to be?"

"Adam," her mom said in a warning voice.

He pushed his chair back from the table. "Look, honey, if you don't want to do this anymore, fine. I'm not going to make you."

She worked her napkin around and around her finger.

"It's just that you've changed," he went on. "You've really come into your own. And it's been a thrill to watch. For all of us."

Have I really come into my own? she thought. *Or have I just turned into your prop?*

"So all I'm asking is for you to come with me to a very glamorous event at the Metropolitan Museum of Art with all of your friends, and speak to a bunch of people," he went on. "But if you don't want to do it —"

"I'll do it," she said. The napkin was wound so tight that her finger had gone numb.

"Great," Adam said. "I'll have Tom and Shanks call you with the details." He stood up. "And now I think I have to go make some fund-raising calls. Dinner was wonderful." He patted his wife on the shoulder, then went to his office.

Emma untwisted the napkin, letting the blood rush back into her finger. She'd made the decision she wanted to make, but something about this still didn't feel right. Her brother picked at his food. Her mom had stopped eating altogether and was taking careful sips of white wine. Something had changed in the dynamic of the Conway household, Emma thought. Something else had come into its own: her dad's thirst to win. And she wondered if her family was going to survive it.

After dinner that night she wrote Lizzie an e-mail: *Dad just asked me to speak at this event hosted by Carina's dad... Said yes, but I think I should back out. Should I?*

By morning, Lizzie hadn't written back.

chapter 27

The speech for the event at the Met came by e-mail a few days later, sent from Tom Beckett's assistant.

Karl Jurgensen event, read the subject line. Sitting in the Chadwick computer lab, Emma clicked on it with trepidation and read the first line.

America's youth is our future, and right now that future needs serious help.

"Ugh," she said. It was almost an exact rehash of the speech she'd given at the University of Pennsylvania: America's youth were out of control, too wrapped up in their cell phones and their video games to buckle down and make sacrifices. *What a joke,* Emma thought, sending the speech to the printer. Sure, her dad didn't want his kids playing video games all day, but she knew for a fact that he didn't blame Sony PlayStation for the country's problems. Why was his campaign doing this? Why were they making him sound like some bitter old-timer who'd fought off grizzly bears on his way to school? It didn't make any sense. She knew her dad wasn't like this.

She got up and went to the printer, where the one sheet sat in the tray, daring her to pick it up. This was going to be a huge mistake, she thought. There wouldn't be press at a private fund-raiser, but her friends would be there, and that was bad enough.

As she was folding the speech in half and about to slip it into her notebook, she saw Lizzie walk into the lab. Lizzie barely looked at Emma as she sat down behind one of the Macs and opened up her Gmail.

Emma wasn't surprised. Things between them had been weird since the event at the University of Pennsylvania, and for the past few days Lizzie had barely said a word to her. Emma had been fine with the semi-silent treatment, but now, as she stood just a few feet away, she thought to herself: *Enough is enough.*

"Hey," she said, walking over. "What's up?"

Lizzie looked at Emma over her shoulder. "Oh, hi," she said. She turned back to her e-mail.

"How are you?" Emma said.

"Good," Lizzie said tonelessly.

Emma wanted to ask her if she'd heard from Todd but she knew that now wasn't the time. "So, I think I told you that I'm speaking at this thing tomorrow night at the Met," she ventured. "Can you come? Carina and Hudson are coming."

"I really don't know," Lizzie said, not turning around. "My mom wants me to help her with stuff."

Emma pulled out the empty chair next to Lizzie and sat down. "Um, are you mad at me?" she asked. "It feels like you're mad at me."

Lizzie let go of the computer mouse. "I just was shocked to hear what that guy said about Todd. Not wanting him around your dad's campaign. And you didn't say anything back to him about it."

"What was I supposed to say?" Emma asked, feeling herself get angry. "When he'd just switched that speech on me and I had no idea what was going on?"

Lizzie shook her head. "The old Emma would have told that guy to go to hell," she said. "And you said nothing. Like it was just...okay."

"Because I was completely freaked out about other stuff!" Emma said.

"Don't yell at me," Lizzie said, getting up and walking away.

"Look, I didn't mean to blow it off — I think that guy's a total jerk, too," Emma said, following her. "I just didn't know what to do in the moment. You know? I would have said something to him later."

Lizzie turned on her heels and faced Emma in the hallway. "I've been a really good friend to you. I welcomed you to this school, I introduced you to people, you name it. But lately it just feels like this is all about you. You haven't been here for me when I really needed you." Her eyes started to get watery. "You've been so busy with this campaign and everything. And Todd has been through enough. He doesn't need to be treated like a criminal on top of it."

"Lizzie, what did I do? I don't even get what you're talking about!"

"Forget it," Lizzie said, wiping her eye with the back of her hand. "Just forget it. Have a good time tomorrow night." She hurried away down the stairs and out of sight.

Emma stood in the hallway for a moment, trying to catch her breath. She'd definitely lost friends before; that was nothing new. And a part of her thought that Lizzie had gone a little overboard.

But nothing had ever felt quite so harsh as seeing the back of Lizzie's head as she ran down the stairs to get away from her.

"So do you know what you're going to say?" Carina asked as the cab drove them down Madison Avenue.

"If you're nervous I can give you some breathing exercises," Hudson said.

"That's okay, guys, I think I have it down," Emma said, looking at all the lit-up boutique windows as they passed. It had finally stopped raining a few hours before, but a thick mist hung in the air, giving the Upper East Side the look of Victorian London — and adding to the dread Emma had been feeling since that morning. For the past day and a half she'd been debating whether or not to come down with a severe case of stomach flu just so she could avoid this night. Her hands felt sweaty as she held the Fendi clutch purse she'd borrowed from her mom. Her speech was folded up inside. Maybe it was a mental block, but she still hadn't been able to memorize it.

"My dad's really psyched to see you speak," Carina said. "He told me. He's been following you on the news."

"That's nice," Emma said in a noncommittal way. "Do you think there are going to be any cute guys at this?" she asked, changing the subject.

"Probably not," Carina said. "I've been to these sorts of things my dad does. There's never anyone under forty. Ever. Though Hudson could probably find someone."

"Shut up," Hudson said, reaching past Emma to swat her on the arm. "I told you guys, I'm over that now."

It was strange for Lizzie not to be there. Her absence could be felt in the car. Even though Emma hadn't said a word to them about the fight, she assumed that Carina and Hudson had heard Lizzie's side of the story, which only doubled the awkwardness.

The cab pulled up in front of the museum, and they all got out. Hudson wore a beautiful strapless lemon-yellow dress with a feathered neckline, and Carina wore a royal blue silk top, black denim leggings, and gold high heels. Emma had opted for a painfully plain black dress, black tights, and heels — and hardly any makeup, due to Tom Beckett's e-mail reminder to look "fresh-faced." The pink hair color was still there, though, and she absolutely defied him to say anything to her about it when she got inside.

"You guys look so pretty," Emma said. "I look so...Ann Taylor, circa nineteen ninety-four."

"You look great," Hudson said, so sincerely that Emma almost believed her.

"Are they really that controlling over what you wear?" asked Carina.

"Oh yeah. The key word is *fresh-faced*," Emma said facetiously. "I.e., boring and gross. So. Should we go?"

Their arms linked, they climbed the stairs to the entrance. Tiny lights hidden in the banisters cast a golden glow on the steps, while bright white spotlights lit up the pillars and arches of the museum's exterior, and became halos in the mist. As they climbed, the churning in her stomach increased. *Don't do this,* she thought. *Turn back. Nightmare scenario fast approaching.* But she kept going.

A fleet of security guards checked them in — her dad's security needs were growing by the minute, it seemed — and they walked into the grand entrance hall, past a reception desk decorated with an enormous arrangement of flowers. Emma felt another warning pass through her. *I don't want to do this,* she thought. *I really don't want to do this.*

One of the museum guards gestured straight ahead. "The event is in the Temple —"

"Of Dendur, got it," she interrupted, quickening her step.

"We came here in seventh grade for a social studies field trip," Carina said as they walked down the hallway. "I hear it's supposed to look pretty cool at night."

"I wish Lizzie were here," Hudson murmured.

Carina didn't say anything.

I do, too, Emma thought. "Maybe someone will be taking pictures," was all she could think of to say.

Slowly, as if she were walking through sand, she turned the corner and entered the main gallery, where the ancient Egyptian temple, lit from below by hot pink and green lights, loomed over a crowd of men and women in black tie. Tall votive candles lined a reflecting pool. A dozen tables covered with ivory tablecloths were lined up beside the glass wall that overlooked Central Park. But the elegance quickly faded as she spotted Tom Beckett moving through the crowd, pumping hands as if he were the one running for president. As he got close she hid behind a waiter handing out grilled shrimp on skewers. The last thing she wanted to deal with was making fake small talk with him. Or hearing about how she had to remove more makeup.

"There's my dad, working the room," Carina said. She pointed to a tall man with a strong jaw and salt-and-pepper hair moving through the room with palpable authority, shaking people's hands and clapping them on the back.

"He looks like he does this a lot," Emma said.

"He does," Carina replied.

"This is gorgeous," Hudson said, staring at the room. "This is where I want to get married. I just decided."

"Um, shouldn't you figure out who you want to get married *to* first?" Carina asked her, helping herself to one of the tuna tartare–covered wontons being passed by a waiter.

"Well, maybe I *have* decided," Hudson said coyly. "Ben and I…*almost* kissed the other day," Hudson said, staring directly at her toes.

"You did?" Emma said, grabbing Hudson's arm. "That's awesome!" Some of the guests turned around and gave her a look, but she didn't care. "I told you to just go for it."

Hudson rolled her eyes. "I said we *almost* kissed. Not the real deal. Not yet. We were alone in the elevator after the photo shoot for the album, and there was this moment when he was looking at me and he kind of forgot what to say. And then he kind of stepped closer and I stepped closer, and we were, like, tilting our heads up, and then we hit our floor and the door opened, and we had to get out." Hudson looked dreamily into her glass of ginger ale. "So, yeah. It almost happened."

"Considering nothing really happens in that story," said Carina, "I kind of really got into that."

Emma thought of Walker for a moment. She had no idea what he thought of her after their fight, but she guessed it wasn't good. They must have passed each other fifty times in the halls without looking at each other or saying hi.

A sound of excitement in the crowd made her look up. Her parents were entering the room, with much waving and shaking of hands. Her mom almost looked unrecognizable with her hair curled in waves and her eyes heavily lined. *So my mom has to put on makeup and I have to take it off,* she thought.

"Emma, are you okay?" Carina asked. "You look a little pale."

"Yeah," said Hudson. "Are you sick?"

"I wish," Emma cracked. "Carina, don't take this the wrong way or anything, but I really don't want to do this."

"O-*kay,*" Carina said.

Just then the Jurg strode over to them and put his hand on Carina's shoulder. "Emma, I'm Karl Jurgensen," he said, offering his hand. "I'm so pleased that you could be a part of tonight's program."

"Me, too," she said, shaking his hand. She gave Carina a quick look that said *Don't say anything.*

"I'm going to go up and say a few quick words and then introduce you, all right?"

"All right," she said, a smile frozen on her face.

"Your parents are over there," he said, pointing. "Would you like to go over and greet them first?"

"No, that's okay," she said with a tight smile. "Whenever you're ready. I'm cool."

"All right, then," he said. "See you in a few minutes."

As soon as he walked away, Carina said, "Okay, say that last bit again. You really don't want to do this?"

"It's not because of your dad, it's because of the speech," she said. She pulled it out of her purse. "It's ridiculous. Just like the last one. It makes people our age sound like morons."

Carina grabbed it and read it. "Yeesh," she said. "You're right."

"Let me see it," Hudson said, taking it from Carina.

Emma watched her dad. He had the same look on his face that she'd seen that night with the donors at their apartment — the same fake smile, the same nervous expression. But there was something harder about his expression now, something more permanent, as if it were a mask that had finally sealed itself to his face. Her dad wasn't her dad anymore. He was any other politician, glad-handing his way through a rich crowd, morphing himself into the person voters expected him to be. Wanting her to morph along with him.

She felt someone tap her on the shoulder. "Emma, are you ready to speak now?" asked a man in a charcoal suit and gray tie. "I think Mr. Jurgensen would like to get started."

Emma eyed Carina. She knew it was too late. "Sure."

"Follow me."

She could feel Carina's and Hudson's concern as she walked away. And she felt something else — something she'd felt in the computer lab during her fight with Lizzie, something she hadn't

236

really felt before. She felt like a fake. She wasn't the girl who went along with things, who did what everyone else wanted, who didn't make waves. She wasn't the girl who stayed quiet when someone asked her to disregard one of her friends.

"Okay, stand just here, and Mr. Jurgensen is going to introduce you in a moment."

Emma watched the crowd part for Carina's dad as he made his way over to her. People seemed to respect — or fear — him in a way that they didn't respect her own dad. Instead of rushing over to him to shake his hand and say hello, they parted and gave Karl Jurgensen a healthy amount of space.

She watched him step up onto the stage and tap the mic. "Everyone, first of all, thank you so much for coming tonight," he said in a velvety-smooth voice. "It's my pleasure to host this little get-together for Senator Conway, who I'm lucky to be able to call a close, personal friend. And with that said, if he wins next year, then you better believe I'm gonna be first in line for movie night at the White House."

Appreciative laughter bubbled up from the crowd. Emma pretended to smile. *Adults always say the same corny things,* she thought.

"Before we sit down to what I hope will be a marvelous meal, I'd like to have him say a few words to you. But first, I've invited his daughter, Emma, who some of you may have already seen stumping for her dad on the campaign trail, to speak." He pointed to her, standing off to the side. "She has become one of her father's most vocal supporters and an astute critic of her generation. She also happens to be my daughter's very good friend. Please welcome Emma Conway."

As the applause began, Carina's dad walked off the platform and gave her a hand up the steps. When she got up there, she faced the lone teleprompter, where the words of her speech were reflected on the plastic screen. For the first time all night, she didn't feel dread anymore.

"Ladies and gentlemen," she said into the microphone. "Thank you for having me. I'm fifteen, as some of you might know, and being fifteen, I'd like to say a few words to you about America's youth."

The words on the teleprompter moved up, and the next line stared out at her: *America's youth is our future, and right now that future needs serious help.*

She swallowed. "But I can't," she said, looking away. "Because the words I'm supposed to say to you — the words that were written for me by my dad's campaign staff — just aren't true. America's youth *isn't* in trouble. We haven't been brainwashed by the Internet or reality TV. We aren't slackers who just want to play with our Wiis and our iPhones all day long. This country isn't going down the tubes because of us. We're the best thing this country has. We're smart, we're spirited, and we know bullshit when we see it."

The crowd was absolutely still and silent. She felt like Remington must have that night he spoke in their living room.

"I'm supposed to talk about how America's young people need to get serious and buckle down and develop a work ethic. But what we really need is to go to college without having to deal with massive student loans for the rest of our lives. And some of us need jobs that just don't exist when we get out of school," she went on. "And some of us need parents who listen to us when we have fears and concerns about our futures. *We're* not the problem. No matter what my dad's campaign manager wants me to say," she said. "Or how they want to water me down."

Out in the crowd, she saw her father grimace. Tom Beckett's face seemed to be almost completely drained of color.

"So, I think this will be my last speech for a while," she said. "Oh, yeah, and vote for my dad. But I guess you guys were going to do that anyway."

She turned to step off the stage. There was no sound except for that of the waiters carrying the salad course to all the tables.

At the bottom of the steps, Hudson and Carina waited for her.

I'm sorry, Emma mouthed to Carina, just as Tom Beckett approached her.

"What the hell was that?" Tom snapped.

And then someone elbowed Tom aside. It was her dad. His mouth had become a thin white line, and he looked the closest that Emma had ever seen him to devastated. "It's over, Emma," he said curtly. "You're done with this."

She felt her friends come to her side, closing ranks.

"No problem," she said. She turned to Carina. "I have to go. I'm sorry."

"It's okay," Carina whispered.

As Emma walked out, trying not to look at the staring faces surrounding her, she grabbed her phone out of her clutch and typed in a text.

Need to see you. Can I come over? 911 situation.

Lizzie wrote back one minute later: *Yes*

chapter 28

Lizzie opened the door for her. Emma stepped into the marble-floored foyer of Lizzie's apartment, too much in shock to even give Lizzie a hug.

"What happened?" Lizzie asked. She was wearing a pair of sweatpants and an old purple sweater, and she still had toilet paper wrapped around her toes from a home pedicure.

"It was another speech just like the one at UPenn," Emma said, taking off her coat. "The same crazy stuff. So I told them all what I really thought. I told them it was bullshit."

Lizzie put her hand to her mouth. "No. You didn't."

"It actually felt really good."

"Oh, Emma, you didn't." Lizzie sighed. "Come into the kitchen. Let me make you some tea."

Emma followed Lizzie into her kitchen and sat down on one of the stools. "I thought you'd be proud of me or something," she said. "I spoke up. I told them all the truth. I was myself again. Isn't that what you were mad at me about with Todd? Not speaking up?"

Lizzie put the kettle on the burner. "Yes, I know I said all those things. But this is a little bit different." She sat on the stool next to her. "Why didn't you just say you couldn't give the speech at all? Don't you think that that would have been the better thing to do?"

Emma listened to the water in the kettle boil. She knew that Lizzie was probably right, as much as she didn't want to admit it.

"I think it's great that you're so outspoken, but sometimes you have to measure the consequences," Lizzie said. "It doesn't always have to be so extreme. You could have just said no, even right before you went on."

The kettle started to whistle. Lizzie got up and turned off the gas. Emma tapped her fingers on the counter as tears came into her eyes. "I guess so," she said. "Maybe it wasn't the smartest thing to do."

Lizzie carried a mug of tea over to Emma. "And I'm sorry I blew up at you about the Todd thing. I'm just going through a hard time, and I took it out on you. I know that there wasn't much you could do about that." She nudged the mug of peppermint tea toward Emma. "I'm sorry. You're an amazing friend. I didn't mean it."

Emma tried to blink the tears away but it didn't work. A big one rolled down her cheek. "That's okay," she said, and then she leaned over and gave Lizzie a hug.

She spent another hour at Lizzie's, and then she finally got in a cab. As it carried her across the park, she saw that the mist had turned into fog. They drove past the Met and Emma looked over at it, wondering just what the fallout of the evening would be for her. She knew now that she hadn't made the most responsible move. Carina's dad would probably never speak to her again, not to mention what her own parents were going to say.

At home she stood in the shower for a long time, letting the hot water run over her face as she thought about each word she'd said. Not one had been negative about her dad. So in the rare event that he ever decided to speak to her again, at least she could defend herself with that.

She turned off the faucet. As she dried herself with a fluffy white towel, she heard the front door open and close. Heavy footsteps moved through the foyer and into the hall. It was her brother.

She walked into her bedroom and put on some pajamas. If she went to speak to him, they would probably have a fight, especially in light of his recent moods. But if she didn't go speak to him, then she would wake up the next morning feeling even worse than she did now. After all, he was the only person who could possibly relate to what she'd been through tonight.

She got out of bed and padded over to his door. "Hey," she said, knocking softly. "Can I talk to you?"

He opened the door. Now she recognized the smell that wafted off him and out into the hall: It was beer. His eyes had the same glassy, unfocused look she'd seen that night a few weeks ago. He was drunk. "What do you want, Emma?" he asked in the same, almost-slurred way.

"Are you okay?" she asked him. "Where've you been?"

He rolled his eyes. "What is it you want?"

"I...I quit tonight," she said. "I'm no longer going to have any part of Dad's campaign. I'm done."

"I'm impressed," he said sarcastically. "I thought you were the political expert."

"I just wanted to say congratulations," she said. "You win. You're still the chosen one, Rem. And you probably will be until the end of time." She backed away from the door. "Unless you'd rather just get wasted. Which seems to be your thing these days."

"You don't know anything about my life," he said thickly.

"You're right," she said. "I don't."

She walked back to her room. Suddenly Emma remembered what Walker had said: *He's in a scene that I really don't want to be a part of.* This was why they were no longer friends. Her brother was turning into a different person. And none of it, she knew now, had been Walker's fault.

chapter 29

The next few days at school drifted by like a movie on a screen. Emma went from class to class, not listening, not participating, just barely able to take notes. Fortunately there were no tests or pop quizzes — she would have almost certainly failed them. Her mind felt foggy, like she was getting over the flu, and the weather had turned chilly and overcast.

Word of her disastrous remarks at the Met hadn't gotten out to the press, which was one thing she felt grateful for. But her mom still hadn't really spoken to her. She floated through the apartment, only speaking to Emma when she absolutely had to. Her dad had flown to Florida right after Karl Jurgensen's party, and he hadn't been back to New York since. Emma knew that in their eyes, what she'd done was irreparable. Fortunately her friends stuck by her, even Carina, who admitted that her dad was "less than thrilled" about her opening remarks.

And there was really no need to continue going to speech club.

The first Monday after the Met event, she sailed past the door to the library on her way out of the building, and she never went back again. Mrs. Bateman didn't press her for an explanation. She didn't even mention it. Emma almost got the impression that she'd been waiting for her to drop out all along. Her brother didn't mention it, either, but then again, they weren't speaking. When she passed him in the hall, they didn't make eye contact. At home they ate at different times. Remington had started swim practice, and now came home after six most nights anyway.

One morning she was putting on her coat in the lobby, getting ready to run to the deli for a bagel, when she saw Walker come down the steps. He was alone and dressed to go out, and as he walked toward her she felt the same shiver she had that first morning she'd started Chadwick.

"Hi," she said, standing in front of him.

"Hey," he said. "What are you doing?"

"Getting ready to go to the deli. Do you want to go with me?"

He looked at her for a few moments. "Okay," he said tentatively, as if she'd just asked him to go bungee-jumping with her.

She knotted her scarf around her neck and led the way out onto the street. It was the coldest day of the fall so far, so cold that Emma thought it smelled like snow.

"So, you finally dropped speech team once and for all," he said as they turned into the wind.

"I'm taking a break from public speaking," she said. "I'm sure you heard about what happened at the Met."

"Just a little," he said. "But we miss you. It's not really the same without you there."

Emma felt something inside her leap up at his words. But she let it go. "Look, I owe you an apology," she said. "What I said to you about Remington. I'm sorry." She stopped walking and faced him. Just behind him was the diner, and through the windows Emma saw the floppy-haired waiter hanging out by the cash register, talking with the manager. "I think I know what you were talking about," she said carefully. "He's kind of turning into a different person, isn't he?"

Walker sighed and looked down the street. "I didn't want to tell you," he said. "But yeah, things have gotten pretty bad with him."

"He drinks a lot now, huh?" she asked.

Walker nodded. "It started last year."

"Last *year*?" she asked.

"That's when he started hanging out with Steven and Chris," he said. "Because of swim team. They're pretty big partiers."

"But last year? Really?"

"Emma, you haven't been here," Walker said. "You've been at boarding school."

"But... what about you two? I thought you guys were friends at the start of the year."

Walker shrugged. "My cousin goes to Georgetown," he said. "When I heard how wasted Rem got on the day he visited, I knew I couldn't really hang with him anymore."

"Wait," Emma said. "He was *wasted* at Georgetown?"

"Yup. He was supposed to meet my cousin for coffee, but he never showed up. Turns out he and Chris spent the whole afternoon in the campus bar, playing darts and pounding beers."

246

Emma thought of Rem's face that night when she knocked on his hotel room door. The way his eyes looked, the way his skin looked. He'd lied to her that night about being sick. He'd lied to the entire family. "He told me he had food poisoning that night. He was supposed to make a speech for my dad's birthday. And instead he got drunk?"

Walker shrugged. "I mean...Yeah. He did." He touched her shoulder. "You okay?"

She still couldn't quite absorb it. "Do you think he has a problem or something? With drinking?"

"I don't know," he said. "I tried bringing it up with him a few times, but he just got mad."

"But Remington's always been so good," she said. "He's always been the responsible one. The perfect one."

"But that's just it, Emma," Walker said. "Maybe he doesn't want to be anymore." His hand was still on her shoulder. "And I think I owe you an apology, too," he said. His brown eyes bored into her. She felt her heart start to beat faster. "I'm hard on you sometimes," he said. "But I guess it's because I like you. I always have."

"Oh," she said. Her heart was beating so fast that she was sure he could tell.

"So...I guess what I really want to ask you is..." He furrowed his brow in an adorable way. "Would you ever want to go somewhere and *not* talk about speech team?"

She smiled. "Sure," she said. "I'd love to."

"Cool," he said, giving her his thousand-watt smile. "That's really cool."

When she got back to school she was on such a cloud that she almost walked straight into her brother at one of the vending machines.

"Hey," he said nonchalantly.

"Oh, hi," she said. She hoped he couldn't tell that she'd just been asked out by his ex–best friend.

"Senator Gibbons just announced he's running," he said. "Four months ahead of schedule."

"Oh jeez. Is Dad freaking out?" she asked.

"It's not like they didn't expect it, but yeah. Gibbons has already siphoned off a huge number of potential voters."

Emma wanted to roll her eyes at the word *siphon*, but she let it slide. At least her brother was speaking to her.

"So Dad's coming home this weekend," he said. "He's gonna try to rest. I'm going up to New Haven tomorrow," he said. "So you'll be with them alone." He offered her a weak smile. "You seem a little out of it. Are you doing all right?"

"Yup. I'm doing great," she said. "But . . . are you doing okay?"

"Sure. Everything's great."

"Rem," she started carefully, "can I talk to you? I know what happened in Georgetown. And I know what's been happening here."

Her brother stepped away from her and sighed. "Emma, you're in no position to lecture me, okay? You practically sabotaged Dad's campaign. If I want to have fun on my own time, then that's my business. Okay?"

"Fine," she said. "Have a good time at Yale."

248

"Thanks," he said halfheartedly. "Have fun with Mom and Dad," he said.

He ambled off down the hall and Emma felt the same internal alarm go off in her stomach. He was in trouble. She could feel it. But Walker was right. There was nothing she could do.

chapter 30

Her dad didn't have much to say to her when he got home, but she was expecting that. Actually, he didn't have much to say to anyone. He went straight to their bedroom and went to sleep. "I don't think either of us knew how much work this was going to be," her mom said in a half-whisper as she made some tea in the kitchen Friday night.

"In what way?" Emma asked.

"All the travel, the handshaking, the speechmaking...It just takes everything out of you. And now that Senator Gibbons has announced he's running, well, it just ratchets the whole thing up a notch." She poured some boiling water into a mug. "You know your father. You know how hard he is on himself."

Her mom looked like she'd lost weight since the night at the Met, and Emma could see tiny wrinkles around her eyes that she'd never noticed before. "I hope you know that I'm sorry," she said. "About the thing at the Met."

Her mom's face darkened. "Oh, Emma," she said with an air of disappointment. "I can imagine you are. But I hope — I really sincerely hope — that you know what a mistake that was. And how much that embarrassed your father and me. You do know that, don't you?"

Emma nodded. "It's kind of all I've been thinking about," she said.

"How's school? Your friends?" her mom asked, stifling a yawn.

Emma shrugged. Talking about school and grades and her friends seemed hopelessly trivial these days. "It's always the same," she said. "Nothing that important."

Just then she heard footsteps in the foyer, and a moment later her dad entered the kitchen. He, too, looked thin and tired, with bluish-black circles under his eyes. "Hi, honey," he said, his voice scratchy. "How're you doing?"

Without even thinking about it, she went to hug him. "Dad, I'm sorry about the other night," she said. "I was just so frustrated. I didn't like what they were doing. To you, and to me. I know I get carried away sometimes — I just hope it didn't cause too much damage."

Her dad cleared his throat. She could hear that he was sick. "I think we all knew it was a temporary thing," he said. "And you did a great job for most of it. We were all very proud. But I should never have asked you to do any of that," he said. "You're fifteen. I should have known better than to try to draft you into the cause. So, I'm sorry, Em."

She stared at him. In all the many times that she'd imagined this conversation, she'd never expected her dad to be the one to apologize to her.

The cordless phone suddenly rang.

"Emma, can you get that?" her mom asked. "If anyone asks for us, we're not here."

She walked over and picked up the phone. "Hello?" she said.

"Is this Mrs. Conway?" asked a male voice. He sounded far away and small, almost as if he were speaking through a tunnel.

"No, it's her daughter," she said. "Who's this?"

"This is Officer John Macaulay," the voice said. "I'm with the New Haven Police."

Emma felt a shiver run through her.

"Are your parents home?" he asked.

"Hold on," she said. She put the phone down.

"Who is it, honey?" her mom asked, peering at her.

"It's the police," she said evenly.

Her mother looked confused. "The police?" she repeated. "Are you kidding?"

"The New Haven Police," Emma said.

She saw this register on her parents' faces. Her father picked up the phone. "This is Adam Conway," he said. He listened for a moment. "*What?*" he asked. "Say that again?"

Her mom sat up on the couch.

"He's in custody?" he asked.

"What is it?" Carolyn whispered.

Adam shook his head slightly, holding her off. "How much was in his system?"

Carolyn shot to her feet.

Adam met his wife's gaze. Emma could see the shocked sadness in his eyes. "I see," he replied.

252

"Oh, no," Carolyn muttered, her hand to her mouth. "Oh, no. Is he okay?"

Her father nodded but stayed on the phone for a few more minutes. "Thank you, Officer," he finally said in a hushed tone. "I'm leaving right now." He placed the phone back in the cradle and let out a deep sigh.

"What happened?" Carolyn asked. She almost sounded hysterical. "For God's sake, tell me."

"Remington was just arrested for disorderly conduct," Adam said slowly. "He was in some bar tonight in New Haven and got in a fight with another boy. The police were called. They say he was intoxicated."

"Oh my God," Carolyn said.

"I have to go get him," Adam said, pulling on his jacket. "I guess I should order a car, since Remington has ours."

"No, call Tom," she said. "He'll send a car." She grabbed the cordless and dialed the number from memory. "Tom? It's Carolyn. There's been an emergency. It's Remington. He's been arrested."

Emma leaned against the kitchen table. There was no way she could have prevented this from happening, but it was hard not to feel like she could or should have done something.

"Tom says he's sending a car right over," Carolyn said.

"He probably just had a couple beers with some students," Adam said. "What a lousy piece of luck."

Carolyn suddenly looked at Emma, as if she'd just remembered that their other child was also in the room. "Who were the kids he was visiting up there?" she asked.

Emma shook her head. "It wasn't the kids, Mom," she said. "There are some things you don't know about him."

"Like what?" her father asked.

Emma paused. She had no idea how to say this. It went against everything she believed in to tattle on Remington, but now she knew that her parents had a right to know. "He's been getting drunk," Emma said. "A lot. Like that night in D.C. Or day, rather. He wasn't sick. He just got too drunk to go with us that night."

Her father looked shocked. "Are you serious?" he asked.

"Walker confirmed it for me," she said. "His cousin was supposed to meet up with Rem on campus. Rem never showed. Then he heard that he went to some bar instead. And I've seen him drunk a couple times since then."

Her mother blinked dumbly. "I can't believe this."

The squawk of the house phone on the kitchen wall broke the silence. "That's the car," her father said. "I better go." He raced to the coat closet in the hall. "Call Tom back. Ask him what we can do about damage control," he said. He shrugged on his coat. "I'll be back as soon as I can."

The front door shut, leaving Emma with her mom, who still hadn't spoken.

"I just can't believe this," she muttered, sitting down on the edge of a kitchen chair. A strand of black hair fell in front of her face and she swatted it away. "He's always been so responsible. So . . . adult. With such good judgment."

"But he's still just a kid, Mom," Emma said. "I've always thought of him as perfect, too. But he's not."

The phone in the office rang. Carolyn picked it up. "Oh, hi,

Tom," she muttered. "Yes, Adam just got in the car. What?" She buried her head in her hands. "Oh, great," she said with a sigh. "Of course it has."

Emma already knew what this meant. The story had leaked to the press.

"Just in time for the Saturday-morning news shows," Carolyn said. "Just tell me: How bad do you think this will be?" She listened. "Just please do what you can to keep any photographers away," she said. "We can't have any pictures of Adam taking him out of the police station."

Emma went to the sink and filled a glass of water. This was going to be terrible. Much, much worse for her dad's campaign than anything she could have said or done. And it was going to be terrible for Remington. He would never live this down. It was always worse for the child who wasn't supposed to mess up. She remembered what he'd said the night of her parents' cocktail party, about having so much responsibility.

Her mom hung up the phone and shook her head. "What a mess," she said. "Tom thinks the press is going to have a field day. And I still can't believe . . . Remington. Of all people."

"Maybe he's just cracking from the pressure," Emma said. "I think he's had to pick up a lot of slack because of me. He's had to be perfect for way too long."

"I was worried about what this campaign might do to you kids," her mom said. "Now I feel like I should have told your father to wait four more years."

Her mom looked so vulnerable that Emma went to her and put her arms around her. "Everything's gonna be okay. This isn't the end of the world. It's really not. I promise you. It could be a lot worse." She hugged her mom hard.

"There were times when I would watch you out there with your father and think that you were a lot more suited to all of this than I am," her mom said. "I admired you for it." She smiled at her. "I really did. I'd think, *That girl has a thick skin. She knows who she is. And if she did end up in the White House, she'd do a helluva lot better job with it all than I would.*"

Emma hugged her mom again. "You would do a great job," she said. "I know you would."

She and her mom hugged for a long time.

"Okay, here's what you do," Emma said. "You go to bed. You don't watch the news, you don't go online, you don't pick up the phone. If anyone calls, I'll deal with it."

Her mom chuckled. "I'm supposed to be the one taking care of you, honey."

"It's okay to switch once in a while," Emma said, helping her to her feet.

That night she stayed on her parents' sofa, drinking Diet Coke to stay awake in case anyone called. Instead of watching CNN, she put on E! and finally fell fast asleep to *100 Worst Celebrity Breakups.*

chapter 31

By Monday morning the news of Remington's arrest had spread all over the country. The pundits were already saying that it was a major stumble for the Adam Conway campaign. CONWAY KID ARRESTED DRUNK, ran the typically blunt headline on the CNN crawl, from Friday night through the weekend.

As Tom predicted, the arrest created a public-relations disaster that didn't appear solvable. A few people were already saying that Adam should pull out, at least before Senator Gibbons crushed him with fund-raising anyway. Emma tried not to read any of the newspapers before school that morning. It all just made her sad.

Remington and her dad had come home in the middle of the night, and the next day her father canceled his flight to Milwaukee. Her parents and brother spent most of Sunday holed up in the apartment, talking about what Remington had done. Emma didn't dare go near her parents' office the entire day, but she pieced together the story eventually. Chris Flagg had been at Yale for the weekend, too, but it had been Remington's idea to start doing shots at the campus bar. Apparently he'd had a fake ID made the previous summer in England. Her parents and her brother stayed in that room for hours. Whatever he was going through, she figured he didn't need one more judgmental face in front of him.

By Monday morning she was ready to go to school, and relieved to get out of her oppressive apartment. She'd already texted her friends about what was going on. Lizzie met her at the lockers. "You okay?" she asked. "How's your brother?"

"Fine, I guess," she said. "I don't think he's coming to school today."

"It wasn't really a banner weekend for me, either," she said. "They found Todd's dad guilty on Friday."

"Are you serious?"

Lizzie's hazel eyes were somber. "Todd's not taking it well. Or at least not from what I hear."

Hudson and Carina joined them. "Hey, Em," Carina said. "We're so sorry to hear about your brother. That's got to really suck for all of you."

"Actually, I think I'm weirdly glad that it happened," Emma said. "At least now it's, you know, a thing. He can't hide it anymore. It was starting to be kind of a problem."

"Maybe he was just way too stressed out," Hudson put in. "He is, like, the smartest kid in the school. And he seemed to push himself pretty hard."

"Will this mess up his college applications?" asked Carina. "I mean, every admissions officer is going to know that this happened."

"I hope not," Emma said. They began to walk toward homeroom. It was weird to walk down the halls knowing that she wouldn't be running into her brother. After all of her personal drama over the past two months, it felt strange to be the one that people weren't worried about.

Emma sat through American Political Structures tracing her name over and over on her notebook. Being the good kid or the bad kid in the family was almost like running for president, she thought. Eventually someone was going to step out of their role and betray everyone else's expectations. But it wasn't fair, because they had never promised to play those roles in the first place. It had just always been that way between her and Remington.

"Emma? Can I speak to you a moment?" Mrs. Bateman asked as soon as class was over.

Emma gathered up her books and walked over to Mrs. Bateman's desk. "Yes?"

"I'm well aware of the fact that you have an ambivalent attitude toward speech and debate," she said, slinging her canvas PBS bag from the seventies over her shoulder. "But as we head into serious debate prep, I would like for you to consider coming back."

Emma looked Mrs. Bateman in the eye. "Why?"

"Because you're good," Mrs. Bateman conceded. "And because without you we're pretty much just a lackluster team." She took a deep breath, as if this had all been very difficult for her to say.

Emma smiled despite herself. "So I'm good," she said. "That's interesting. I really never thought you'd admit it."

Mrs. Bateman scratched at an indeterminate place underneath her steel-wool hair. "Nobody ever gets better if they don't think they need to," she said.

"I'll think about it," Emma said.

"And may I remind you that debate is much more about ad-libbing than speech was," Mrs. Bateman said. "But something tells me that you'd be quite good at it. And personally, I'm getting tired of giving you all of these invitations." She walked away, leaving Emma to digest her words.

When Emma left the room and walked into the hallway, she knew that she'd made the right decision. And almost like a sign from the universe, she spotted Walker coming out of a classroom.

"Hi," she said, walking right up to him. "Can I walk with you for a second?"

He gave just the smallest nod of his head. "Fine," he said.

"So I'm sure you've heard," she said.

Walker nodded.

"I can't stop thinking that I should have done something."

"No. You couldn't have done anything, Emma, believe me."

"But I knew. You told me. I could have tried to —"

"What? Not let him go visit Yale?" Walker shook his head. "There wasn't much you could do, Emma. Which is why I waited so long to tell you. If I couldn't get through to him...then how could you?"

They walked in silence down the hall as Emma let this sink in. "I guess you're right."

They turned down a hallway that led to a back stairway. "So," he said, stopping to look at her. They seemed to be alone, and Emma's heart began to race again. "What are you doing on Friday?" he asked. "Do you want to go see a movie or something?"

She smiled. "I'd love to. And by the way, I'm going to be on the debate team."

He held up his hand and gave her a high five. "Awesome," he said. "Except for one thing."

"What?" she asked, stepping closer to him.

"Now I'm seriously never going to be able to concentrate," he said. "Not with you so close to me."

Walker took her hand and slowly drew her closer to him. Time seemed to stop as he leaned down. His lips brushed softly against hers.

That was it, she thought. *My first kiss.* It only seemed right that Walker Lloyd was the one to give it to her. His fingers were warm and smooth as he squeezed her hand, and when he smiled at her, she knew that this was the guy she'd been waiting for.

chapter 32

"So let me ask you: One snake wasn't enough?" Remington asked, taking Archie out of his terrarium and letting him slither across the carpet. "You had to get him a buddy?"

"We all need companionship in our lives," Emma said, taking the smaller garter snake from the tank and letting it slither next to Archie. "Isabella can kind of be like his girlfriend."

"Snakes don't need to be in relationships," Remington said.

"Well, I don't think they're going to be signing any prenups or anything like that," Emma wisecracked.

Outside the window, the snow fell thick and fast over the front lawn of their house on Lake George. She always liked it when it snowed on Thanksgiving up here. It made her feel like they were even farther away from their regular life. Downstairs she could hear her dad helping her mom in the kitchen — he'd actually been granted the entire holiday weekend off by Tom Beckett. His campaign had taken a beating in the past few weeks, ever since Remington's arrest, but a few days earlier a story had been leaked about Jim Gibbons's possible affair with an intern, which had put smiles back on everyone's faces at Conway for America. Emma had stopped following the campaign too closely, and so had her brother. Ever since that night in New Haven, he'd thrown himself into his swim team and debate practice. As far as she knew, he hadn't touched any alcohol since that night, and most weekend nights he stayed home to finish his college applications.

And a funny thing had happened. Slowly, she and Remington were becoming friends again. He started coming by her room after dinner to chat, and soon they were taking the subway to school together. When they passed each other in the halls they said hi, most of the time. Even he and Walker had started hanging out again, once Walker made sure Remington knew that he and Emma were very much an item.

"So, do you want to hear something crazy?" Remington asked suddenly. "I think I'm going to put off going to college next year."

"You mean to be with Dad?" Emma asked, drawing a throw blanket closer around her on the living room couch.

"No, to travel," he said. "There's this program down in the Galapagos Islands. It's an environmental research project kind of thing. I just heard about it. I think it would be cool."

"Yeah, definitely," Emma said. "Have you talked to Mom and Dad about it?"

"Not yet," Remington said. "What do you think they'll say?"

"I think they'll be super into it," Emma said.

"Yeah?" he asked.

"Yeah. I think you should do it," she said. "College will be here when you get back. But I'd miss you. It wouldn't be the same not having you in the country for a year."

"You could always do a semester abroad," he said. "Chadwick has programs all over the place. Maybe one in Ecuador?"

Emma realized she'd never thought of taking part in one of those programs before; she'd always assumed that they were for the nerds in her school. But suddenly she remembered that she'd been doing pretty well in Spanish so far this semester, and said, "I'll look into that. Why not?"

"I think it might be good for both of us to get a little break next year." Remington kicked off his duck boots and put his feet on the coffee table. "Sorry if I was a major jerk to you this term."

Emma held Archie in her hand. She was tempted to agree, but only for a moment. "It's okay. I was kind of a jerk, too. I think we're even."

"You weren't a jerk," he said. "You tried to smack some sense into me, and I wouldn't listen." He looked at her. "You're not a bad little sister, you know that? As far as little sisters go."

She smiled. "Why does that still kind of sound like a put-down?"

"Just because I'm your older brother. I'm supposed to be annoyed by you."

She smiled. "Let's stop thinking of supposed to, and let's just start being us," she said, as their parents called them down to dinner.

chapter 33

It was a little cold outside for Pinkberry, but that didn't seem to matter to Lizzie, Carina, Emma, and Hudson as they huddled around a white plastic table, digging into their yogurt.

"This chocolate is sooo good," Carina said, offering a loaded spoon to anyone who wanted a taste. "Emma, here. Taste it. You have to."

Emma took the spoon. "Yum," she said. "But I hate to tell you, I think I'm getting the flu."

Carina's face fell as Lizzie and Hudson laughed.

"Just kidding," Emma said, giggling.

"Ha, ha," Carina said.

"So, when does the album drop?" Lizzie asked Hudson, who had finished almost half of her pomegranate yogurt with blueberries.

"In two weeks," Hudson said with a half-smile, half-grimace. "The week before Christmas."

"So, are you ready?" asked Emma.

"Not really," Hudson said. "And I have news for you guys: I don't think I'm going to be in school for a couple months."

Emma, Lizzie, and Carina all looked at one another. "Seriously?" Carina asked. "You're leaving us?"

"It's just while I promote the album," Hudson said. "They've got me doing a tour up and down the East Coast, then going out to L.A., and then to Europe."

"No way," Emma said. Hudson's life sounded like the coolest thing in the world.

"That sounds amazing, H," Lizzie said. "But when would you come back?"

"I'm not sure right now," Hudson said. "Probably after spring break."

"Wow," Lizzie said thoughtfully, stirring her yogurt. "This is really happening for you."

"About time," Carina added.

"But we'll miss you," Emma said. "Mrs. Bateman's class definitely won't be the same without you."

"And there's one more thing I have to tell you," Hudson said. "Ben asked me out the other day. We're officially going out."

"Woo-hoo!" Emma yelled, giving her a high five. "That's amazing!"

"Finally," Carina said. "Has he kissed you yet?"

Hudson nodded. "Uh-huh."

"Yes!" Carina yelled, causing some of the other customers to turn around and stare. "You both are so shy I thought it might never happen." She clasped her hands and looked up to the sky. "Thank you, God."

"I actually kind of asked him out," Hudson said. "Or at least, I dropped some serious hints that I was into him." She looked at Emma. "Thanks, Em. I could never have done it without you."

"You're totally welcome," Emma said, running a hand through her blue-streaked hair. She'd celebrated the end of exams with another bottle of Manic Panic at Ricky's, and so far nobody at school or home had complained.

"And I want to hear what's going on with Walker Lloyd," Carina said, turning to Emma. "How many dates have you guys been on?"

"Just three," Emma said, feeling herself blush. It was still hard to believe sometimes that she had a boyfriend.

"And your brother's cool with it?" Carina asked.

"My brother actually couldn't be happier about it," she said. "And, weirdly, my parents. The last thing I expected them to approve of was my boyfriend."

"Well, when you date one of the smartest guys in school, that's kind of inevitable," Lizzie said. "I think it's awesome you guys are together."

As Lizzie said this, Emma couldn't help but notice how sad she seemed. She and Todd were still taking a break, even though his dad's trial was over and he had returned to school.

"Don't worry, Lizbutt," Carina said. "Everything's going to be okay."

"No, I'm fine," she said, shaking her head. "Really. I'm okay with it now. We're actually becoming friends again. But it has been totally awkward. I just hope we're past all the weirdness by the time we come back from Christmas break."

Suddenly they heard the sound of a cell phone chiming. Emma lunged for her bag, along with the rest of them.

Lizzie pulled out her phone. "It's from Todd."

"Read it," Carina said urgently.

Lizzie clicked on the message and stared at it.

"What does it say?" Hudson urged.

"I miss you," Lizzie read aloud.

"Holy shnit," Carina said.

"Wow," Hudson said.

Lizzie swallowed. Emma could see that she was trying to fight off a smile.

"What do you guys think this means?" she asked.

"It means he wants you!" Emma said. "He misses you. Write him back right now and say you miss him back!"

Lizzie looked doubtful. "Really?"

"Yes!" Emma said. "He wants another chance! Don't over-think this!"

Lizzie picked up the phone.

"What do you want, Lizbutt?" Hudson asked. "What do *you* want to do?"

"What do you *think* I want to do?" Lizzie said, starting to type. "I want to see him." She typed for a few moments.

"What are you saying?" Emma asked.

There was another chime as Lizzie got a new text. Her eyes filled with tears.

"What did it say?" Carina asked.

"I love you," Lizzie read.

"Damn straight he does!" Carina said.

Lizzie started to laugh, and then Emma, Carina, and Hudson joined in. As Emma giggled into her yogurt, she realized that this, right now, was the happiest she'd ever been in her life. Maybe she would never fully belong in her own family, but she'd made another one for herself. And this one was just as strong.

acknowledgments

Once again, I am so grateful for my agent, Becka Oliver, whose enthusiasm for this series — and for me — makes me feel like the luckiest author in the world. Enormous thanks also go to Cindy Eagan and Elizabeth Bewley, my genius editors, for all of their support and insightful suggestions. Tracy Shaw designed another gorgeous cover — thank you, Tracy! And JoAnna Kremer's copy-editing improved the manuscript tenfold — thank you! I'd also like to thank my sister and friend, JJ Philbin, for being my first reader. And for always reading everything so fast. She has two kids and a busy writing career of her own, so I have no idea how she does it.

The following books gave me much-needed insight into the world of presidential campaigning: *Game Change* and *The Way to Win*, by John Heilemann and Mark Halperin; *Notes from the Trail*, by Alexandra Kerry; *The Audacity of Hope*, by Barack Obama; and *The Audacity to Win*, by David Plouffe.

Many thanks also go to my friend Michael Oates Palmer, for answering endless campaign-related questions.

I am also grateful to the following for schooling me on the principles of speech and debate: *You Can Write Speeches and Debates*, by Jennifer Rozines Roy and Johannah Haney; *The Complete Book of Speech Communication*, by Carol Marrs; *Speaking with Confidence*, by Wanda Vassallo; and the website www.middleschooldebate.com.

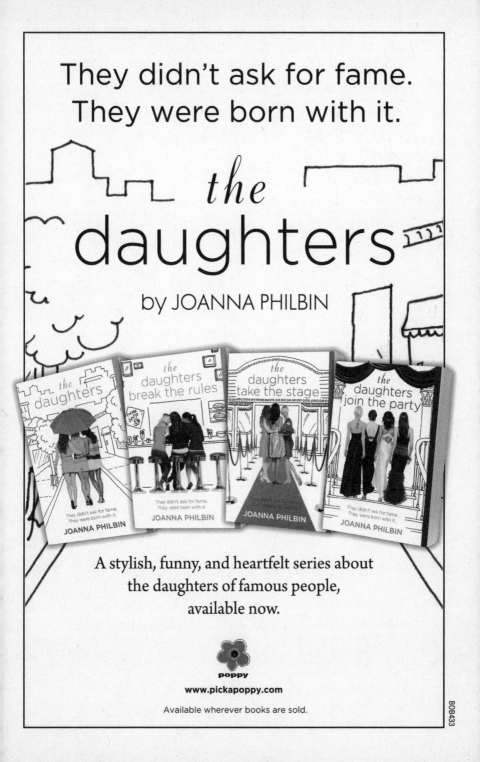

Don't miss any of the books in the
New York Times bestselling
MONSTER HIGH SERIES!

THE GHOUL NEXT DOOR

WHERE THERE'S A WOLF, THERE'S A WAY

Drop Dead Diary

FINAL BOOK COMING MAY 2012!

What if a beautiful dress could take you back in time?

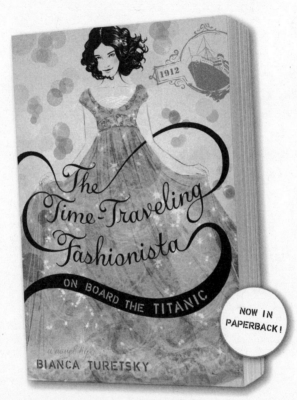

When Louise Lambert receives a mysterious invitation to a traveling vintage-fashion sale, she discovers that beautiful dresses can *transport* you to a whole new era. . . .

In Louise's first time-traveling adventure, she becomes a movie starlet on board a luxury cruise ship. Louise is living the high life until she discovers the boat's name: the *Titanic*.

"Will capture readers with its **honesty** and **heart**."

—*Publishers Weekly*

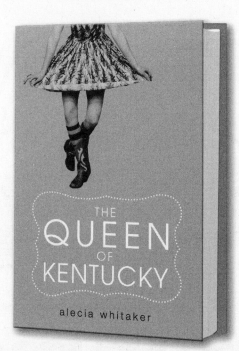

Fourteen-year-old Kentucky girl Ricki Jo Winstead,
who would prefer to be called Ericka, *thank you very much*,
is eager to shed her farmer's daughter roots and become part of
the popular crowd at her small-town high school. But her best friend
and the boy next door, Luke, says he misses "plain old Ricki Jo."

Where does Ricki Jo belong, and
what will it take for her to find out?

poppy
www.pickapoppy.com

Where stories bloom.

poppy

Visit us online at
www.pickapoppy.com